**He stood still, afraid to move
in the deafening silence.**

He could hear her heart beating within her chest. He wondered if she could hear the racing of his own heart.

"It must have been the wind." Miranda's words broke the quiet.

The disappointment he heard in her voice prompted him to step forward. He stopped himself before he reached the bed and took her in his arms. It would do no good to frighten her to death. Calling back his concentration, which had scattered to the four winds upon hearing his name, he whispered a comfort prayer. He completed it with an urgent command for her to sleep.

The sun's rays now crested the treetops. He needed to be gone. But still he didn't move. He waited until Miranda slid back down in the bed and her breathing relaxed before he allowed his desire to overcome his common sense.

He approached her slumbering body. The purity of her face, still marred by a score of tear-tracks, looked beautiful beyond belief. Although he felt the rays of the sun heat his skin, he had one more thing to do: a safety prayer to keep Gabriella out along with any henchmen she might send to do her dirty work.

That done, Zacke leaned down and brushed her lips with his own. The sweetness pulling at him threatened to drop him to his knees. He fought the urge to lie at her side. It would mean his death—but to die in Miranda's arms would be worth the agony.

Praise for Faith V. Smith

"I really enjoyed the twist Ms. Smith added to make this traditional vampire story unusual. The hero is sexy and heroic with loyal friends, fighting the truly hateful antagonist alongside his charming sidekicks. The love story between the hero and the bright feisty heroine is touching, endearing and inspirational. Filled with intrigue, the story has all the components necessary for a tantalizing adventure."

~*Maureen Sevilla*

"Smith covers plenty of ground in her latest novel—the first in a series—infusing charming Southern flavor into an action-packed vampire tale. It's not the same old bloodsucking story, and Zacke and his merry band of vamp (and mortal) brothers are a fabulous addition."

~*Lauren Spielberg, Romantic Times Book Reviews*

"In KENSINGTON'S SOUL, author Faith V. Smith writes a wonderful romance between the conflicted vampire hero, Zacke, and the spunky mortal heroine, Miranda. The well drawn characters reveal loveable personalities, inner demons, and secret desires. Smith expertly paces the conflict and passion, blending supportive minor characters and a formidable antagonist into a satisfying climax. The Savannah setting provides a wonderful backdrop to the story's eeriness, history, and sensuousness. Readers will fall in love with Zacke and Miranda. Thank goodness you won't have to say goodbye to them after you close the book. KENSINGTON'S SOUL is the first in Smith's Bound by Blood series. Highly recommended."

~*Jennifer Akers, www.MyShelf.com*

Kensington's Soul

by

Faith V. Smith

Kensington's Soul

Cover Art by *Rae Monet*

The Wild Rose Press
PO Box 708
Adams Basin, NY 14410-0706
Visit us at www.thewildrosepress.com

Publishing History
First Black Rose Edition, 2009
Print ISBN 1-60154-553-3

Published in the United States of America

Dedication

I never thought when I researched *Kensington's Soul*
that my soul mate would fly away to Heaven.
I dedicate this book to Rick,
who believed in me and loved me
through the good times and bad.
To my darling daughter, Amanda,
who put up with my vents until this book was
finished. Love you baby!
A special thank you
to Callie Lynn Wolfe, my awesome editor
who loved Zacke and his friends as much as I did.
To Rae Monet who created the ultimate cover.
Also, a special thank you to Mark Johnson,
the awesome cover model, and to Casey Winters.
Your help and blessings mean so much!
To my family and friends thank you for your insight,
your time spent critiquing this work
and for the love you shared with me.
To God, I give you the praise and the glory!

Acknowledgments

Jim and Jennifer Salandi/The Ballastone Inn
The Pirate's House Restaurant
Savannah Carriage Tours

Through the ages and into the new millennium he craved peace. He'd given up on love, having lived centuries without the emotion, and he'd grown accustomed to being alone. Besides, no woman would ever care enough to look beyond the creature he'd become. His soul had been stolen from him but he'd take a stake through the heart before he'd allow them to steal his humanity.

Chapter One

Evil moved on the droplets of mist that hung in the night air as well as those bathing the ground. A skittish moon dipped behind a cloud and shrouded the tenement section of Savannah in darkness.

Newly formed shadows helped to obscure Zacke's silhouette as he leaned against the wall of a desecrated church. Sidewalk preachers once toiled here, trying to turn the tide against the dregs of evil. Now it served as a handy bolt-hole for drug dealers, prostitutes, and sometimes even murderers.

He rotated his shoulders in an effort to ease stiff muscles while he watched and waited for the depraved carriers of sin to come to him. If an inevitable battle ensued, then it would be welcomed. At least this time, good would triumph over evil.

His ears picked up the heartbeats of his prey, which hastened as they approached his hiding place. His nostrils burned with their stench.

The taller of the men glanced back as he passed the church and made the sign of the cross on his chest. The man's companion smirked but moved a bit faster than before, their combined footsteps resonating into soft thuds on the uneven pavement.

Zacke contained his disgust; the man lacked morals, but when frightened called upon a higher power.

Zacke smiled. It wouldn't be long now.

"Did you bring the money?"

The boy shuddered. "No, Jake. I couldn't get it. I need more time." His words sounded as if he had a hard time getting them out.

A few months back, Zacke had arrested the seventeen-year old runaway for prostitution. The D.A. dropped the charges after Matt agreed to help trap the pimps who once drugged and beat him into submission.

Zacke's presence at the meeting ensured another witness to back up Matt's story. He hoped to clear the boy's name and reunite him with his anxious parents.

Zacke turned his attention to Jake Archer, a well-known criminal element in Savannah.

"I told you what would happen if you didn't fill your quota this week. I paid you good money to get out there and drum up johns. Consider this a small taste of what you'll get in the future if you don't do your job." Jake motioned Tyler Brown forward.

The boy whimpered and moved back until a corner of the alley wall cradled his trembling body. When Matt dropped to his knees and started begging, Zacke curled his fingers into a fist. He hated the legalities that kept him from killing the sadistic animals before him. Words alone would not imprison Jake and Tyler for long; he needed to catch them with a weapon.

His nails lengthened into talons as he thought of the crimes both men had committed and how they had gotten away scot-free. He gulped the sultry night air in an effort to calm his rage and remember why he had chosen his particular career.

His vision blurred and then cleared into a blue haze magnifying the scene around him.

Tyler moved toward Matt and placed a serrated blade against his throat.

Zacke felt the low humming in his vocal chords before the growl formed on his lips. The twenty feet separating him from his prey fell away like inches. He caught Tyler's wrist and heard the bones crack. The dagger fell to the pavement with a clatter, almost drowning out the man's cry of pain. His hand moved to encircle Tyler's throat, changing his high pitch whine into guttural choking.

"How does it feel to fight with someone your own size? Would you like for me to finish the lesson you had planned for the boy?"

"I suggest you let him go before I blow a hole in your back."

Zacke allowed a grin of satisfaction to touch his lips. He kicked back with his right leg, still maintaining his hold on Tyler.

"Mother Mary—"

"I suggest you find another line of work after you get out of jail." Zacke applied a bit more pressure and then eased Tyler's limp body to the pavement.

He turned and faced Jake, who bent at the waist, gasping for breath, with his arms wrapped around his body. His mouth opened and closed like a fish on a hook, and his pristine suit now showed stains under the arms.

Zacke smiled before seizing Jake's chin.

"It's time you learned a lesson as well, Mr. Archer. The next time you want to practice your trade, it will be behind bars. I wonder how you'll like being on the receiving end for a change."

"Who are you?" The question came out in a rush of air.

"Someone who doesn't like you or your lifestyle."

The purple-tinged face looked up and sneered at Zacke. "You may not like my line of work, but I bet a thousand bucks would change your mind."

"You do realize that you're adding bribery to your already considerable list of charges?"

"But if you take the bribe, you'll have to let me go." Zacke released Jake who backpeddled a few feet.

Jake's eyes brimmed with derision and satisfaction. "So, do we have a deal?"

"Not in your lifetime or even mine. I suggest you save your plea bargains for court."

Zacke's stomach roiled as he thought of the sundry technicalities that could kick Jake loose and put him back on the streets of Savannah. How easy it would be to save the city the cost of a jail cell by killing the piece of offal and his cohort.

His chest expanded with the indecision and turmoil rocking within. Zacke shook his head to banish the temptation. He would not betray the creed he swore to uphold.

The air currents around Zacke moved. He caught Jake's wrist before it could complete its downward swing. A dagger, smaller and more expensive than the one Tyler had planned to use on Matt, shone in the waning light.

He resisted the urge to break bones this time. Jake needed to learn a stronger lesson than pain—a lesson he would not soon forget.

Zacke pulled Jake's arm forward until the knifepoint touched the skin beneath Zacke's collarbone. He forced the blade downward, opening a two-inch gash.

Jake's eyes flared.

Good! He had his attention. He then twisted Jake's wrist and cut a thin line into the man's paper white cheek. Next, he flung the weapon against the alley wall where it broke in half.

Jake's eyes bulged when Zacke took Jake's trembling hand and brought it up to touch the laceration. He moved the palm in circles before releasing it.

"Look at your hand, Jake. Your blood stains it like your sins stain your soul. Now look at my wound."

Zacke unbuttoned the top two buttons of his shirt, baring his skin and the self-inflicted wound. He watched confusion coat Jake's face as he gawked at Zacke's almost healed injury.

"How did you do that? What happened to the cut?"

Zacke's laughter filled the alleyway and sent rodents and felines scampering for cover.

Jake stumbled back. "What are you?"

"Something that exists only in your worst nightmares." Despite his anger, Zacke deliberately kept his tone soft. "It would be to your benefit to remember my words. If by some injustice you end up back on the streets, I'll be watching. And next time you step over the line, I will not hesitate to kill you."

Zacke's lips parted, showing incisors that lengthened in his rage. "You or your flunky will not be able to run or hide from me. Do you understand?"

Jake's eyes rolled back in his head, and he slumped to the ground.

Zacke turned and went to Matt who lay in a fetal position. Bile at what the boy had endured warred with the sympathy hindering his vocal chords. "You are safe now, Matt."

When the boy didn't respond, Zacke squatted beside him. The boy's whimper enraged Zacke. His hand shook with the emotion. His threat to kill Jake had been a scare tactic but right now, it would be so rewarding to tear him limb to limb. He took a deep calming breath and reached out to touch the back of Matt's head. He allowed his hand to linger for a moment before he eased Matt into sleep.

He regretted he couldn't do more.

A moment later, he rocked back on his heels and rose to his feet, unclipped the cell phone from his belt, and punched a button. It rang twice before a voice answered.

"Gideon Hawks, Savannah P.D."

"Gideon, I need a pickup in the alleyway behind St. John's church."

A sharp inhalation followed his words. "What

kind of pickup?"

"A P.D. van and one ambulance."

"Sheesh, don't tell me you're hurt."

Zacke chuckled at the note of disbelief in his partner's voice. "Sorry to disappoint you. I want the ambulance for Matt. He needs to be checked out before his folks pick him up. Besides, a shower, some food, and a good night's sleep in a clean bed won't hurt him."

"You got that right. The boy looks as undernourished as a baby chicken. Who do you need the van for?"

"Jake Archer and Tyler Edwards, his faithful servant."

"Oh man, you really did it. You actually caught their butts."

Gideon's chortle of delight was almost deafening.

"Yes I did and now, I'm heading home."

The click of his phone joined the soft breathing in the alleyway. Jake and Tyler remained down for the count, and Matt was probably enjoying his first restful sleep since he had hit the streets.

The wail of sirens broke into the night not long before he saw headlights. Only a moment passed before the rescue and police vehicles pulled alongside him. He nodded but didn't speak to the attendants.

"Great job, Zacke."

"Thanks, Joe. Make sure you get them to the station in one piece. We don't need them screaming police brutality—even though they'd deserve what they got. You also might want to have Tyler's wrist looked at. He had a little accident."

He watched the grinning uniformed officers escort a dazed and handcuffed Jake and his injured partner in crime to the van.

After the paramedics checked Matt's vital signs

and placed him on the stretcher, Zacke helped load him into the back of the emergency vehicle.

Soon he stood alone in the darkness. It had been a good night, the battle, although brief, satisfactory. But, Zacke knew his peace would be fleeting. He felt the darkness inside his heart and soul returning; evil lurked in the air like a nasty germ waiting to spread its contagious spores onto the inhabitants of Savannah. He might be a vampire, but there were men and women with darker sins staining their souls.

He shrugged his shoulders. Wickedness had outlived kings, queens, and presidents; it could wait a bit longer.

The earth dropped away as he took to the night sky and soared into its darkness.

Chapter Two

Thud, whop, bump.
"Shoot! Double shoot!"

Miranda James steered her late model Ford Mustang onto the exit ramp and prayed she wouldn't ruin the wheel rim. She should have had the tires changed before leaving Atlanta. The right one had been almost bald—now it was probably flat as a fritter.

Yep, she should have taken the time but in truth, she'd been running late. Not exactly a new trait for her, but tonight she wasn't in the mood for delays.

She decreased her speed and looked for a place to pull over. Maybe her luck was changing; straight ahead loomed an empty lot. Now if she could just get the tire changed, she might make it on time for orientation.

Two months earlier, she'd been offered the position of trauma surgeon at Savannah's newest hospital. It had taken her years to find such a dream job, and she intended to make the most of it.

Miranda parked her car in the first available space and then cut the motor. The small desolate lot adjoined an equally deserted gas station. Boards plastered shattered windows and broken bottles, scraps of paper, and garbage littered the sidewalk in bordering the storefront.

The sky sparkled powdery blue, but soon twilight would add a navy cast. She dismissed a shiver that had nothing to do with the car's air-conditioning.

She couldn't afford to wait any longer. She seriously doubted this part of town housed a knight in shining—or even tarnished—armor. Her cell phone rested on the passenger seat—useless without the battery charger Miranda had forgotten to pack. That left her one option.

She pressed the trunk's access button on the underside of the dash before unlocking her door and exiting the vehicle. The aggressive shove she gave the door to close it didn't relieve her anger, frustration, or apprehension.

Miranda moved to the back of the car and started a frantic shuffle and push. She dislodged her laptop, suitcase, and a box of books before finally unearthing the metal ring in the center of the trunk. She tugged on it but couldn't lift the lid of the storage compartment.

Dang it! She'd have to unload most of the back end to get the blasted spare and tire iron out.

Forty-five minutes later, just as the sun fell toward the horizon, she pulled her suit jacket's wrinkled sleeves down. The smudges of grease on the eggplant polyester came in second to the rip in her pantyhose and a giant stain of Lord-knew-what on her skirt. She forced her gaze from her ruined garments and glanced at her wristwatch.

Wonderful. She had thirty minutes to get to the hospital. Even if she flew like a jet, she'd never get there in time to change her clothes. Maybe her lab coat would hide the damage. She gave the trunk lid a hard slam before moving to the passenger door. Her gaze caught the stuff she had stacked on the backseat. No way did she have the energy to move everything. It would have to stay there until later.

A look at her dirt-encrusted nails made her cringe. Somewhere inside her suitcase lurked a nail file. If she found it now, she might be able to pry loose some of the crud before her appointment. As she reached for the door handle, a large dirty hand caught her wrist. Her heart stopped and then jumpstarted into an irregular rhythm.

"Hey pretty lady, what ya doing out here by yourself?"

Miranda turned slightly and then wished she hadn't. The fumes emanating from the man made her want to gag. Dirty socks would be refreshing compared to his breath and body odor.

She refused to panic. The man could be harmless. Maybe one of the homeless that roamed the city streets.

She summoned a slight smile from the vicinity of her feet—where her heart now resided. "I'm sorry. I didn't see you come up. Can I help you with something?" She managed a polite tone in spite of the fact she wanted to scream.

"Yeah, you could help me with something. Give me the keys to your car."

The keys to her car? Terror ripped through her limbs, turning her knees into liquid. Carjackers killed people. She fought a wave of dizziness. She focused on the backseat; her gaze picked out and then stayed riveted on her white lab coat.

Rage replaced her fear. Without her car, she couldn't get to the hospital. She'd miss her orientation, which could mean losing the job she coveted before she even had the chance to start it.

Miranda straightened to her full height and balanced her weight on her heels. She'd be daggone if she'd allow him to turn her already crappy day into a complete disaster.

She closed her eyes, breathed a prayer, and then rammed her left elbow into his solar plexus.

"Awww."

She jerked her hand free. She turned, faced her nightmare, and then smashed her hand into his nose. A bright spurt of scarlet finished off her suit.

Her self-congratulations, however, fell short when she saw a shadow in her peripheral vision.

"Look what she did to my nose, Harry."

Miranda ignored the whiny tone of her previous attacker and fought the urge to collapse. If she fainted, she couldn't keep her eyes on the knife her new assailant held.

"Stick it, Mikey. You deserved what you got. Letting a woman beat you up." Knife Man cut his eyes toward Mikey. "You shoulda waited for me."

Miranda heard the sneer in his voice.

"She was fixing to leave. I just wanted to stop her."

"Well, she ain't going nowhere now." Harry's gaze shifted back to Miranda. "You just don't know how to handle a real woman."

Try as she might she couldn't make herself disappear.

"And this here is a real woman." He followed his words with a quick perusal of her body.

What she wouldn't give to be able to twitch her nose like Samantha or blink like Jeannie. She bet they'd look real cute as pigs.

"I found a buyer for the car while the woman was cleaning your plow. They won't be ready for it for about an hour. That gives us plenty of time to have some fun."

Miranda cursed the blasted organ in her chest when it threatened to run away and leave her behind.

"We get to play with her?"

"Yep. And after we have our fun, we'll leave her body for the cops to find."

Miranda hid her trembling hands behind her back; her stomach churned and nausea coated her throat and tongue. She couldn't be sick—at least not yet. She forced her cotton candy legs to move and edged to her right. She needed to get around the car to the driver's side. The keys were still in the ignition. If she could just get in the car, she could hit the automatic door lock and drive off.

Harry stalked her movements as she rounded the back of the Mustang. When her back pressed against the ridge of the trunk, she exulted in the fact she had made it halfway to her goal. A glimmer of hope ripened in her chest. The heel of her shoe slipped on what felt like loose gravel, and she looked down.

A mistake—the knifepoint now pressed against her throat. Her breath smothered in her lungs. Her imagination went into overdrive. She could smell the metallic odor of her own blood; she saw the crimson flow as it poured from her slashed throat.

"Did you really think I planned on letting you just waltz away, lady?"

Miranda hoped her silence would mask the horror stinging every nerve in her body.

"Sorry to disappoint you, but the only dancing you'll be doing is with me." He made a repugnant gesture with his tongue, accompanied by several thrusts of his pelvis.

Her knees didn't ask for permission before they buckled. Filthy hands clawing at her waist preempted a close call with the pavement. The shove he gave her almost snapped her backbone in two as the lock on the top edge of the trunk bit into her spine.

The leer on his lips—which were moving way too fast toward her own—caused the fast food she had wolfed down to make itself known for the second time.

When he moved back without kissing her, she hoped he had changed his mind. And when he removed his grip from her waistband, she felt giddy with relief.

The first brush of her skirt being pushed up her

14

thighs dissipated that hope. Fear returned two-fold; her insides quaked and her limbs trembled anew.

His hand edged under her skirt and touched the lace trim of her panties. She closed her eyes to shut out what would happen next. A light breeze caressed another area of skin that should have remained covered. She opened her eyes in time to see the knife shear off the last button of her jacket. She held her breath when he slid the blade beneath the lace of her bra. She willed her chest to cease all movement, as he stroked her nipple with his thumb.

Miranda's worst nightmare of being chased by Freddie Kruger didn't compare to what she felt right now. She willed herself to faint, something she'd never done before in her life, but she was denied total oblivion. She wouldn't be able to escape the violation of her body with an old-fashioned swoon.

Instead, she would have a front row seat to her own rape and execution.

A feral growl sounded off to the right. Her attacker released her and moved several few feet away.

A blur of black streaked from behind the gas station. Miranda caught back her scream as the dark shape leapt at Harry.

She blinked to clear the tears and Savannah sweat from her eyes. A man stood where the shadow of darkness had been. She watched as he disarmed both her assailants before handcuffing them together.

Only his profile was evident as he spoke into a cell phone. She couldn't hear his words, but the rumble of his voice caressed her ears and helped ease some of her fright.

He finished his call and turned to face her. Miranda tried in vain to pull her slack lips together. Her mother always preached it was rude to stare, but her mother never warned her she'd meet a man like this.

His above average height complimented a mouth-watering build. Hair, as black as a raven's wing, hung well below his collar, and rested against the impossible broad width of his shoulders. His waist tapered into lean hips.

She had to remind herself to breathe. Her gaze traveled the length of his denim-clad legs to the tops of his leather sneakers before she allowed herself the pleasure of looking at his face once again.

The ice-blue spheres staring back at her sent a fresh chill coursing through her already frigid body, but the smile he gave her warmed her considerably.

Good gracious. Even his teeth were perfect— although his canines seemed a bit longer than the others. The sensual cast of his lips sent additional heat fanning through her blood and finished thawing her cold limbs. She must be delusional from the attack. She checked her pulse—it was within normal limits. Although she felt a bit dizzy, her vision seemed fine. But no way a man could possibly look this good.

He moved so swiftly, Miranda knew she must have been lost in her thoughts. One second he was several feet away, and the next he stood right in front of her.

"Are you all right?"

A simple enough question, but she had a hard time forcing a reply through her suddenly dry lips. "I think so. Thank you. He would have raped me if you hadn't stopped him."

"Or worse, Dr. James."

Miranda tried to still her trembling hands. "How do you know my name and who are you?"

For a moment, the man standing so near seemed taken back by her questions.

"My apologies for not introducing myself. Zacke Kensington. I'm a detective with the Savannah P.D.

My partner ran your plates through the Georgia DMV and gave me your name."

Miranda pulled the remnants of her jacket tighter to hide her exposed skin from his gaze and a night that had suddenly turned glacial. "Could I see some identification, Detective? Don't partners usually work together?"

"Forgive me." Mr. Tall, Dark, and Hot pushed a hand inside a snug jean pocket and pulled out a piece of plastic.

Miranda looked it over and felt her cheeks heat. "I'm sorry, but this is a new town for me and after what..."

The detective slid the ID back into its receptacle. "It's I who am sorry, Dr. James. I should have thought. I should also have told you that my partner is back at the station, doing paperwork on a case."

The detective touched Miranda's shoulder and warmth seeped into her chilled bones. "I regret I didn't get here sooner. I'll call an ambulance."

"I don't need an ambulance and unless you have supernatural powers, I don't think you could have known ahead of time I would be attacked." Miranda forced a smile. She wondered about his mixed old-world speech and sporadic use of modern day contractions. "However, I do need to get to the Savannah Trauma Hospital. I'm already late."

A quizzical expression appeared in his blue gaze.

"I should have been there thirty minutes ago for orientation."

The detective's expression remained puzzled.

"I was just hired as a trauma surgeon. And I really need to change my clothes."

"I'm sure the hospital will take into consideration what has happened. I'll be happy to drive you and explain the circumstances to your employer."

Miranda looked around but didn't see any other

vehicles in or around the vacant lot. "I appreciate that, Detective, but it's not necessary." She motioned toward the handcuffed pair. "Don't you need to stay here with them?" And can you tell me if you will have to impound my car? And if you do, how do I get to the hospital? Is your car parked somewhere else? I don't see it."

A smile touched lips that she found utterly sinful.

"No, to your first question. There will be a wagon by for these two in a few minutes. As for your other questions, since there wasn't any damage to your car, you can keep it. But, I will need your version of what happened. As first officer on the scene, I can fill in some of the report but there are a few details only you can supply. I am on foot patrol, so I don't have a car."

"Oh, okay. And about the report, can it wait? I really do need to get to the hospital." Miranda stepped away from Detective Kensington and staggered.

"Dr. James, my driving you wasn't just a suggestion."

Miranda found herself leaning against the detective as he walked her around the back of the Mustang to the passenger door. After the near rape, she should feel revulsion by his touch but she welcomed the protective gentleness he displayed while he assisted her into the car. Her body was beginning to throb in places she knew would be black and blue come morning.

After closing her door, the detective moved around to the driver's side. He adjusted the seat before he gave her a smile that brightened the dark interior of the car.

The ride took only a few moments. Detective Kensington asked a few pointed questions about the attack and then remained silent until they arrived.

The detective didn't pull into the front entrance of the hospital but circled around the building to the Emergency zone and parked the car in one of the visitor's spaces.

He used the same gentle touch he had before to help her from the car. She bit back a gasp as he scooped her into his arms. "I can walk you know."

Her rescuer ignored her comment, bumped the door closed with his hip and carried her to the Emergency Room entrance. Instead of continuing inside, he sat Miranda down carefully on a low wall buffering the drive. The man then lifted her hand to his mouth and kissed it. Lightning raced up her arm, sending shock waves into every corpuscle.

Subsequent to the last hour, any sane woman would be quaking in her shoes. And even though she probably should be frightened, the warmth of his touch set off emotions of a different type but still... "I really think that..."

His lips caressed her forehead. For a brief moment, after the detective pulled back, Miranda thought his gaze held regret before his lips covered hers. White-hot heat scorched her body. A faint wave of dizziness assaulted her. Miranda's breathing slowed, her eyes closed, and she fell into a tunnel of oblivion.

****

Malevolent eyes glowed red in the darkness. She had found Lord Kensington again. After transforming him centuries before, he'd refused her offer to share eternity together. He belonged to her. And she'd destroy anyone who stood in her way.

Chapter Three

Zacke opened his eyes but made no effort to leave his bed. Heavy drapes covered the windows, hiding twilight shadows that painted the sky. He shuttered his eyes and concentrated on the air around him before his mind probed further.

The only vibrations he picked up came from the surf that pounded the beach a few miles away. At the moment, the world around him remained undisturbed and that tranquility spoke volumes. The sanctity of his home had remained intact during his unholy sleep.

Most days, even in the superficial death sleep that claimed him after sunrise, he continued to be aware of what went on around him though today had been different. His slumber, so deep that without the safety spell, which he preferred to call a prayer, he would have been vulnerable to any who sought to do him harm.

Zacke sat up and then slid to the edge of his king-size bed. Scrolled posts rose at each corner and held a canopy, but no bed curtains. The heavy draperies had reminded him of the shroud in which he'd been buried in centuries past.

His days of sleeping in a crypt were over.

Zacke discovered the three-story brownstone he now lived in by accident. He and Gideon had been checking a lead in a drug case when he spotted the vacant house. The "For Sale" sign in the weed-choked grass drew his attention.

After a tour with the anxious-to-please real estate agent, Zacke had purchased it. A smart move.

The old cemetery he had used for sleeping was in the process of being renovated as a historical landmark.

The previous owners of his new home had refurbished the entire house before the husband's job had transferred them out of state. The master bath had been an ingenious design. A sunken tub and glassed-in shower sat in the center of the room.

Zacke enjoyed the feel of hot water as it hit his body. The numerous jets embedded in strategic spots helped to relieve job tension but did not alleviate the disgust he felt for himself and mankind, in general.

A revulsion and rage grew even more relevant since the night before.

Scumbags had put their hands on Miranda. Restraint and years of training his mind prevented him from killing them. Last night he'd felt a crack in the cold core of his heart because of Miranda. He'd kissed her and still didn't know why. Or for that matter, why he denied himself an elicit taste of the sweetness he knew he would find if he deepened the kiss.

Centuries had passed since he'd allowed himself to experience lust. In his younger days, his women had been willing and with considerable experience in the bedchamber.

Miranda James was an innocent.

He felt it in her body language when he kissed her hand. He'd also read it in her thoughts. The beautiful doctor was as virginal as a newborn babe, an old-fashioned trait that endeared her to him even more.

Still, he should not have kissed her. Not her hand or her lips. The woman had almost been raped for Heaven's sake! But Miranda's courage and sensual looks awakened a sexual appetite he'd buried long ago, an appetite that could feed his thirst for blood. It could also threaten his vow of never hurting another innocent. His urges must be kept in check, or his hunger could prove dangerous.

Zacke's nails bit into his palms as he contemplated what would happen if Gabriella became aware of his error in judgment. Thankfully, his life had been free of her presence for decades. Hopefully she was dead, for if she still breathed, she would strike out and make Miranda suffer before she died a horrendous death—if death proved to be the end of her punishment.

He ground his teeth together at the thought of the tortures Miranda would suffer at Gabriella's hands. He swiped his tongue against incisors grown long and tasted the sweetness of his own blood.

A reminder that he needed to feed.

He took the immortal way out, used his mind to dry his body and transferred naked to the kitchen. He could eat as mortals did but not often and only particular foods.

His digestive system also allowed him to enjoy an occasional soft drink, tea, or wine, but he limited his intake. He preferred to save those luxuries of a past life for social events—also a rarity for him.

Gideon knew the truth of Zacke's unwanted heritage, but pledged to keep his secret. Other mortals might not be as lenient if they knew such a creature walked amongst them. Zacke had neither the time nor inclination to deal with a populace stirred to violence by what they couldn't understand.

A vial of liquid set on a shelf in the almost empty refrigerator. He gave it a gentle shake and moved to the microwave—a clever invention in his opinion. Once the vial lay inside the cubicle, he programmed the numbers on the front display.

While his dinner heated, he took a 60cc syringe and a 20-gauge needle from the cabinet over the stove and used his teeth to tear the cellophane. The timer sounded, and he retraced his steps to retrieve the life, or in his case, death-sustaining fluid.

His incisors lengthened, and his nails grew into talons as the liquid filled the plastic tube. He pressed the plunger lightly to remove the air bubbles. His rapid heartbeat ran a poor second to the dizziness that made his head spin as he prepared to inject the blood into his jugular vein.

The prick of the needle stung before the sweetness he craved raced through his veins. Although not the given mode for his kind, the injection achieved the same results. It would stave off the desire to drain a mortal's blood. It was also better than feeding on animals. Something he'd detested but had to do until the last few years. Zacke could have swallowed the human blood but his first taste after he had been transformed had been disastrous.

A stray drop ran down his neck. He caught the crimson morsel on his finger. The red color blurred before his eyes as he remembered a day long ago. A day when his blood stained the cold, hard ground.

Zacke disposed of the syringe with more force than necessary before walking to the sink. He pulled back the curtains covering the window. The sky, a masterpiece of orange and crimson, signaled the coming night and his need to get to work.

He transferred himself back to the third floor to get dressed.

Briefs, a navy T-shirt, and a pair of jeans from the closet were a thought and then a reality as they covered his body. The sneakers hiding under his bed received a brief glance before encompassing his feet.

He tied his hair back with a leather band and descended the stairs. He didn't stop to lock the door, but he did mumble his habitual safety spell. The spell also came in handy for protecting mortals as well as property.

He cast a look of regret at his new toy, a black convertible. Although fast, his mode of travel would be faster. He needed to talk to Gideon before they hit the streets.

Cloaking his body, he took to the sky; exultation enveloped him when the night wind caressed his face. He welcomed the clouds, a reminder of a higher being's handiwork, dancing above him.

His destination, the brick building that housed the police department, appeared below. Marked and unmarked patrol cars lined the parking lot. His gaze searched and found Gideon's truck as his partner exited the vehicle. Zacke watched Gideon, with a perception that still amazed him, raise his hand to the Savannah skyline and wave before entering the building.

Zacke dove for the ground but pulled up from his dive. He ignored his conscience and duty, then turned his body in the direction of Savannah's Trauma Hospital.

****

Miranda tied off the last stitch on her third patient of the day. This one had been a ten on a one to ten scale, ten being the easiest. A multi-car pileup on I-16 right outside of Savannah had kept her busy after her morning orientation.

She was grateful her new boss had waved away her apologies for missing yesterday's meeting. After making sure Miranda was okay, she had instructed her to report to the hospital at six that morning.

Her new position entailed being on hand in the emergency room for triage as well as surgical duties. The twelve hours she'd been there felt like twenty-four. Her back felt like it needed to be stretched and her feet swelled more each moment she stood on them.

A perforated liver and an amputated leg had kept her in surgery for hours, but both patients would survive. She had managed five minutes at midday for a sandwich and a diet cola before receiving a page to return to the surgery suite.

However, her caseload had helped to dispel some of last night's memories, at least the ones she recalled.

With the latest and hopefully the last surgery of the day behind her, Miranda stripped off her gloves and washed up at the deep sink in the prep room. When finished, she exited backward into the hospital corridor, straight into a solid object.

"Sorry. I should have been watching where I was going."

She considered that enough of an apology and didn't bother to look up. She needed to get to her office to write up her surgical notes. After that, she hoped to beat a hasty retreat to her apartment. She sidestepped around whomever she had bumped into.

A hand gently caught her arm, halting her attempted escape.

"Look, I said I was sorry. I really need to—"

The hand moved, cupped her chin, and tilted her head back.

The air left her lungs in a whoosh.

Her rescuer of the previous night held her captive in more ways than one. What was he doing here? And why did he have to look as mouthwatering as a piece of pecan pie?

While she, of course, looked like something the cat had dragged in.

Life was so unfair! Twice in less than twenty-four hours, she managed to find herself in the company of a man that made the most handsome movie star look like day-old bread and both times, she had been at a disadvantage. Not like it mattered. He would never be interested in her. They had only just met, and she certainly hadn't been at her best. Besides, even if by some remote possibility he was pursuing her, she didn't have time for a man in her life.

"How did you get up here? The O.R. wing is off limits to non-medical personnel." *Oh great, Miranda, snarl at the man who saved your life. Way to go.*

"My job does have some privileges."

The look he gave her with those extraordinary eyes of his made her weak in the knees. The smile that accompanied it could have restored vision to the three blind mice with its brightness.

"They told me downstairs you were in surgery. I planned on leaving a note at the desk but decided not to. I thought I would see if you were finished for the day."

The detective's hand, which he had lowered after her oh-so-rude question, moved to the small of her back. She'd never felt the need to be guided by a man, but she actually enjoyed the feel of his palm against her spine as they walked toward the bank of elevators.

When the doors closed and they were alone, she pressed the button for the fourth floor. Only then did she glance toward her companion. His eyes were still a deep azure, but they didn't glow with the same intensity she remembered from the night before.

Miranda pulled her gaze away from his face. She really should stop staring at the man. "So, you never said what brought you here."

"You did."

"Me?" Her body melted at the thought he wanted to see her, but her mind reeled her insane hope back in. "Did you need something more concerning last night? Do I need to what—swear out a complaint?"

The smile that creased his lips deepened, shooting a tingle of awareness straight to her center core. The man could make a lot of money doing toothpaste commercials. Not to mention the sex appeal oozing off the man was positively dangerous.

"No, swearing out a complaint is not necessary.

Since I witnessed the attack, I filed the charges."

"Well, then I don't understand..."

"I am here because I wanted to see *you*."

Miranda closed her mouth and strived for a tone that would not convey the damage his words caused her nervous system. Again, her mind threw caution at her like an amber traffic light. She chastised the persistent optimism. She couldn't attract a man like Detective Kensington.

"Look, Detective, I appreciate you stopping by, but there's no need to check on me. I'm fine."

"My name's Zacke, and I'm not here just to check on you. I wanted to ask if you would have dinner with me."

"Why?" Miranda lowered her gaze to the floor. She didn't want to see pity in his eyes, but what other reason could he have for asking her out?

"Because I admire your courage, and I would like to get to know you better."

Miranda raised her head. The detective appeared earnest.

"I'm off this weekend. We could go out Saturday night if you have no plans."

"Uh, yes, that sounds good. Just so you know, I'm on call and might have to leave if I get beeped." She looked closely into his eyes to see if he might change his mind.

Zacke's eyes darkened, and she received a more close-up view of his irises when his head dipped forward and his face drew even with hers.

My word, did he mean to kiss her again? She loved the idea but didn't relish a repeat fainting spell. And that would probably happen. The man's lips were lethal, no matter where he put them and with fatigue beating a refrain inside her body, Miranda doubted her defense mechanisms would be any help against his touch.

Even if she wanted them to.

When Zacke only brushed a strand of hair out of her eyes, Miranda felt the boil of disappointment churn inside her stomach.

"I'm on call, too. I'm willing to chance it if you are."

Miranda must have nodded her head, but it seemed like minutes before she could get her mouth to open. "Do you need my address?"

His soft laughter warmed her suddenly chilled limbs. For the life of her, it seemed every time the man showed up, her body temperature either dropped to subzero or heated to a thermal blast.

"I have it already, from when we ran your license plate. But if you want to tell me again, I'll be glad to listen."

The teasing glint in his eyes was contagious. As she watched, the amazing man bent slightly at the waist in an old-fashioned bow.

"Wow, I don't think I've ever seen anyone do that except in a movie."

Zacke's body tensed and with a quick snap, he straightened to his full height. Had she hurt his feelings? Offended him? She hoped not.

The elevator lurched to a stop, forestalling her apology.

"I'll pick you up at seven Saturday night."

Zacke's words broke the silence Miranda's runaway mouth had evoked.

The opening elevator doors drew her attention; she turned back to voice an apology.

He was gone!

The man had simply disappeared. Impossible. He couldn't just vanish into thin air. Miranda moved forward until she stood square in the middle of the doorway. The doors tried to close, and she gave them a hard shove before doing a quick hop, skip, and jump out into the corridor.

She searched both directions of the hallway but

saw no trace of the missing detective. His Houdini act posed another question on her list of what puzzled her about the mouth-watering man.

****

Zacke, his mood a blend of anger and excitement, took to the night sky again. Miranda's agreement to go out with him filled him with jubilation. Not only did he want to spend the evening with her, he wanted to taste her lips, strip her naked, and plunge himself into her virginal body.

His teeth lengthened with the intensity of his passion, and that simple act further fired his anger. He should have ripped the useless appendage inside his mouth out. A date with Miranda should be taboo. He knew better; any contact with him could throw her right into Gabriella's claws. His nemesis wouldn't hesitate to tear an innocent to shreds— figuratively and literally.

Gabriella had awakened. He'd felt the air vibrate with her evil while he chatted with Miranda. Zacke's hope she had met her death, burned to ashes, and died with the realization.

His blood quickened with dread—the city he called home had been free of others of his kind for over a decade.

This new threat to his turf had caused him to go into full alert in the elevator. But his abrupt exit, although justified, had not been worthy of Miranda.

Zacke descended undetected to the dark alley behind the station. He made his way through the back door, passing several cells filled with some of Savannah's undesirables and arrived in the office he shared with Gideon to find his partner on the phone.

"282 East Savannah Drive? Yep, got it! He's here and we're on our way." Gideon dropped the phone back into its cradle.

"Where are we going?"

"And a good evening to you too, Partner. You're

late. I saw your sorry carcass fly over more than an hour ago."

Gideon's lips smiled but his eyes looked somber. "Forget about me. What's happened?"

"It's bad Zacke—*really* bad. A couple of teenagers making out in the alley on East Savannah stumbled over a woman's mutilated corpse about fifteen minutes ago. The kids are on their way to the hospital; they're pretty shook up."

Gideon fiddled with the pencil in his hand. "Dr. D's at the scene but says he won't touch anything until we get there."

"Any details?"

The pencil snapped in two. "Not yet. All I got out of the captain is the body looked like a pack of wolves had mauled it. There ain't any wolves in Savannah. Wild dogs, maybe. What do you think?"

Zacke felt a coldness seep into his bones that had nothing to do with his chemical makeup. "I think we need to get over there and find out."

****

"I can't be definite on the time of death yet. I need to get the body back to the lab and do an autopsy."

Zacke watched as Delbert Stewart, forensic coroner for the city of Savannah, turned the body over. The corpse wouldn't have to be opened up to look inside—someone or something had already done it.

Dr. D raised eyes that held more than a bit of shock—something unusual for the experienced M.E. His usually flushed face looked pale, and his hands shook when he stripped off his gloves.

Zacke sympathized with the good doctor. This was not a scene for the weak of heart, mind, or stomach. The gruesome sight of eviscerated wounds had already resulted in his partner losing his dinner.

The violence enacted here had been malicious

and without a shred of conscience.

The paramedics loaded the body onto the stretcher and into the medical examiner's van. Zacke returned Dr. D's wave and then walked to where Gideon sat slumped against the tailgate of his truck.

"You okay, Partner?"

Gideon stayed silent. His face had taken on the appearance of cotton; the horror of the last few minutes filled his dilated pupils.

"You want me to drive?"

"Not in this lifetime or even the next." Gideon slowly peeled himself off his metal resting place.

He still trembled, but Zacke felt relieved that his question had galvanized Gideon into acting more like himself. "Your faith in my driving ability wounds me."

"Yeah well, tell it to someone who cares. Even sick, I wouldn't want to risk a repeat of last time. You almost drove us off the Savannah Dock. Didn't ya mama teach you not to drive like you had wings?"

Zacke chose to overlook the subtle reference to what most mortals thought vampires were. "Point taken, but remember, where I come from cars had yet to be invented."

"Oh jeez, Zacke. I'm sorry. I forgot for a moment."

Zacke's laughter rang hollow to his own ears. "That I'm almost as old as dirt? It's not important. We have more imperative things to worry about."

Zacke's jaw clenched as he reviewed the poor woman's body in his mind. He shook off the morbid thoughts of how she must have suffered before dying. "Listen, I want to swing by the hospital for another look at the body before we go back to the station and write up the report."

If possible, Gideon's face blanched even more; his mouth opened and closed a couple of times.

"Tell you what, I'll wing the trip to the morgue

myself, if you handle the captain."

"You know, I think I feel better already. I'll talk to Captain Myers, and you go see Dr. D." Gideon's words rushed forth in a panic.

Zacke's laughter wasn't forced this time. He welcomed it and its effectiveness in dispelling a bit of the morbid air clinging to the alley.

****

High above the Heavens a shriek rent the silent night. The satisfaction in the kill appeased her but disappointment prevailed at Lord Kensington's uncommon reaction. Why hadn't he shown more emotion? Her former lover hated to see mortals die. No matter. She would leave another and another until he lost his calm manner. She had plenty of time, and it would be amusing to pit wits with Zachary. He had been the only man in her centuries of existence to offer more than a token battle of resistance.

Her laughter seared the darkness, its macabre sound causing a shiver to cross the shoulders of angels and mortals alike.

Chapter Four

Miranda smoothed the navy material of her sundress over her hips. Her breath escaped in a sigh of relief. All she had to do now was add earrings and brush her hair. A good thing, too. Her last trauma case had taken longer than expected.

She needed a break from the hospital; the week had been full of death as well as jubilation over the patients who had survived. She needed the time out, but she felt the beginnings of a migraine waiting to happen. She didn't know if it was from nerves or fatigue. If not for the significant fact Zachary Kensington had saved her life, she would just call and cancel their date.

No! That was a lie.

She might be tired and not quite herself, but she wasn't dead. The man made her heart beat so fast it could break speed records, and one look from his unique eyes made her insides drown in a sea of want. He'd certainly left his mark on her.

For the life of her, she didn't know why he hadn't actually kissed her for real and wasn't sure if that was a good thing or not. Most of her relationships with men had fizzled after one or two dates. It had taken her a while, but Miranda had learned that a life without male companionship definitely bit big time, but it was better than getting her heart broken. Something that Detective Kensington could probably do without any effort at all.

The doorbell chimed and Miranda jumped, causing her earring to fall to the floor. She dropped to her knees to search for it amidst the chaos her quick change had caused.

"Ouch!" She removed the metal post attached to her kneecap and pulled the long skirt out from under her knees then tried to get to her feet. She toppled backward narrowly missing the box of books she needed to unpack.

A few seconds later, she inserted the earring and clipped the errant post in place. Another hasty glance in the mirror did nothing to reassure her. She grimaced at the face looking back at her. She didn't look like the type of woman a man like Zacke would go out with.

She wondered if he regretted his moment of insanity.

****

Zacke kept his eyes off the door as he waited. He could use his gifts to probe Miranda's thoughts. Lord knew he wanted to, but he would not spy on her. Instead, he'd play by the rules he had learned in his birth century. He wanted to see her as a mortal man would see his woman for their first date; as he had seen the women he'd courted centuries before. Not as a voyeur or through the eyes of the loathsome creature he had become.

He heard the rattle of a chain and then a bolt being drawn back. The creak of the door signaled his wait had ended.

His first glance of Miranda more than made up for his hard fought self-control. The casual disarray of her auburn hair twisted seductively against the cream of her shoulders. The material of her navy dress grazed the slight swell above the bodice and clung to her slender curves. Her eyes mirrored the hue of the material, beckoning to him like a twilight sky. A soft peach that matched the polish on her short nails colored her lips. Did she know what power she held in her grasp?

"Hi, Zacke, sorry it took me so long to answer the door."

Her words came out in a breathless rush, brushing the air between them. The sweetness of her exhalation tormented him. "You have no reason to apologize. I owe you one for leaving so abruptly the other evening."

"I wondered where you went, but that's okay. Would you like to come in for a minute?"

Miranda looked everywhere but at him as she waited for his answer.

"Actually, I made dinner reservations. We should leave now."

She hesitated before giving a slight nod. The shadows of relief in her eyes made him wonder if the thought of being alone with him made her nervous. Maybe he should have given her more time after her recent ordeal.

Zacke moved back, and Miranda stepped out into the hallway. She locked the door and then twisted the knob to make sure it was secure before looking up at him in expectation.

The hand he placed on her spine as they walked down the dimly lit hallway trembled slightly. The woman affected him in a bad way. It would be Heaven to touch her and Hell trying to keep his hands from caressing her curves.

The Savannah skyline resembled an artist's canvas of colors. Blue, almost the same shade as her eyes, mingled with seductive purple and tawny pink. Zacke knew no earthly artist could hope to rival the creator's masterpiece.

"This is your car?"

Zacke chuckled at the awe in Miranda's voice as she gaped at the two-door Lexus SC. "Yes, do you like it?"

"It's awesome. Is it brand new?"

"I bought it a couple of months ago."

Zacke opened the passenger door. He'd not bothered to lock the car. His safety spell would prevent mortals from stealing or damaging his new plaything.

Miranda drew her skirt up as she slid onto the seat and then eased her bare legs inside the car. He silently and vehemently cursed the demons hiding in his loins, tempting him to follow the swathe of material with his hands.

"So, uh, you never said where we're going for dinner."

Her tone had reverted to apprehension. Zacke wished he could just take her into his arms and reassure her she had nothing to fear from him.

If only he could be certain of that himself.

"I made reservations at the *Pirate's House* on East Broad. I thought you would enjoy the historical atmosphere."

"That's great. It's on my to-do list. When I visited Savannah a few years ago, I couldn't get a reservation."

Miranda's eyes glowed when she turned to look at him. "Did you know that Captain Flint is supposed to have died upstairs at the Pirate's House when it was a tavern? And it's rumored his ghost is still there?"

"Are you telling me you believe in ghosts?"

She arched an auburn brow. "Of course not, but it is sort of exciting to think the place could be haunted."

A shard of electricity engulfed his hand as he caught hers. His amusement faded. Would she show that same look of excitement if he disclosed he was a creature destined to roam the earth forever? He grimaced and then cursed silently when the glow faded from her eyes and her face took on a look of uncertainty.

"Is everything okay? I tend to run off at the

mouth on subjects that interest me. I—"

"You did nothing." Zacke searched for an explanation. "I was thinking about a case."

"I guess it didn't turn out like you wanted. I mean by the look on your face."

"No, but sometimes they don't."

"Do you want to talk about it? Sometimes that helps."

"No, but thanks." He forced a smile to hide the repulsion he felt over his current case. Not one shred of evidence had turned into a concrete lead.

Zacke slowed the car and then braked at the next traffic light. A quick turn put them on the street adjacent to the restaurant. Relief beat a tattoo in his chest; hopefully, he could keep his mind strictly on Miranda.

****

Miranda's nervousness disappeared during dinner. Zacke queried her preferences and then ordered. Savannah crab cakes, served with mixed baby greens and tomato chutney to begin with, followed by the house salad. She'd chosen the honey pecan fried chicken, and Zacke a New York strip loin cooked rare. The baked potatoes and homemade bread that accompanied their entrees had been to die for. She polished off every morsel on her plate. When she questioned Zacke about his lack of appetite, he cited a late lunch.

"Would you care for some dessert?" Zacke's eyes held laughter as he beckoned the waiter.

"Are you kidding me? I'm stuffed." Miranda's laughter flowed. "I ate as if it were my first and last meal. Honestly, Zacke, the food was fantastic. Thank you."

Zacke reached out, captured her hand, and then lifted it to his lips. The kiss he placed on the inside of her palm before releasing it singed her skin. The desire she had put on the back burner flooded back—stronger than before.

"It is I who should thank you for a lovely evening."

Her face positively stung with heat at his words.

"You have no idea, do you, that you turned the heads of half the men here when we walked in?"

"Don't be ridiculous. I'm just ordinary."

Laughter escaped from Zacke's insanely seductive lips and the gaze from his equally seductive eyes scorched her with its intensity.

"You are not ordinary, Miranda James. You're one of the most stunning women I have ever seen. You are seduction bundled with an ingenuity and innocence that is so rare these days."

His words staggered her. His opinion differed vastly from what she thought of herself. Sure, she'd dated off and on since she turned sixteen. Who hadn't? But nothing serious and nothing remotely sexual. The boys and then men she had gone out with had never even tried to get her into bed. Now, four years past thirty-something, this incredibly sexy man thought she was desirable.

It had to be the wine. She must have misunderstood him.

"No, you heard me correctly, Miranda. I meant what I said. I want you as a man wants a woman."

Miranda's heart stopped. Had she spoken her thoughts out loud? Zacke leaned over and pressed his lips to hers, silencing her question before she could ask it. The kiss, soft and gentle, left her bewildered; it felt almost platonic.

"I want you, but there is a lot we need to learn about one another before I take you to bed."

The look he gave her sent a warning galloping through her nervous system; he reminded her of a predator on the prowl.

"But when I do, I assure you it will be something we both will remember."

****

An hour later Miranda stood inside her apartment—alone. She wasn't quite sure what had happened, but Zacke had walked her to the door, and after another brief touch of his lips, he left.

He'd started to withdraw from her after receiving a phone call on his cell. His words had been clipped when speaking to whomever, but he'd been politeness itself when apologizing for the interruption—almost too polite.

She kicked off her shoes and flopped on the threadbare sofa. The starkness of her still unpacked apartment struck her anew. Loneliness gaped at her from every inch of the cluttered space. Her new home had come furnished and it was close to the hospital—which she wanted. Her first thought on viewing the third-story, two-bedroom flat had been it would be more than ample for her needs. Now the place felt too pocketsize to hold both her and her thoughts.

Zachary Kensington and what he did to her with his words and actions didn't relate to any experience she'd ever had. The man seemed to be able to read her mind. Were her thoughts that transparent? Did she have a large scarlet V—for-virgin—engraved on her forehead? Was that why he didn't kiss her for real?

Miranda slipped down and rested her head on the cushion that matched the striped pattern of the sofa. The two glasses of wine she had consumed with dinner ran sluggishly through her veins. She felt both mellow and sleepy.

With any luck, she might get a full night's sleep without a call from the hospital. And if she couldn't have Zacke staked out next to her on the couch, then she could dream about him.

Or maybe she would just dream about the luscious dessert menu at the restaurant. Yes, dreaming about sweets would be a lot less dangerous then dreaming about Detective Kensington.

****

"This time the body was left in the Old Bonaventure Cemetery. The groundskeeper heard a scream and when he went to investigate, he found our victim."

Gideon's words were low as they walked out of the station together, but Zacke heard the warning behind them. A mausoleum at Bonaventure had been his place of residence before buying his home. There would be numerous police personnel on foot combing the area for evidence.

"They won't find anything of mine. I travel light." Zacke tried to calm Gideon's fears.

"How can you joke about this, Zacke? If one shred of anything is found to tie you to that cemetery, there will be a whole slew of questions."

"Nothing will lead them to me. Now give me the blow-by-blow on time and cause of death. Has Dr. D been to the scene yet?"

"No, he claimed no way this side of Hell would he go out there unless you and I meet him at the gates of the cemetery."

****

Hell was exactly what the woman had been through before perishing from the gaping hole in her chest. Zacke's stomach churned; a reminder of why he seldom ate food.

"Lord in Heaven!" Gideon managed to groan before staggering away.

Only Zacke and the M.E. remained beside the body. After a hasty examination of the torso and face, the doctor sat back on his haunches, his pallor decidedly worse than a few days before. This time his gaze held both anger and shock.

"Who in all that is holy would do this?"

"I think that's your answer. *No one* with a shred

of holiness could do this."

Blood formed a dark viscous circle under the victim's back.

"I'm going to take pics back at the lab, but I can tell you this much, her heart is missing." Dr. D shook his head, then rose and walked toward the paramedics.

The implications of what Delbert Stewart revealed galvanized Zacke's brain. Both crimes in the last week had been horrific, but this one bordered on sadistic. Even with his unholy curse, he would not mutilate a body in this way. Something about the murders set off warning signals. His uneasiness escalated into full-blown alarm.

Zacke decided to take a second look at the corpse.

He didn't spot any footprints near the body, nor did he see any evidence that would prove the sex of their perp. Nothing littered the crime scene that shouldn't have been there.

Zacke rotated his shoulders. His exasperation caused his teeth to ache. He might as well see if Gideon, who still held onto his newfound friend—a trashcan—was ready to head back to the station. He cast one last glance at the poor soul, stopped, and bent to get a closer look. Something white lay almost hidden under the body. How had he missed that?

He pulled a pair of gloves from his back pocket. He didn't have to worry about leaving his fingerprints behind, but he didn't want to invoke questions about his non-conformal habits.

He eased a folded piece of paper enclosed in plastic from under the woman's thigh. Blood obscured the writing on the front. A quick swipe with latex unearthed an old-fashioned script—one he hadn't seen in years, but the letters were too smudged to make out the name on the front.

Zacke knew he shouldn't tamper with evidence,

but maybe it would shed some light on what had happened and that would justify his breach in procedure.

Dearest Zachary,

It's been such a long time since our last meeting. I haven't forgotten the promise I made. You belong to me, and I will not tolerate anyone taking my place in your affections. It would be a deadly mistake to assume I would. I hope you enjoyed my gifts to you.

I will be in touch,

Gabriella

His hand trembled as he pocketed the note. Although it shed light on the killer, how could he show it to his captain? Myers would never understand how one of his men could end up as a motive in a murder investigation. Why should he? Zacke didn't understand it himself.

Gabriella had no hold on him. He'd never been nor ever would be her puppet. The brief liaison they had shared ended almost four hundred years ago, his rejection of her continuous pursuit the reason he now lived his life as a monster.

"Zacke, you okay? I swear if I didn't know better, I would think you were off your color."

Gideon's observation wasn't far from the truth.

Zacke felt as if the fluid running in his veins had stopped. "You're more right than you know, Gideon. I need to talk to you if you don't have any plans."

"Sounds serious. Your house or my hole in the wall?"

"Make it my place. I need to do a quick flyby at the south end of town. Do you mind doing the paperwork? I should be finished by the time you get to the house."

"Naw, you got it. I'll head back to the station now. I'll talk to the captain, too. You can consider that a gift for not laughing at me for puking up my guts again."

Zacke groaned. "Could you use a word besides *gift*?"

Gideon's puzzlement showed in his slack-jaw gape, but Zacke didn't have time to fill in the blanks. His car sat right behind Gideon's vehicle, but he made his way to a secluded section of the cemetery. He intended to fly, and he wanted no detection by mortal eyes.

The night air felt cool with just a hint of rain from the clouds suspended above him. The sultry weather he and Miranda had shared on their way to dinner now a distant memory.

He followed the path a crow would fly—straight to Miranda's apartment. A safety spell would protect her home against Gabriella's powers. The spawn of Satan had probably not yet realized her fledgling's skills had grown in the centuries she'd spent underground. He anticipated and welcomed the chance to enlighten her as soon as he caught up with the witch who had stolen his birthright—and his soul.

His gaze sought and found Miranda's form through the brick barrier. He envied the sheet wrapped around her and wished he could share the closeness and the night hours with her.

His senses told him no one had disturbed the peace of her apartment. He would make sure no one did.

"Protect and keep all I hold dear. Be it home, hearth, or a precious loved one's soul. Keep at bay evil when dark shadows call for all who walk in the light of Heaven's glow; may they be protected by the Lord of all."

****

Gideon's truck took up part of Zacke's double carport. The rusty bucket of bolts, his partner called a truck, sat well out of reach of the waterworks that had started on Zacke's way back from Miranda's.

The downpour had gotten harder after he picked up his car.

His soaked shirt stuck to his skin, and his hair dripped a river down his neck. If he were still a mortal, he would be courting his death by cold. At least he didn't have to add that to his list of worries.

Zacke pulled under the carport and parked. Only his partner would deem the ten-year-old wreck worthy of a dry spot. It burned more oil than the Middle East could produce and was the most uncomfortable form of transportation Zacke had ever been subjected to.

Travis Tritt blasted from the stereo system and assaulted Zacke's ears as he entered the house. He followed the strains of music and found Gideon seated in the living room, a beer held in one hand, his other one keeping time with the beat.

"I see you made yourself at home."

Gideon's eyes snapped open and the beer went flying. Zacke's gaze went lucid as he transported the can away from Gideon's reaching hands.

"How many times have I told you not to sneak up on me? You scared the life out of me, Zacke!"

"On the contrary, if I had, you would be dead and not talking when you should be listening."

"Sorry. What's going on? Does it have anything to do with the vampire in distress act you pulled on me back at the cemetery?" Gideon rubbed at a spot of beer on his blue jeans before looking Zacke in the eyes once more.

"Yes, it does. There's something you need to know."

Gideon removed his ball cap, turned the bill around to face backward and replaced it on his head. He sat forward in the recliner. "Okay, you got my full attention. Shoot."

Zacke took a deep breath before he spoke the name of the woman he despised. "Gabriella's back."

Chapter Five

"Gabriella, as in fangs and claws Gabriella?"

"Yes."

"Whoa, that ain't good."

"And not healthy for anyone associated with me, I'm afraid."

Gideon inhaled and exhaled several times. "Okay, how do you know she's back?"

Zacke pulled the note from his hip pocket and tossed it over. "Read this and then if you want to find a new partner, just tell me."

His partner pulled a pair of glasses from his shirt pocket and read the note. "My Lord, she's admitting to killing those women."

"Yes, and she plans to kill again."

"We have a big problem."

"Not we, Gideon. Me. You are not involved in this."

"How can you say that? I'm your partner, part of this investigation."

"Not anymore. I'm not willing to take the chance that Gabriella will get her hands on you."

"Hey, I ain't gonna let you walk into that woman's trap without backup."

Zacke dropped a hand on his partner's shoulder. "Your heart is in the right place, but I want to keep it where it belongs—in your chest. Gabriella Sanspree plays for keeps. She did back in 1623, and she hasn't changed."

He headed for the kitchen. He needed something a bit stronger than alcohol.

Before Zacke could warm up his syringe, he

found his partner dogging his footsteps.

"Oh man, do you have to shoot up while I'm here? I hate it."

"Well, you know my options. Shoot up or..."

"Forget I said anything, your way is fine with me."

Zacke resisted the urge to present Gideon with a glimpse of his fangs. He had done just that not long after revealing his secret. Gideon's comical reaction had amused him for several days. The same amount of time it had taken his friend to get over it.
Tossing the syringe in the trash, he grabbed a beer from the fridge and handed it to Gideon.

"Don't spill it this time."

"Yeah well, don't creep up on me with your Barnabas Collins impression. I saw all the reruns of *Dark Shadows* when I worked second shift."

"My, my. It seems you *have* been doing your homework. Just don't make the mistake of confusing Gabriella with the vampire, Angelique. They are no more alike than a lion and a kitten."

Zacke caught the slack-jawed Gideon by the arm. "Now, if we are finished with soap operas, I have something a bit more substantial to tell you."

Before Gideon could reclaim the recliner, Zacke propelled him to the sofa. He seated himself in the coveted chair and ran a hand through his hair.

"You know what Gabriella is and what she did to me, but you don't know how or why. Before I tell you, I want to make sure you and Miranda remain safe."

"Miranda? The woman you rescued from the carjackers?"

"Yes, and the woman I took to dinner tonight before you called me."

"So, you're seeing her as what, a man or..."

Zacke raised a brow.

"I mean instead of as a case. It wasn't a slur on

your exceptional background."

"Yes, as a man. But I don't know how long it will last. I will have to keep my talents from her but still find a way to protect her from Gabriella."

Gideon popped the top on the can and took a hefty swig.

"You think Fang Woman will go after Miranda."

"Yes, I'd bet on it. She has a penchant for not liking competition. Miranda would be an easy target for her."

"Yeppers, but how are you gonna protect her twenty-four seven? I mean you have to do your sleep thing, buddy, and she has to work."

"I hope it will not come to that. I expect Gabriella will confront me first. I will warn her to stay away from Miranda, but I doubt she will heed my counsel. Gabriella has never tempered her actions with reason."

"So tell me what went on way back when." Gideon set his beer on the coffee table and waited for his partner to speak.

Zacke's features changed as Gideon watched. Never one to show emotion, his friend's face now took on two expressions he could have done without. Disgust and anger narrowed his eyes, and the blatant view of incisors made Gideon want to make the sign of the cross over his heart and run for the nearest church.

After a moment, Zacke shrugged his shoulders.

"I was almost forty when I met her the first time. Newly widowed, Lady Sanspree needed a fresh husband. Husband number three was thirty years her senior. Their marriage lasted a year. I assume her appetites for carnal pleasure killed him."

Zacke's cheeks acquired a faint tinge of red. Gideon had never known him to be embarrassed.

"I arrived back from Scotland a few days prior to our meeting at court. Beautiful did not suffice to describe her. She had long raven hair and the most intense amethyst eyes I had ever seen. Gabriella knew how to entice even the most bashful of men. I, as one would say in this century, was a pushover."

Gideon could not stand it a minute longer. "So you got it on with her."

The smile Zacke gave him did not reach his eyes. "We went to bed and stayed there for several days. For me, our relationship was nothing more than a pleasurable interlude. And then, I received orders to return to Scotland. There had been some trouble with one of the border lords and a highland laird. Some dispute over *reiving*."

"Hold it a sec. What is *reiving*?"

Gideon welcomed Zacke's laughter. His partner had sunk too far into an unnatural funk.

"*Reiving* is where clans steal cattle and sheep from one another. It is often done to carry out a feud, but this time it had escalated into the death of a clansman."

"So, I take it she didn't like you leaving."

"No, she had a temper tantrum in front of the king. Told him I dishonored her."

Zacke got up and walked to the window. "When the king laughed at her, she said that she would make both of us sorry. Of course, she didn't follow through with her threat to the king. But she more than made up for it with me."

Gideon followed the same path to the window. He dropped a hand on the shoulder of a man that had saved his butt several times over. "Look, you don't have to tell me the rest of it. I know she's dangerous. I promise to watch my back and to safeguard Miranda."

The sadness and gratitude he glimpsed in Zacke's eyes humbled Gideon. This man was not a monster. He was the best friend a guy could have.

A good man with a warm heart.

He had seen his partner give money to the homeless roaming Savannah's streets and witnessed the countless times Zacke had spirited away an abused wife or child.

Zacke held Gideon's gaze for a moment more before he turned to stare out the window at the night sky.

"Thank you, my friend, but I need to tell you the rest.

"Gabriella hired mercenaries to lie in wait until I crossed the border into Scotland. I didn't have time to draw my weapon before they were on me—slashing and gouging. Within moments, it was over. I lay in a pool of my own blood."

Zacke shuttered his eyes; the images were as strong tonight as they had been initially. "I lost consciousness. I could already hear what sounded like the harps of Heaven when Gabriella shook me awake. The smile on her face caused what blood I had left to freeze. She told me that I would be hers forever. And I would pay dearly for slighting her."

Zacke's hands trembled. The grasp of the window ledge stopped the outward signs of his relived horror, but not the swirl of emotions on the inside.

"She bared her teeth, and I saw the feral creature she truly was. I wept and prayed for deliverance. When she sank her fangs into my throat, I was ready to die. I believed in God and hoped to wake in Heaven. Instead, I awoke to an eternity of Hell here on earth. She has tormented me even in her absence. I look at myself, and I hate what I am."

He faced the man at his side. "Gideon, I will defeat her, but I need to know you are safe and that Miranda will not fall into her hands. Gabriella will strike at those closest to me. She did it before. She will not hesitate to do it again. I'll not have the blood of more innocents tainting my descent into Hell."

"Okay, whatever you want, man. Just tell me what I need to do."

****

Miranda stumbled over the still unpacked box of books, quick-stepped to regain her balance, and grabbed her briefcase as she flew out the door. Turning off the alarm had not been smart. Her eyes refused to stay open, and she'd fallen back into a peaceful doze—something she'd not been able to do last night.

She had slept in fits and starts. Her hopes of dreaming of dessert and Zachary Kensington had not materialized. Instead, she'd dreamt nightmares. Haunting apparitions taunted her. She couldn't escape the ghastly creatures—fangs and claws extended as if to snag Miranda and pull her down into a pit of darkness. Red eyes glared and goaded her with images of flames. She tried to flee, but they followed her—chasing her into an old cemetery. The gravestones lying haphazardly on their sides had given her a glimpse of what laid beneath the soil.

"Thanks, Mac." She accepted the large vanilla-flavored coffee one of the operating room techs brought her. It was a half an hour into her shift. Thank God, the on-call doctor had covered for her.

"You okay this morning, Dr. James?"

"Yes, just a bit tired. I'll be fine once we get started. Why don't you pull the surgery orders while I make a heartfelt thank-you and apology to Dr. Stone?"

"Sure thing. See you in a few."

Jarrod Stone waved away her explanation and apology. The seasoned resident blew her a kiss before hitting the elevator button. The automatic doors swished closed and swallowed up his goodbye wave.

She jumped at the light touch on her shoulder.

"Sorry, didn't mean to sneak up on you ma'am. Here are the notes on your morning caseload."

"Seems as if this is a day for apologies, Mac, don't worry about it. And forget the ma'am. Call me Miranda. It's going to be a long day."

****

The day passed in an endless reality of torn ligaments, gunshot wounds, and victims from a bus wreck. By the time her shift ended at seven, Miranda's body ached for a hot bath and a peaceful night's sleep.

The sun rested just above the horizon when she made her way to the parking area. Rick, one of the security guards, had promised to walk her to the car. With her nightmares fresh in her memory and the news that there had been a second murder, she welcomed the gesture. Unfortunately, the burly and soft-spoken guard had been called to another part of the hospital at the last moment.

She arranged her keys so that one protruded from between each of her fisted fingers. The makeshift weapon alleviated a bit of her concern evoked by the long walk to her vehicle. The next time her tardiness forced her to park at the far end of the lot, she'd make certain she moved it closer during her break.

Her footsteps echoed off the pavement. She hiked the strap of her briefcase higher on her shoulder and walked faster. The parking lot seemed to grow in length.

A faint sound from behind her caused her heart to flip-flop.

Should she turn and look? No. Ten more steps and she would be at the car. She increased her pace to a slow jog. With her head down, she inserted the key, turned it, and pulled the key out.

Running footsteps galvanized her movements.

She jerked on the door handle. The door slammed into her arm and knocked the keys out of her hand. She bent and grappled for the elusive pieces of metal and managed to grasp the ring.

Before she could straighten a pair of dusty boots stepped into her range of vision.

Her heart didn't flip-flop, this time; it stopped.

When a hand touched her shoulder, she froze, but only for a moment. No way would she give someone else a chance to attack her. She swung her briefcase into the man's legs. His swaying form didn't fall, but it did allow her time to straighten to a standing position with the coveted keys poised to gouge his eyes out.

"Dr. James, hold on a minute."

Miranda stiffened upon hearing her name. A firm hand caught her arm in a gentle grip. Only then did she dare to look up.

Brown eyes met her gaze. The bit of humor she saw within them did more to relieve her fear than anything else. That relief transferred itself into tears.

"Dr. James... Miranda, please don't cry."

"How do you know me?" Her question came out as a croak. The sniffles that threatened to clog her airway reduced after he handed her a clean handkerchief.

"I didn't mean to startle you."

"Startle me? You scared me out of my wits."

"I apologize. Zacke will have my head for frightening you."

"Zacke? He sent you?"

"Yes. He wondered if you would meet him for dinner."

"Why didn't he ask me himself?"

"He had an errand to run but will meet you there."

"What are you, his personal messenger?"

"Hardly. I'm his partner. Gideon Hawks, at your service."

Her fright continued to lessen and excitement took its place. She would see Zacke again. After last night, she hadn't been so sure.

"Thank you, Detective Hawks. I'm sorry I tried to—"

"Blind me?"

"Well, yes."

Miranda echoed his laughter. At least he didn't hold a grudge. That would never do if she and Zacke were to continue seeing one another.

"Don't worry about it, Dr. James."

"Please, call me Miranda. After crying buckets all over you, I think we can dispense with formality."

Again Zacke's partner laughed. She wondered how two such different people became partners. Something else to ask Zacke when she saw him.

A bit unsteady, Miranda opted to ride with Gideon to the restaurant. It would be nice to have company while she waited.

And if she gleaned more information about the man who fascinated her, then all the better.

****

Zacke awakened before the sun dropped behind the horizon. This time of the year darkness came late. He wanted the extra time to finalize his plan to confront Gabriella.

If she ran true-to-form, she would not wait long before making her next move.

Sadness dragged at his limbs, making him slow to leave his bed. He wanted more than just friendship with Miranda. He couldn't explain it, but something about her shyness pulled at him deep inside. Their first date had been hard on him in more ways than one. Her innocence made him want to protect her, as well as draw his beast forward. He wanted to explore his awakening feelings. He wanted a second date and a third. For the first time in forever, he wanted a lasting relationship, but that wasn't something he could pursue unless he stopped Gabriella.

He strived to focus his thoughts. He needed to know where Gabriella rested. Never an early riser, as a mortal, she took advantage of sleeping until the noon hour, and he suspected her habits had not changed.

Yes—there she is. He saw her in his mind's eye, the connection still strong.

Her body lay in deep repose on a slab of marble. He scanned the surrounding area.

Shock tightened the coil in his gut. She had taken over his old resting place, no doubt to taunt him.

His years of being a creature of the night had been fraught with battles. Others of his kind challenged him. It had been that way since the beginning of time—man and creature tearing at one another to prove who was the superior. And in all wars for supremacy, someone had to die.

Zacke planned to survive.

****

His descent into the mausoleum was quiet and uneventful. For those blessings, he thanked his Heavenly father, even though he knew his soul was consigned to Hell.

Ebony locks of hair curled over Gabriella's shoulders and rested upon her crossed arms. The brows she had so proudly arched when attempting a conquest were the same dark color. Her skin, pale in life, appeared alabaster in living death. The lips she had used to entice Zacke had a bluish tint. He knew she'd paint them red, her preferred color, when she awoke.

He caught himself before he reached out to touch her. Her power pulsated even in slumber—

almost as if she knew he was there.

As he watched, her dark lashes flickered—the red of her pupils impaled him. After he broke their hypnotic shackle, they changed to their birth color of amethyst.

"So good of you to visit me, Lord Kensington. It saves me the trouble of finding you."

"I'm not here to be of assistance to you, Gabriella. I think it's time we had a talk."

Gabriella slithered off her stone bed. As she stretched, she brought her arms up and behind her head, thrusting her more than ample breasts forward.

Zacke turned away from the sight of her cleavage pushing against the low V-shaped neck of her satin gown. The crimson color contrasted with her skin and hair, cementing the fact that Gabriella still dressed for seduction.

"There are a lot of things I would like to do with you my darling Zachary—talking is not one of them."

"Talking is all you will get from me."

"I remember a time when you begged me for more than trivial chit chat."

"Those days are over. You have nothing I would ever want again."

Zacke moved away from the claws that swiped a ferocious arc toward his face. A low, vicious hiss escaped her lips. He had struck a nerve.

"Are you sure there is nothing you want? I would have thought you would beg me to stop leaving you my little gifts. Or don't you care about your pathetic mortals anymore?"

"I care, Gabriella. But I will not *ask* you to stop the killing. You *will* stop or face my wrath."

"I, who made you, should be frightened?"

Her laughter caused an uneasy shiver to bore into Zacke's spine.

"That was a long time ago and unlike you, I

have not been sleeping the years away. I don't know why you have resurfaced here and now, but your fight is with me—not the poor souls you have tortured to death."

"Oh, but they were so easy, Zachary. Should I tell you how they begged for mercy right up until the last moment?"

"No, you can tell me why you are here. Not the dribble you left in your note. You don't want me, Gabriella."

"*Au contraire*, I do want you. You owe me."

"For what? Turning me into the despicable creature that you are? I owe you nothing, except pity. You were a monster as a mortal and you haven't changed."

Gabriella's eyes glowed, turning her orbs into a pool of blood. The teeth she bared were longer and sharper than he remembered; a miniscule drop of crimson clung to her lip, which she had bitten.

"Save your worthless pity, Zachary. I do not need it. But your latest conquest might."

Zacke's heart, dead during the daytime sleep but a pulsing, beating organ at night, stopped. His vision blurred as he reached inside Gabriella's mind. The contempt she felt for him played a distant second to the fury and hatred she held for Miranda.

His incisors lengthened as he witnessed the depravities that Gabriella planned to unleash upon Miranda. He could not allow the rage that beckoned him full reign. To kill in anger would put him on the same level as her and what hope he had of redeeming himself in the eyes of Heaven, if that was a possibility, would be gone.

"What do you want from me?"

"I want you to stay away from your little doctor and to—"

"I will not come back to you, Gabriella. That is not on the table. Why should I stay away from

Miranda? You have offered me nothing in return."

Gabriella's lips curved into a snarl. "Fine, I'll amuse myself without killing if you stay away from the mortal."

Zacke felt a piece of his heart shatter, but he had no choice. "All right, after tonight, I won't see Miranda again."

He waved away her hiss. "I've already made plans to meet her, and I will not stand her up."

"Go, fly to your little mortal. Enjoy the last hours you have with her. I will be watching. And make sure you do not renege on your promise or the next body you find will be hers."

"I honor my word; have no fear on that score. But I will not hesitate to kill you if you break yours."

"Promises, promises. That is all you ever give me, but I will let that suffice for now, darling." Gabriella blew a kiss at Zacke before her body shifted into a ribbon of crimson smoke.

Zacke allowed her only a moment's head start before taking to the sky himself. The smoke trail shimmered and twisted on a path straight to the heart of the city. As he neared the restaurant where he would meet Miranda, he spied the laughing features of Gabriella for the space of a second. Then the evil mirage disappeared along with the smoke.

His meeting had not gone as well as he would have liked, but Gabriella had been warned. His promise to keep his distance from Miranda had erected a temporary barrier against Gabriella doing her harm.

But Lady Sanspree had won a victory. The emotions he had begun to feel for Miranda would have to be put on hold—until he could find a way to stop Gabriella forever.

Chapter Six

Miranda chewed on her fourth breadstick—still no Zacke. Gideon had been politeness itself, but she wanted to see his partner. She needed to see him. He had turned her insides to mush and made her yearn for a life that didn't consist of just her career. She wanted to see if he returned the stirring of attraction.

"And there we were, me and Zacke, waiting for the perp to run out of bullets. I don't mind admitting, I was scared speechless, but Zacke, on the other hand, remained as calm as all get out."

"Is he always calm?"

Gideon froze for a moment before he answered. "Calm as in never getting flustered?"

Miranda nodded her head.

"Yeah, you could say that. I've only seen the man come unglued a couple of times. It ain't a pretty sight, but most of the time his feathers stay unruffled. And that comes in handy in our line of work. A body can get shot, stabbed, you name it—if they ain't careful."

"Has Zacke ever been hurt in the line of duty?"

Again, Gideon's facial expression stiffened.

"Naw, you can't hurt Zacke. We call him the invincible man."

His answer intrigued Miranda, but she knew what a bullet or a knife could do. She didn't want to see that happen to Zacke or his partner. Maybe thinking the way Gideon did helped to keep the possibility of something horrendous happening at bay.

She felt a chill settle lightly on her arms. She didn't know how she knew but Zacke had finally arrived.

"I see you've been telling tales again, Gideon."

Zacke stood behind Miranda, caught Gideon's eyes and gave a slight jerk of his head. He would have been amused at the startled look in his partner's eyes, but the situation defied hilarity. He didn't relish having to blow Miranda off with a fabricated excuse.

"Well, you know me, Zacke. I love talking about everyone but myself." Gideon's laughter sounded forced and a bit uncomfortable.

"Hello, Miranda. I apologize for being late."

He couldn't stop himself from bringing Miranda's hand, the one not grasping the breadstick, to his lips. Miranda's effusive gestures while she talked were charming—as long as he stayed out of her line of fire.

He watched color tint her cheeks when he purposely blew into the palm of her hand. Her reaction sent a surge of desire to his loins. She had a way of getting to him like no other woman ever had.

"Oh, that's fine. I mean you being late and all. I understand about work and stuff."

The mild breathlessness of her words made him wonder how she would sound after he made love to her. Or would she lie there next to him unable to speak at all? He would give all the years of his existence to find out.

The futility of thinking along those lines caused a pain within his chest. Since his kind were reputed not to have hearts, he ignored it.

"I hope Gideon has not been filling your head with the nonsense he spats at work."

"Hey man, just keeping the lady occupied until you got here."

"Well, now that I am here, don't you need to be

elsewhere?"

Gideon's look of disappointment almost made Zacke laugh.

"I reckon I could get a doggie bag for my chicken wings. Of course, I'll have to fight my dog for them, but what the heck."

Zacke turned slightly away from Miranda. He allowed just a bit of his incisors to show.

"On second thought—I need to lose some weight. Nice meeting you, Miranda."

Gideon received a full-blown smile this time.

"Hey, she told me to call her that. Explain it. Will ya, Miranda? I'm out of here."

Gideon hurried toward the exit, mumbling, "Sheesh, you would think he was Count Dracula."

No, but I can introduce you to him, if you like.

When Gideon paused and then missed his step, Zacke knew his words had transferred into his partner's mind.

Miranda's face appeared a study of confusion as he sat in the vacated chair.

"He didn't have to leave that quickly. I wanted to thank him."

Zacke didn't like her disheartened expression.

"I'm sure he didn't mind escorting you here. I'll pass along your thanks."

"Thank you, but I had a second reason to thank him. He was so sweet when I made such an idiot of myself at the hospital."

Zacke's curiosity pricked. "A woman who fights off carjackers and works in your profession could never make an idiot of herself."

"Well, I did, and royally. With the person committing those murders still on the loose, my nerves were a bit on edge walking through the parking area. I heard something behind me, it rattled me so much I dropped my keys."

He watched Miranda shred the paper napkin in

her hands. He reached out and removed the tiny bits. "Why don't you tell me what happened next?"

"Well, I didn't know him from Adam's housecat, and I tried to stab him with my keys. He was so nice about it, but I feel terrible."

Zacke owed Gideon a favor and an apology. Something he knew his partner would hold over his head for quite some time.

Miranda's eyes glistened. She grabbed a new napkin and wiped her eyes, before picking up the butter knife again.

"I'm sorry. I'm not usually a water-pot. As a doctor, I would diagnose it as sleep deprivation and nerves. Both contributed to the nightmares I had last night."

Before he could ask Miranda about her nightmares, the waiter approached their table.

Zacke gave their order: a Caesar salad with vinaigrette dressing, for Miranda, and two glasses of red wine.

"Aren't you having anything to eat? I thought we were doing dinner?"

He waited until the waiter headed for the kitchen before stating, "Last minute change of plans, I have to do some work so..."

Zacke ran a hand through his hair, looked away from Miranda before turning back. "Would you like to tell me about the dreams? Sometimes just talking about them can make them less frightening."

"Don't I wish? And just because I tell you about the dreams doesn't mean you're off the hook about having to leave early."

Miranda's slight smile caused Zacke's heart to ache. How on earth could he tell her he couldn't see her anymore, when it was going to kill the light in her eyes and his soul?

He took the butter knife away from her before she stabbed him in the face.

"Sorry, I guess you notice I talk with my hands."

"Yes, and as endearing as that is, I think you should stay away from pointed objects when conversing."

His words chased the shadows from Miranda's eyes, and her laughter delighted and saddened him. For so long he'd lived without joy, and now he would be forced to give up that delicious sound.

"I seldom dream, but last night it felt as if I was inside the dream and whenever I thought it was over, it would start up again. The last time was the worst. I could hear an eerie laughter high above me. It actually woke me up. Don't get me wrong, I'm glad it did but it still gave me the creeps."

Miranda took a sip of her drink.

"Are you sure you were awake?"

"Oh yes, I remember looking at the alarm clock. It was barely five o'clock."

Zacke's heart thudded in time with his apprehension. Had Gabriella cast a dream sequence on Miranda? Not likely with his safety spell in place, but she could have transferred her thoughts without penetrating the boundaries of the spell. It could just be a coincidence but the description of the laughter was reminiscent of the vixen's character. She would have thought it extremely amusing for Miranda to be frightened. He wished now he had issued a stronger warning—one that would prevent her from disturbing Miranda, in any way, at all.

"Well, I'm certain you will rest a lot easier tonight."

Zacke planned to make sure nothing or no one disturbed Miranda in her slumbers. A peace spell would take care of that. And keeping his promise to Gabriella would be even more helpful.

"I hope so. So why don't I quit monopolizing the conversation and we talk about you for a change. Other than the fact you're a detective and you rescue damsels in distress, I'm clueless."

"Miranda, I'm afraid you would be bored with my life. I have no siblings, and I'm a workaholic. In fact, I really need to be…"

"Oh, but I would love to…"

Zacke caught her hand and carried it to his lips, stalling the words in her dry throat. Miranda loved the delicious thrill his touch created in her bones. She resisted the compulsion to throw herself into his arms—that wouldn't do in a public place.

"Do you have any siblings or parents?" Zacke's voice disturbed her fantasy.

"You do that rather well."

"What?"

"Change the subject. Fine. I'll concede the fact that you don't want to talk about yourself—for now. But I can't promise I won't plague you in the future."

Miranda didn't receive the smile she'd hope for from Zacke. When he didn't acknowledge her comment, she decided to answer his question.

"No, I don't have any brothers or sisters, and my parents died in a car accident my first year of med school. Their deaths are the reason I'm working as a trauma surgeon. I'd planned to study hematology and do research, but I changed my mind after a drunk driver hit their car. They were still alive when they were transported to the nearest hospital. The doctor on staff did all he could, but I found out later if they had received care at a trauma hospital, they might have recovered."

"I'm sorry, Miranda. I know that had to be an awful time for you. I wish…"

Miranda waited for Zacke to finish his sentence but instead he signaled the waiter.

Was this the end of their date? Could she even call it a date? He hadn't asked her out himself.

"Miranda?"

The low tone of his voice seeped into her ears

and ended the question session within her brain. The blush she felt heating her face made her want to crawl under the table.

"I'm sorry, my mind trailed off onto something else. A habit that gets me into trouble."

Zacke rose to his feet, a dark frown marring his handsome face, and held out his hand.

"I'm sorry, but I have to cut our evening short. I need to take you back to your car and then get to work."

****

The ride back to the hospital, although quiet, went much too fast for Miranda. Before she could get up the courage to say anything or to ask if she had done anything wrong, they pulled into the hospital lot.

"Come, I'll see you safely locked in and then follow you to your apartment."

"Would you like to come in for a few minutes when we get there?" The moment the words left her mouth, she could have bitten her tongue in two. The man had already told her he had to go to work. Could she be any more transparent?

"I'm sorry, Miranda. I have a backlog of work waiting for me at the station."

"I, uh, guess I just assumed you could do it later."

Zacke looked down before answering.

"With the extra workload due to the murders, I volunteered to catch up on the case notes. They really should get done as quickly as possible"

Had she heard a note of impatience in his voice? "I understand. I think that most of my job consists of paper trails."

"I hope that you'll also understand after tonight I will be tied up indefinitely due to work."

He was blowing her off! She shouldn't be surprised but it still hurt.

She absolutely refused to cry. He wasn't worth the effort it would take to repair the aftermath of a crying jag.

"Fine. If you'll excuse me, I really need to get home."

"Miranda, I'm..."

"Really, Zacke, I have to be at work, early." She didn't wait for him to help her out of the vehicle. She ran to her car, jammed the key in the lock, and fairly ripped the door open in her haste. She was inside before Zacke could exit the driver's side of the Lexus.

She watched him walk toward her in the slow seductive way that never failed to cause her heart to pound. She shook her head. He couldn't have been more explicit—he wanted no place in her life.

Miranda turned the key in the ignition and put the car in gear. She pressed the gas pedal and sped out of the parking lot.

Zacke watched the car's taillights disappear. He unclenched his fist. The thin line of blood in his palm surprised him. He hadn't felt his nails lengthen.

He hurt Miranda—something he'd vowed he wouldn't do. He found it ironic that in order to protect her he had to make her hate him. He'd read her thoughts before she peeled out of the lot. He shared her pain. Her confusion tore at his soul. But he couldn't help her—except by leaving her alone.

Zacke returned to his car. He had nothing to do except go to work. If he deserved any sense of salvation, for his deeds on this earth, he hoped God would allow him a chance to make things right with Miranda after he destroyed Gabriella.

****

Miranda tossed the shards of glass into the garbage can. Dang it, she'd broken the only coffee cup she had. Now what?

She needed caffeine. Her continuous tossing and turning had all but destroyed the bed covers.

Thoughts of Zacke had vanquished any hope of the sandman's visit.

Handsome, sexy as heck, and get lost Miranda, Zacke.

She shouldn't have been surprised at the outcome of their short-lived relationship, but it still hurt. He made her feel safe and protected—when he wasn't making her hot and bothered.

Miranda's nostrils twitched. Wonderful, the coffee was ready. She decided to forgo her usual two spoonfuls of sugar. Black would better match her mood. The java tasted just as good in the plastic cup she'd unearthed from a box.

Zacke's total turnaround had been a blow. Sure, by no means beautiful, she still didn't need a sign warning others to look at their own risk.

Her personality had always been studious, but her profession required more than just a hit and miss with the books. So what if she didn't come across as a mover or shaker. She still managed to have a good time when she went out. And none of her few and far between dates had complained she was dull as ditch-water, or at least not to her face.

Maybe it *was* Zacke's caseload. Those gruesome murders had made headlines across the country. He had to be under a lot of pressure to find out who had killed those women. Maybe she had overreacted.

Miranda finished her second cup of coffee and glanced at the clock on the microwave. Her sigh sounded loud even to her ears. Time to get busy and put the confusing detective out of her mind.

Exactly a half-hour later, she had showered and dressed. The hot water had soothed her tired body and the sunshine shining through her bedroom window lightened her mood.

When she pulled into the hospital parking lot, Miranda congratulated herself. She had managed to put Zacke out of her mind for exactly two minutes of the five-minute drive.

A few moments later, she stepped into the elevator and pressed the button for the surgical floor. As it lumbered and creaked upward to the sixth floor, she ran through her mental list of things to do.

The soft lurch as it stopped caused her to look up—not her floor. A woman stepped through the open doors. Expertly made-up and with her hair professionally styled, Miranda couldn't help but wonder if this was the type of woman Zacke preferred. Her business suit, a bold red, matched the lipstick and nail polish she wore. A bit too much for Miranda's taste, but it suited the woman's dark hair. She bet Miss *Thin Thighs* didn't have to watch what she ate to fit into a size four.

Miranda chastised herself for staring.

"Which floor?" she asked. She hoped the smile she offered did not smack of plain-out envy.

"The rooftop, if you would be so kind."

"Sure, no problem."

Miranda pressed the button. She must be meeting some bigwig for breakfast. The top-floor of the hospital housed a lovely restaurant. Not at all like the utilitarian cafeteria in which the employees had their meals.

The ding of the elevator signaled Miranda's floor. While she waited for the doors to open, she turned to the woman once again.

"The next stop should be yours. Have a nice day."

She shifted her briefcase off her shoulder and grasped the handle. The doors creaked opened. As she stepped out the woman's words reached her ears.

"I plan on it. I only hope your day is just as pleasant, Dr. James."

Miranda looked down to where her name badge

should be. *Great.* She had left it at home on the dresser. So how did the woman know her name?

She turned back to ask but the doors had already closed.

An eerie sound of laughter waffled from the elevator. It sounded remarkably like the laughter in her nightmare. Miranda's heart stopped for the space of a moment before she moved toward the hustle and bustle of the surgical suite. She had better get a grip on her imagination. Too many caffeine fixes after two sleepless nights played havoc with her mind.

Chapter Seven

Zacke used the bottom half of his tank top to mop the sweat from his forehead. He had taken up running in the last six months. Something he would not have dared to try as a fledgling creature of the night. It seemed that the older he got the more time he could spend in the sunlight. Late afternoon suited him best for his five-mile run. The rays of the waning sun provoked no harm to his vampire skin.

How he hated that word—*vampire*.

So many stories had circulated about his kind over the centuries. Most had been more fiction than fact but all with the underlying thread that he and others like him were monsters.

Although in the last few years, the younger generation seemed to think the idea of dressing up in gothic costumes with fake fangs a tremendous rush. If they only knew the truth.

Running would never take the place of a cry to arms from his king or a good sword battle but it did help him believe he was once more just a man.

Another mile and he would be back at the house. Three minutes later, he rounded the last corner onto his street.

His vision picked up Gideon as he walked down his porch steps. His hair, minus the ball cap, although not quite as long as Zacke's, still defied department regulations. They both had gotten around that clause by working undercover. The night shift captain ignored them as much as possible. He was more concerned with getting cases solved than their appearance.

Gideon looked up and waved as Zacke drew closer. Working with Gideon was one of the more pleasant aspects of his job.

Zacke stopped in front of the house and waited for his partner's usual comment.

"I still ain't figured out how you can run and not be gasping for breath. It ain't human."

"Right you are, but you ought to try it."

"Why? I'll just let you chase down the bad guys, while I drive the truck."

Gideon's laughter almost swallowed Zacke's chuckle.

"Come on in. I need to get cleaned up, and you can tell me what got you up an hour earlier than usual."

"Couldn't sleep. Yeah, I know that's unreal for me. It's been seven days, and even though you and I both know who's behind the murders, the captain doesn't." Gideon moved to the refrigerator and snagged one of the beers Zacke kept on hand just for him.

"Be back in a few, and—"

"I know, don't spill it." Gideon's tone smacked of chagrin.

Zacke ran up the stairs to the master bedroom.

He turned on the shower taps and stripped off his clothes. He sniffed the air and frowned. Although unusual for him to perspire like a mortal, he had started that unattractive body function right after he had started running. Maybe it had something to do with being out in the sunlight. He tossed the clothes into the hamper and stepped under the hot spray of water.

It had been a quiet week.

Even though the captain had not asked for any additional meetings, Zacke knew it would not be long until he did. So far, Gabriella had kept her word, but the captain wanted the murders solved.

And he was not the type to believe in vampires. He would probably have both him and Gideon take a psych eval—that is, after he stopped laughing.

The water began to run cold and he turned it off. He wracked his brain for a believable explanation for Captain Myers but came up with nothing. He'd also hit a brick wall with his search to find ways not to think of Miranda.

He had to keep her safe and find a way to stop Gabriella for good. That would solve his problems for the moment, and then he would think once more on how to decipher the tangle of his soul's redemption.

Despair rocked him as never before. Tired of the existence he'd been forced to endure for several immortal lifetimes, he wanted out.

Death seemed the only alternative and before he met Miranda, he would have welcomed it. Now he wasn't so sure.

When and if he was blessed enough to die, his spirit would spend the rest of eternity in Hell. His already condemned soul screamed in defiance at the injustice.

Zacke shrugged off the morbid thoughts and dressed hastily in jeans and a T-shirt. If he knew Gideon, he would be having a fit for food right about now, and he needed to feed also.

****

Forty-five minutes later, Zacke fought the urge to kiss the pavement outside the station. He should have taken to the air instead of riding in Gideon's vehicle of torture. The two miles of grinding gears to the fast food restaurant and then to the station had made him wonder if he would exit the truck with all his parts intact.

"Come on Zacke, it wasn't that bad."

"Compared to what?"

"Sheesh, compared to a lot of things."

"Maybe a stake through the heart. Seriously,

that contraption you drive should be condemned or considered a dangerous weapon." Zacke didn't allow the smile that begged to be released touch his lips.

Gideon rolled his eyes; a signal that meant Zacke was about to receive a sermon on the pride of southern gentlemen and their pick-up trucks.

"A truck ain't a contraption. It's a palace on wheels. How many times do I have to...?" Gideon's voice trailed off when the rear door to the station house opened.

"Kensington, Hawks, the captain wants to see you both pronto."

"Thanks, Jeff." Zacke caught the door and held it open, calling back over his shoulder. "You coming, Partner?"

"Do I have a choice?"

Zacke's chuckle rumbled low as Gideon moved past him and down the hall to Captain Myers office. He had a feeling it would be the last time he would feel like expressing amusement that night.

****

"Take a seat, Detectives." Captain Myers didn't so much as look up from the paperwork he shuffled through when they entered the room. His uniform appeared fresh as if it had just come from the cleaners, and his attitude rivaled the starch in his shirt.

Zacke watched his superior push his spectacles back up the sliver of nose that had earned him the nickname "No nose." The thick soda-bottle lenses turned his green eyes into a wavy blur. He'd left off the regulation hat he habitually wore, and his receding, gray-flecked hair stood on end. Not a good sign.

Zacke exchanged a look with Gideon. The silent question from his partner had Zacke shrugging his shoulders. He still had no idea what to tell the captain.

"I haven't had a report from you on the Slash and Maul cases in over a week. What is the status of the investigation?"

Zacke didn't care for the name Myers had tagged to the murders. It just created more fodder for the press.

"Our investigation is ongoing, Captain. We are following all the leads we have."

"That isn't acceptable, Detective. I have the governor and the mayor breathing down my neck every time I step foot outside this station. I need more." The captain removed his horn-rimmed glasses and pinched the bridge of his nose between his thumb and forefinger.

Definitely not a good sign.

He fixed a clear and determined gaze on Zacke, a reminder that at one time, their captain had served in the military. His good ol' boy persona dropped away.

"I want something concrete on my desk in the next forty-eight hours. Is that understood?"

Before Zacke could say yes sir, Gideon opened his mouth.

"But Captain, that ain't enough—"

A knock on the door interrupted whatever else his partner was going to say.

"This had better be good," Captain Myers mumbled before snapping, "Come in."

"Sorry, Captain. But, the sergeant on desk duty wanted me to let Zacke and—"

"Well, get on with it."

Sam Gibbons had been with the Savannah P.D. for several years. Zacke knew he wouldn't interrupt a meeting like this one without good reason.

"Jake Archer and Tyler Brown are being released. Someone posted their bail. And Zacke, you have a visitor in the front lobby."

Zacke's heart jumped. *Miranda?* He was

halfway out of his chair before Captain Myers spoke.

"Dismissed, for now. But I want that report on my desk soon, detailing what you know and the leads you have. Is that clear?"

"Yes, sir." Zacke didn't wait to see if Gideon followed. The news about Jake and his henchman didn't make him happy but he'd expected it. His concern lay with whoever awaited him in the lobby. As he moved down the hallway to the front of the station, he tamped down his desire to transfer himself there.

He could hear Gideon's footsteps behind him but for once, he had no desire to wait on his partner. He hit the threshold to the lobby almost at a run and stopped just inside the doorway. He scanned the room for any sight of Miranda's auburn hair, but the only woman in sight was a well-dressed brunette. The bright red of her clothing provoked an image of another time.

She turned to face him and the red material dissolved into a blur and then centered inside his head. His senses climbed to high alert.

"Detective Kensington, I wonder if you could spare me a few moments of your time."

Zacke heard her words, coated to seduce the surrounding officers, who already appeared to be under her spell.

"Gabriella, I wasn't expecting to see you tonight or any night."

Zacke reached out and closed Gideon's mouth. He then sent a gentle urging to his partner's mind and the men that still loitered in the lobby. He wanted Gabriella's attention on him, not Gideon or the others.

He needn't have worried. She didn't even glance at the departing men. Her eyes glowed—not red, but soft lavender.

He knew better than to trust the friendly smile

on her lips, and he refused to look at the siren sway of her hips as she moved to his side.

He resisted the urge to snatch his arm from the grip of her red-coated nails.

"Why, Zachary, you wound me with your callousness." The tip of her nail, which lengthened considerably as he watched, dug into the flesh of his forearm.

This time he did move his arm and his body from her reach. When a scant two feet separated them, Zacke answered her accusation. "A callous attitude is all you deserve, Gabriella. What are you doing here?"

For a moment, her smile slipped but she recovered quickly. A moue of her crimson painted lips preceded her next words. "I see that you are in a testy mood, Lord Kensington. I hoped to pass a few pleasant moments with an old friend without the animosity that has been so prevalent between us. Now you have ruined it and my peace offering."

Peace offering, my incisors. Zacke wondered what trickery Gabriella had up her sleeve. "You are trying my patience, Lady Sanspree. I suggest you dispense with the idle chitchat and tell me what you're talking about."

"Very well. I wanted to tell you that I know you have been upholding your end of our bargain. I will continue to uphold mine; in fact, I might even take my enjoyment elsewhere for a while."

Gabriella paused for a moment, as if waiting for him to acknowledge her words. He didn't. The gaze she fixed on Zacke radiated coquetry and smugness.

"Although, after seeing the innocent Dr. James, I admit it will make it harder to leave, even for a short vacation."

Zacke's heart exploded, as did his rage. Gabriella had visited Miranda. How or when did not matter.

She had lied, and she would pay for it.

He vaguely noticed that the hand he reached out to encircle her throat had talons. His gaze splintered into a kaleidoscope of blues. The lighter colors darkened until he could see nothing but a haze of azure.

His incisors grew and stretched the inside of his mouth—he could taste the sweetness of blood. Looking at Gabriella evoked hatred so strong he could almost feel the bones of her neck snap beneath his grip.

The look of surprise on his prey's face fired his blood. The fear that skittered across her purple orbs heightened the power he felt having her at his mercy. It would take only a moment to put out the flame of life—or—death within her. Then he would remove her head and heart to ensure she could not rise again and steal another's soul.

"Zacke, stop it."

He ignored the low but insistent voice in his ear. He shrugged off the hand that caught and clung to his arm. But the voice persisted.

"I mean it, man. She ain't worth it. Look at me."

Zacke turned his gaze to the ashen-faced man standing at his side. He'd never even heard Gideon return. Horror pulled Gideon's features together in a mask of disbelief. His partner's brown eyes dilated and as Zacke watched, Gideon flinched.

Zacke followed the path of his partner's eyes downward and saw droplets of blood forming on Gideon's forearm.

His mind reeled with shock. He released the arm he hadn't realized he held and then turned back to Gabriella. He loosened his grip just a bit and the color that had seeped into her face from his stranglehold fled.

He slowed his breathing and closed his eyes. As he calmed down, the ice-blue glow engulfing his vision faded to a softer aquamarine. When he was certain his rage had abated to a simmer, he pulled Gabriella toward him. With her face inches from his, he removed his hand from her throat. He then placed both hands, with considerably shorter nails, on her shoulders.

"You had better thank the God you do not believe in for divine intervention. He is the only reason I do not cleave your head from your neck and take your diseased heart from your body."

"As if you could, Zachary. I made you. You are powerless against me."

Zacke called on all that was holy to keep him from following through with his desire to end her existence. "You delude yourself, Gabriella. I am the stronger one now. My power does not come from evil nor does it come from feeding on innocents. It comes from what little bit of good I manage to do. That is what makes us different."

"Different? You are deceiving yourself. You are a creature, my creature. What goodness you perceive in your self-righteous mind will come undone when you lash out and kill in rage. You almost did tonight, my darling. It will happen and when it does, you will need me."

Gabriella reached up and stroked his face with her hand. He suppressed the shudder that ran through his body as the soft skin glided across his cheek. He received no warning before her nails slashed into skin.

"That is enough, Gabriella." Zacke captured her hands. When she moved to attack him with her teeth, he allowed her a glimpse into his mind. Her stunned look gratified him.

She needed to know he would give up everything he had to keep her from harming Miranda.

"Fine, keep your little friend. She probably wouldn't provide much amusement anyway."

"You will stay away from her. We had a bargain, and I kept my end."

"Yes, and I will continue to keep my part of our bargain—for now."

Zacke did not like the implications of her words. "You will not kill another innocent or you will regret it."

Gabriella's eyes narrowed. "I have one regret and that is our bargain. I will, however, extend the peace offering you threw in my face." Her macabre smile revealed her fangs. "I think it is time we played a game. You are familiar with *Hide-and-Go-Seek*, are you not? Well, you have forty-eight hours to find and try to stop me. If you fail, I will kill again and again. And Zachary? Enjoy your time with Miranda. I foresee regretting that promise also. When I do, I will have her."

Her lips grazed his throbbing cheek before she moved past him and out of his reach.

He turned to follow her out of the lobby and came face to face with Miranda. A Miranda whose features were bleached white except for twin spots of color staining her cheekbones.

A hapless and stunned Gideon offered no help. Zacke reached out and touched her arm. She recoiled and backed away from him.

As he watched, she turned and fled down the hallway toward the exit and the parking area. He couldn't allow her to leave—not just yet. Miranda was too upset, and he would bet his last syringe of blood that Gabriella had seen her also. She had staged her last movement too well, and it had been aimed not at him but rather to hurt an audience of one.

"Miranda, wait!"

She ignored his words and continued to run. Zacke caught up with her in the parking lot.

"Get away from me."

"Please, listen to me, Miranda."

"Why, so you can feed me another lie?" She tried to move past him.

"No, so I can explain."

"Explain what? That you blew me off for your girlfriend in there? Why didn't you just tell me I was nothing more than a two-night—stand—oh wait, I wasn't even that."

Zacke had no inking of how to answer her. Her reference to his not taking her to bed implied she might have been willing. Would she laugh in his face if he told her how much he wanted to do just that? "Miranda, I want to talk to you. Please?"

"No, I don't think so, Zacke. I came here to see if I could help you with your workload. Maybe do some paperwork but silly me, you seem to be handling your extra duties just fine."

Miranda hands moved back and forth over the material of her lab coat. Zacke wondered if she even realized she was wrinkling its starched crease.

"I understand you have to work, Zacke. But I don't like being put on the curb like a piece of trash, especially when you led me to believe we were going to be more than friends."

The catch in her voice tugged at his heart. "I do want that one day but..."

"And I suppose you think I'm dumber than dirt? Do you think I'm so pitiful or needy that I don't see that you were just stringing me along? Did your girlfriend just get back into town? How convenient that I just happen to be here to fill in the gap. But no more, not in this lifetime."

Zacke reached out to touch her cheek but Miranda moved back. His chest ached. "I am—"

"Save it. I don't want to hear anymore."

His hands fell to his sides. A quick scan of the area told him Gabriella had left—his reason for keeping Miranda from leaving now gone.

Miranda walked away, taking his heart, which should not have felt pain with her. He wanted to kick something, tear someone, or something to shreds. His teeth ached, and his blood turned colder than English winters at the thought of losing the one woman who could turn his dark existence into light.

Chapter Eight

Miranda's eyes caught the lighted dial of her alarm clock. Another hour had crawled by. The numbers flashed at her before blurring into a red glow. Surely, they matched the bloodshot state of her eyes. Behind her maligned eyelids, her eyes throbbed and burned and her nose felt like a wad of cotton. She had used half the tissues from the full box sitting on her bedside table.

Now after hours of crying, she felt almost numb. A stray tear slid from the corner of her eyes every now and then, belying her anesthetized state.

She had only herself to blame. She'd done the unforgivable, the unthinkable, and the unbelievable. She had fallen in love.

Oh, yes, I knew it was foolish—I only met the man last week. Sure, he saved my life but that doesn't mean he was doing more than his job. I should have known better. Stupid, stupid to fall for someone as sexy as Zacke is. Why couldn't I have been content with just my career? How could I possibly think love was for me?

Tell that to her treacherous heart or her mind— both of which she lost the day Zacke entered her life.

She cringed anew over her behavior the evening before. But it had been a shock to see Zachary in the embrace of that woman. He'd been holding her hands, and the kiss she gave him was unmistakable. It carried the stamp "he's mine" and Zacke hadn't made any effort to pull away.

"Darn it! He'd lied to me." In fact, probably all he had told her had been lies. Of course, he hadn't said he loved her—not in so many words—but he had referred to the fact he wanted to be more than friends. He had plied her with wine and wooed her with a silver tongue. "The only truth he spoke was wanting me in bed. Ha, well that certainly wasn't going to happen."

Oh, but she had to give him credit. He used his job as a cop to advantage—an excellent ploy— rescuing damsels in distress. And it had worked like a well-oiled machine. She had fallen under his spell.

God bless America. She had believed him, hook, line, and sinker. He had almost reeled her in, until she spit out the hook. But there wasn't a chance this side of Hades of that happening now.

I'm not stupid, I know if you can't run with the big dogs, you need to stay on the porch.

She planned to stay as far away from the man as she could.

****

Zacke stood in the shadows of the room. He had learned how to cloak himself with darkness not long after his transformation. His invisibility came in handy when he pursued criminals.

Tonight it served no purpose but to rend the useless organ from his chest.

He had spent the night standing guard. He could keep Miranda safe from Gabriella, but who would keep her safe from him? He'd hurt her. Her loud sobs dwindled to soft weeping, but both would linger in his mind for centuries to come. He despised the pain he brought to her, and he hated his inability to do anything about it.

He had lost her.

Even if he could convince Miranda he didn't love Gabriella, he had nothing to offer her.

He brought only misery to those he cared about. His father had lamented over his death and his mother had turned into an old woman before his eyes. He lost all but two of his childhood friends to death.

Zacke could blame no one but himself. His actions had been the catalyst; his lust his downfall. Gabriella could not have turned him into an immortal creature if he had not succumbed to her seductive lure.

He would cause Miranda no further harm. She would have his protection until she was no longer in danger but after that—

The shrill ring of her alarm cut into his thoughts. Miranda moved one slender arm from under the bed coverings and slapped at the clock. She grew still and he wondered if she finally slept.

The sun edged over the horizon and Zacke knew it was time to leave. He moved toward the window.

"Zacke?"

He froze.

Miranda couldn't possibly see him but could she somehow sense his presence? Why now and not before? He turned back toward the bed, afraid to see the look of distrust and possible horror on her face.

She sat up, her lovely body reclining against the headboard. Her hair, a tangled mass of copper, framed her face. Black lashes, spiked from tears, outlined her blue eyes dimmed by her sleepless night.

He stood still, afraid to move in the deafening silence. He could hear her heart beating within her chest. He wondered if she could hear the racing of his own heart.

"It must have been the wind." Miranda's words broke the quiet.

The disappointment he heard in her voice prompted him to step forward. He stopped himself before he reached the bed and took her in his arms. It would do no good to frighten her to death. Calling back his concentration, which had scattered to the four winds upon hearing his name, he whispered a comfort prayer. He completed it with an urgent command for her to sleep.

The sun's rays now crested the treetops. He needed to be gone. But still he didn't move. He waited until Miranda slid back down in the bed and her breathing relaxed before he allowed his desire to overcome his common sense.

He approached her slumbering body. The purity of her face, still marred by a score of tear-tracks, looked beautiful beyond belief. Although he felt the rays of the sun heat his skin, he had one more thing to do: a safety prayer to keep Gabriella out along with any henchmen she might send to do her dirty work.

That done, Zacke leaned down and brushed her lips with his own. The sweetness pulling at him threatened to drop him to his knees. He fought the urge to lie at her side. It would mean his death—but to die in Miranda's arms would be worth the agony.

****

Miranda sipped from the hot cup of coffee before setting it down and dropping her head in her hands. Lord above, she was tired. She awoke with fatigue swamping her limbs—almost as if she had taken a sleeping pill.

She gulped more of the hot brew. She still had half a shift to go. During the first half, she stayed busy enough to keep thoughts of Zacke at bay.

Her last thought before falling asleep had been of him. With him she felt safe and loved. Which didn't make any sense—the man was responsible for her sleeplessness in the first place. But she'd swear she'd felt his presence.

Of course, her brain could just be on overload. What other reason would she have to think she had tasted the seductive lure of his lips?

"Dr. James, our GSW is here." Miranda looked

up to see Mac standing in the doorway.

"On my way, Mac." Miranda left her office and thoughts of Zacke behind as she ran toward the emergency room.

****

Zacke awoke to the piercing trill of his cell phone. Something's wrong.

Only one person had access to his private number.

The ringing stopped.

He tried to move his limbs but failed. He concentrated on his phone and willed it to come to him. He pressed the button for recent calls. Gideon's number flashed.

Horror embraced his mind as one word screamed inside his brain. *Miranda.* Had something happened to her? He hit the callback feature and waited an eternity for Gideon to pick up.

"Is Miranda safe?"

Zacke heard Gideon suck in air so forcibly he started choking. He waited impatiently for his partner to get his breath back.

"Zacke?"

"Yes. Now, tell me, is Miranda safe?"

"She was when I checked about thirty minutes ago. And by the way, so am I. Thanks for asking."

Relief coated his laughter at Gideon's exasperation. "You're welcome. So, what's going on?"

"Sorry. I know you need your beauty rest, but Captain Myers is on a rampage. They found another body—same MO. He called me when he got your voice mail. After tearing a strip off my handsome hide, he said to get in touch with you. He wants us both on the scene, now. I tried to put him off. I told him you might be out following a lead, but he didn't buy it."

Zacke didn't reply. Gabriella had lied again. Why he was surprised, he didn't know, but he'd *hoped* she would keep her word. He'd called it wrong. Mingling with mortals had corrupted his instincts when it came to Gabriella. He wouldn't make that mistake again. He must think as a creature, not a man—something he could never be again.

"Earth to Zacke. Did you hear what I said?"

"Yes. I need a bit of time to wake up. Give me the address, and I'll meet you there."

Once the information he needed was stored in his memory banks, Zacke disconnected the call. He attempted and then managed to move his body off the bed. His legs trembled so badly he almost fell. He needed a shower, and he had to feed. Without both, he would never make it out of his house, let alone face the sun or the crime scene.

A scant fifteen minutes later, he was ready to go. His limbs still trembled like a newborn calf, but doubling his ration of blood should give him strength and help protect him from the sun's rays, as would the long sleeve shirt he wore. Dark shades covered his eyes and with the air-conditioning running in the car, he should be fine. He just prayed when he stepped out of the car, he wouldn't fall flat on his face.

****

Doctor D's medical van sat next to Gideon's truck. This time Gabriella had tossed the body in a dumpster near the back of a popular shopping mall. Security would be harder to enforce. Probably one of the reasons Myers had been adamant about no delay. The other being, three murders in less than two weeks would probably make the national news. Not good for the department, and political suicide for a captain who hoped to become chief.

Zacke stepped out of the car and moved toward the crime scene. So far, so good. The sun heated his skin, but he could handle it—for a bit.

Gideon waved to him. From the looks of his pale face, he had already lost whatever junk food he had consumed that day. The truth be known, Zacke's own internal organs were doing flip-flops, further proving that sometimes a liquid diet came in handy.

He traversed his way through street cops, emergency personnel, and the beginning of a media circus. Gideon lifted the yellow tape, which proved ineffective in keeping the curious back.

"You okay, Zacke?"

"I'm alive as much as I can be. How about you?"

"So far, but I ain't fond of the eat and purge diet your ex-girlfriend has me on."

Gideon's softly spoken words, held an underlying meaning.

"Did she leave a note this time?"

"I wouldn't exactly say a note, but she did leave her calling card."

Zacke followed Gideon to where the body lay. After a grim look at the detectives, Dr. D went back to examining the young woman's body. Gideon pulled back the sheet covering the woman's lower back.

From the looks of the symmetrical letter "Z" etched just above the woman's buttocks, Zacke identified one of Gabriella's claws as the weapon.

He had little doubt that she wanted to mark her victims with his guilt. Remorse ate at him like a wolf devouring a lamb.

His knees buckled and for the first time in his inhuman life, he experienced the equivalent of dry heaves.

****

Two hours later, Zacke found himself at the station filling out paper work—Gideon's orders. His partner had been adamant. Zacke was to stay inside until the sun went down. And here he sat behind a desk, waiting for his partner to call him. He resisted the urge to snarl at his impotence. He hated waiting for someone else to do his job.

His first thought after almost puking up his guts had been for Miranda. Gideon left to check on her as soon as Dr. D loaded the body in his van. But before he peeled out of the parking lot, he had given Zacke a piece of his mind.

Zacke would have argued with him, but Gideon wore his "don't mess with this southern boy's face." Then he did something no one else had ever done. He had gotten in his face and yelled. "Don't be stupid, man. Stop being a hero for once and look after yourself. You have to be strong to help Miranda."

The truth of his words filtered into Zacke's dizzy head and slowly registered. He had to focus on what needed to be done—stop Gabriella before she killed again.

To do that he had to regain the strength the sun had sapped from him. He would follow Gideon's orders, but not knowing if Miranda remained safe played havoc on his nerves.

When his cell phone rang, he had it to his ear before a second ring started.

"She's fine, man. I spoke to her for a minute."

"Did you tell—?"

"No, I told her I had a friend in the hospital and just wanted to say hi."

Zacke hated that Gideon had to lie to Miranda. But he didn't want her even more upset. He had caused her enough distress for a lifetime.

He tried but couldn't stop himself from asking, "Did she mention me?"

"No, but she had an emergency coming in."

Zacke applauded Gideon's efforts to spare him. At times, his partner could read him like a well-loved book. The events of the past night had not been mentioned, but he knew Gideon picked up his emotional turmoil concerning Miranda.

"Give her time, Zacke. She'll come around when you explain to her what—"

"Explain what? That my ex-girlfriend as you so eloquently put it, is a murderer. That not only is she a vampire but I'm one also?"

"Well, sheesh, that ain't exactly what I meant."

Zacke sighed. "I'm sorry, but I would prefer not having this conversation over the phone—or even at all—"

"Have it your way, Zacke. I'm headed back to the station now. Do yourself and Miranda a favor. Tell her the truth."

Before he could reply, there was a click and then a buzz as Gideon hung up.

The seldom-used coffee mug he kept on his desk, exploded into pieces as it hit the brick wall across from him.

He left the shards of glass where they settled. He would wait no longer. Sunset neared, and he needed to find Gabriella before she awoke.

Chapter Nine

Gabriella smoothed the folds of her skirt over her hips and awaited her prey. She expected her quarry to arrive any minute and then she would put her plan into operation. It had been a pleasure to toy with her latest victim; just a bit of torture had loosened the woman's tongue. The men she sought frequented the Silver Lady Club.

She despised the depraved morals of this century's inhabitants. In her day, women and men alike had chosen their bedding partner in a more discreet manner. Taverns existed, but only women of ill repute and their favorites had frequented them. Still, the several she had visited, recently, had aided her in choosing her victims and would continue to do so.

The young women she'd killed had either been looking for a one-night stand or a lasting relationship.

She chose Savannah for her coming out for one reason—Lord Zachary Kensington.

From the beginning, he resisted the ties that should have bound them after she'd transformed him. He repudiated her claim of ownership and his refusal to become her mate angered her. He had spurned her plans for unholy wedlock and rebuffed all her thought commands. His will to defy her appeared even stronger than before.

Zachary's strong will had been one of the traits that drew her to him in the first place. And his handsome and youthful looks helped to make up for years of suffering an arranged marriage and then marriages to old men so she wouldn't have to live on the streets. She knew Zachary thought she killed her first husband, but she was innocent in James's death.

Innocent, but not sorry he had died.

He had been a tightwad and abusive. Claude, a man she had met while at court, had taken care of that problem for her. He'd also changed her life by transforming her into a vampire. She would have been content to live out eternity with Claude, but the wastrel had been careless. His last victim's husband had taken his head.

Such a pity. Claude had been excellent in the bedchamber, almost as good as Zachary. Her next two husbands had died by her own hands and fangs.

Gabriella took a sip from her glass of beer. She forced herself to swallow. Compared to the aged wine and ale she had been served at court, it tasted putrid. But it allowed her to blend in with the mortals around her.

"Hey baby, how about you and me getting out of this joint?"

Gabriella turned to her left and looked at the man leaning against the bar. His come-hither posture blocked her view of the door. She kept her gaze on the man's hopeful expression as she set her glass down on the bar's polished surface.

Mortal men were so transparent with their lust.

She reached out and caressed the man's jaw. He wore a suit and tie, which made him more acceptable than some of the less formally dressed patrons. His dark hair reminded her of Zachary's. His clipped mustache accentuated lips she might consider worth exploring, if she had the time—which she didn't. His blue gaze stared back at her, clouded with his slightly inebriated state. She pursed her lips in a mock kiss before extending her fangs.

The man jumped back as if scalded, slamming

into the couple standing behind him. Gabriella laughed when the woman's partner pulled back his fist and plowed it into the face of her rejected suitor.

Two minutes later, her view of the door was once again clear, and the man's unconscious body had been removed from the floor.

The door's bell signaled another arrival, and she took out her compact and lipstick. She liked some of the advantages of this day and time. It was much easier opening a tube instead of crushing berries to color her lips.

She angled the compact toward the door and applied color as she watched the two men approach. They strutted within a foot of her barstool.

She returned the makeup to her bag, twisted her body on the swivel seat, and managed to slide off the stool, right into the arms of the better-dressed man.

"Oh, I am so sorry."

As Gabriella had hoped, the man wrapped his arms around her waist and held fast.

"Nothing to be sorry about, lady."

"That's so kind of you. I'd really like to make up for my clumsiness. Would you allow me to buy you and your friend a drink?"

"How about I buy you a drink?"

Gabriella nodded but resisted the smug smile that threatened.

The man released her waist but captured her arm. "I think we'll be more comfortable in the back."

She allowed herself to be led to the rear of the bar and then seated in a booth, her body wedged between the men who slid in on either side of her. She wrinkled her nose. The air reeked of cigarette smoke, perspiration, and cheap cologne.

After the better-dressed man placed an order for drinks, Gabriella propped one elbow on the table. She pursed her lips once more, but this time without any evidence of her fangs.

"My name is Gabriella." She caught her bottom lip and worried it with her teeth. "I don't usually drink with strange men."

"We can take care of that right now, pretty lady. My name is Jake and my associate here, is Tyler."

****

Zacke dove and twisted through the dark sky. The time spent inside the police department's confining walls had helped. His strength was back to normal, the nausea gone, and the slight headache he'd developed after hearing from Gideon a thing of the past. However, his hunt for Gabriella so far had been fruitless. He'd stopped at the mausoleum right after he left the station. His old abode smelled of death and the slight scent of her perfume but was devoid of her presence.

The night wind caressed his body as he moved with it. He welcomed its soothing touch after the day's sultry heat. He headed toward a small graveyard on the outskirts of the city. Although it fell at the bottom of his list of places Gabriella would seek as a haven, he still needed to check it out. Hope dwindled to reality with the knowledge that he might not catch her in her lair or at all this night.

He landed inside the gates of a private family plot. Most of the departed souls lay buried underground in coffins, with the exception of one petite aboveground crypt. Given his knowledge of Gabriella's taste, he really didn't think this would be her choice of a resting place.

The door hung on its hinges but rested flush against the threshold. He placed one palm against the rotting vegetation covering the iron handle and pushed. The door splintered and then caved in onto the stone floor. His nose wrinkled from the burst of putrid air expelled out of the crypt's moldy interior. Cobwebs without inhabitants strung a canopy of silver across the ceiling and the corners of the tomb, but no footprints marred the dust-covered floor.

His fist slammed into the mildewed side of the tomb. Rivulets of crimson ran between his fingers and spattered a floor strewn with the bones of rodents long dead.

Despair carved a wound inside his heart. He had to find Gabriella before she again sought revenge for his imagined wrongdoings. The she-demon would bask in delight as she enlightened Miranda to the circumstances of his origins. He could only imagine Miranda's reaction to his creature-state. But Gabriella would not stop there; she would torture Miranda before she killed her. He scrubbed his face with his knuckles. Gabriella's bargain was broken, and now, there was only one way he could ensure Miranda's safety.

His frustrated roar startled two bats that had entered in his wake. The winged creatures left their newfound home and flew back through the doorway, escaping to the sky.

Zacke followed a moment later—a new destination taking root in his mind.

****

Miranda moved around the cubicle comprising her kitchen and winced when she jammed her hip into the refrigerator. Another bruise to add to the many she'd accumulated since moving into the apartment. She missed the large homey kitchen of her parents' home. She had kept the house after their deaths but rented it out before moving to Savannah. The tenant's lease would be up in less than a year, and Miranda didn't know if she would renew it.

She turned off the soup simmering on the barely operable range. Maybe she should resign her position at the hospital and move back home. Distance might make the heart grow fonder, but it would also prevent her from running into Zacke unexpectedly.

She poured the fragrant liquid into one of the two bowls in her cabinet and crushed some saltines on top. Who was she kidding? Out of sight—out of mind would just not cut it when it came to Detective Kensington. She could run to the ends of the earth and still not escape her attraction to the man.

Miranda pushed the bowl away—her appetite vanished. She wished her thoughts of Zacke would leave just as quickly.

The hand she propped under her chin shook slightly. She would have to get her thoughts under control. She couldn't allow her personal life to interfere with the care of her patients.

Sleep would help but she didn't want to go to bed just yet. She needed to come to some decision about what to do—move or stay here. She hated the idea of giving up her job.

Her eyelids seemed to have a will of their own, and she couldn't prevent them from closing over eyes that felt like sand granules had invaded them. She should get up and go to bed, but her legs would not cooperate. Lord, she was tired. She would just rest a minute.

****

Miranda awoke suddenly. Her head thrust forward and almost connected with the table. She wondered if the stiffness in her neck came from the sudden drop in gravity or from the position in which she'd slept.

She glanced at her watch—almost midnight. She'd slept two hours. She shook her arm to get rid of the pins and needles, before standing up. After dumping the congealed soup into the sink, she turned on the tap and splashed cold water on her face. Giving the tap a hard wrench to turn off the water, she stood for a moment before heading for bed.

The living room's darkness surprised her because she knew she'd left the lamp on. The bulb must have burned out.

She started toward the doorway of her bedroom but stopped. Goose bumps dotted her arms. She should have turned down the air conditioner before she fell asleep.

She checked the thermostat; it was *down*. A memory teased her mind. She'd felt this way before—her first meeting with Zacke and again in the restaurant, right before he'd arrived.

I'm losing it. There's no way I can conjure the man up out of thin air. "Oh, Zacke, why didn't you just leave me alone? Why did you claim you wanted more than friendship when you didn't mean it?"

"But I did mean it, Miranda."

Miranda's heart beat a staccato rhythm inside her chest. Could her fatigued mind be playing tricks on her? If so, she didn't find it funny, not in the least.

A hand touched her shoulder. Her body jerked before she twisted around to find herself staring at a man's shirt buttons. Her gaze strayed upward and came to rest on the face of the man she had sworn to forget.

Her last coherent thought taunted her with its truth—she *had* lost her mind, and all the therapy in the world wouldn't bring it back.

****

"Miranda, wake up!"

The voice calling her name seemed to be coming from directly over her head. Maybe she was dreaming. She didn't remember coming to bed but she must have—she was lying on it. The voice sounded like Zacke's, so it had to be a dream—or a nightmare. Either way it didn't matter. She'd sworn off the man and this auditory delusion was just her heart's way of getting even.

"Miranda, please."

The rasped words sounded desperate. Could it be concern she heard in the figment's voice? Ridiculous! She might have fallen over the edge into the abyss of madness, but she still had enough sanity to know one pertinent fact. A man who brushed you off like you were yesterday's news wouldn't be worried—even in a dream.

Besides, he's not here anyway.

Something cold landed on her forehead covering her eyes, Miranda jerked forward, banging her forehead into something solid and hard. "Ouch!" She reached up to pull whatever attacked her face away and encountered a hand. This time her careening jerk caused her to topple sideways. Her flailing hands connected with what felt like a nose before gravity spilled her onto the floor.

"For the love of—"

The imaginary voice stopped, but before Miranda could get her limbs untangled or open her mouth to tell it to go away, hands snatched her up and held her against an incredibly muscular chest. The bands of steel that held her felt achingly familiar.

"Zacke?"

"What do I have to do to convince you I am here?"

Miranda, for the first time since her impromptu fainting spell, opened her eyes. She lifted one tentative and trembling hand to touch his face.

"I take it you now believe I am real?"

The humor she heard in Zacke's voice rivaled the twinkling in his eyes. For a moment, she allowed herself to forget all that had happened, until her pragmatic mind barred the hope in her heart. "Yes, and if you don't mind, I would prefer you put me down."

The ice she forcibly injected into her tone found its mark. The muscles in Zacke's jaw tightened before he placed her back on the bed. He moved with a panther's grace to the chair across the room.

The distance he placed between them helped Miranda to breathe again. The man was entirely too sexy for her own good. As much as she wanted to throw herself back into his arms, she refused to oblige her wanton desire. She had some questions, and he had better have the right answers.

"Why are you here and more importantly, how did you get in?" She watched Zacke's face. Would she be able to tell if he lied to her? Probably not.

Yet, his presence must have some meaning, didn't it? So absorbed in her thoughts, she almost failed to see the slight grimace that touched his features.

"I am here because I couldn't stay away."

"Sure, and it snows in Savannah in July."

"Miranda, I have reasons that I can't explain right now, but I am here because I *want* to see you."

His voice held sincerity, but could she believe him? She'd fallen for that line before.

"Yeah, right. Then explain why you were kissing that woman."

Zacke's lithe body moved just a bit. Oh, Heavens, surely he wasn't getting up. She couldn't think straight when he stood near her. When he only sat forward, Miranda couldn't decide if she felt relief or disappointment.

"In the first place, I wasn't kissing her, *she* was kissing me."

"Oh, but—"

"Yes, there is a difference. If I need to explain it to you then it will be a hands on explanation."

Shards of fire played tag in her blood. She knew she would be lost if he touched her. But if he kissed her with those lethal lips of his, she would melt like butter in a hot frying pan. Something she wasn't prepared to have happen—at least not at the moment. The man still had some serious sweet-talking to do to get out of the hole he had dug for himself. And she still wanted to know how he got inside her apartment.

"All right, let's say I believe you didn't instigate the kiss. You certainly didn't stop it."

"It was only a kiss on my cheek. Believe me, I would have stopped her if it had been more."

"Who was she? I spoke to her in the elevator at the hospital, but I assumed she was one of the doctor's wives."

"She is an old acquaintance. Someone I had hoped never to see again. She doesn't matter. You're the one I care about."

"I really want to believe you Zacke, but you still haven't told me how you got in here."

"Would you believe I picked the lock?"

"Why didn't you just ring the doorbell, like a normal person would do?"

"You were asleep. I didn't want to wake you."

"Fudge. How could you know that? Please don't expect me to believe you have x-ray vision like Superman."

He closed his eyes and leaned back in the chair.

Probably to think up something to substantiate his outrageous lie, Miranda thought. When his laughter reached out and caressed her ears with its fullness, she began to doubt *his* sanity.

"I'm so glad you find something humorous about this. I personally think you've lost your ever-loving mind."

He stopped chuckling and the look in his eyes grew so intense, she wouldn't have been surprised if the room ignited from its heat. The air-conditioning she had turned down would feel good against her suddenly warm skin.

"I apologize, Miranda, but you caught me off guard with your super-hero remark. When I knocked and you didn't answer, I assumed you were asleep. So I went around back and climbed the fire escape."

"That still didn't give you the right to break and enter my apartment."

"A B&E would mean I had to break something to gain entrance. I'm not guilty of that. I merely opened the window you left ajar in your bedroom and climbed in."

His tone had lost its laughter. The fault was hers, but she couldn't afford to let his actions slide.

"Rest assured, I'll make certain the window is not only closed but locked next time."

"That would be a good idea. There was another killing this afternoon."

Miranda's outrage took a backseat to the implications of his statement. Her gaze moved to the window he had closed. She *had* been foolish. After her experience in the parking lot, she had made it a priority to check all the windows and the door before she left home and after she returned. But tonight her emotions had interfered with her common sense.

She allowed herself to be enthralled by two small birds that had lit on the windowsill earlier that evening. She opened the window just a bit to place some crumbs on the sill. Their feathered antics had taken her mind off Zacke for a bit. When she left the room to fix dinner, she had failed to close and lock the window.

Miranda turned her gaze to his. "What exactly do you want from me, Zacke?"

"I want you to tell me you'll see me again."

"And if I don't?"

"I'll leave you alone."

Miranda moved from the bed. Her insides quaked like a preacher delivering his first sermon. What should she do? If she told him to stay away and he did, then she would be cutting off her nose to spite her face. She wanted to see Zacke. More than that, she wanted to know what it felt like to make love with him.

The thought of all that muscular body exposed caused her to pull up short on her way to the kitchen. Her face felt like a ribbon of fire touched it. The heat traveled downward, leaving her in a mess of want. Her dad's words, "If you can't stand the heat stay out of the kitchen," rang in her ears.

She pressed an ice-cold glass of water against her forehead. It helped drown some of the heat in her face. Now if she could just get the rest of the flames doused, she could concentrate on what she should tell Zacke.

Water sloshed from the glass when two identifiable arms slid around her waist. Zacke pulled her back to rest against a chest she had grown to appreciate. A skin-tingling breath caressed one side of her neck before moving to her ear. The gentle tug of his lips on her lobe sent a pulse of desire straight to the center of her body. Lord above, did the man sit up at night thinking of ways to entice her?

Zacke reached out and rescued the glass of water from her trembling grip. The sensual brush of his fingers against hers caused an erotic earthquake to erupt inside Miranda.

He turned her to face him. She hid her face against the softness of his shirt. He gently cupped her chin and raised it. She was lost to all but the lips descending to claim her own. He nipped her bottom lip, and she opened to the probing touch of his tongue. She met his caress with one of her own. Fire ignited and then burned a trail of passion straight to her core. When he finally released her, she feared she wouldn't be able to breathe normally again.

"Now do you believe me? Will you give us another chance?"

Miranda held on to what bit of pride she had left. She waited all of ten seconds before she whispered, "Yes."

She confirmed her answer as her lips sought out and laid claim to his. If the man was the King of Seduction, then she needed a bit of practice to be Queen.

Chapter Ten

Zacke opened his eyes but didn't make the effort to leave his bed. He noticed the darkened room's interior. It could be close to sundown; or an unpredictable summer storm pended.

Not even the possibility of thunder, lightning, or the torrential downpours that usually accompanied the humidity could dampen his spirits.

Tonight he had a date with Miranda. He wouldn't have blamed her if instead of listening to him, she had told him to get the Hell out. But thank God, she had listened.

The closer he stayed to Miranda until he found Gabriella, the better. He'd almost lost her through his own stupidity, and Gabriella's show-stopping scene had only made it worse. Miranda needed to know she could trust him—with her life if necessary.

Zacke pushed the silk sheet off his lower body; he had never grown accustomed to the feel of cotton-polyester blends. He smiled at the thought of how Miranda would look on the black sheets with her auburn hair and pale skin.

The physically incapacitating desire that lengthened his sex astounded him. His constant craving for Miranda threatened to shatter his control. Their first kiss had been all he expected and more. She returned his desire in spades, but she might not appreciate him jumping her the first moment he had her alone. A cold shower would put out the flames that burned within him, or at least he hoped.

He had bribed Gideon to cover for him if they

got a call with the promise of a new music CD.

He planned to take Miranda to a restaurant that boasted a view of the Savannah River, and he hoped the seductive atmosphere would aid him in wooing her spirit as well as her body. After dinner, he had arranged for a horse and carriage drive though the old section of the city. A moonlight and roses tour could not hurt his cause.

As he moved through the ordinary rites of preparing for his dinner engagement, his mind touched again on the number one reason Miranda would be smart to avoid him—Gabriella.

After her latest victim, she had been quiet. Too quiet. No doubt she bided her time, but three days had passed without a peep from her. He prayed, when she struck again, he would catch her in the act. If she still hovered over the poor soul, he could justify killing her and not worry about the consequences or his conscience.

But enough of Gabriella. He had a lady waiting, and he didn't plan on being late. A black suit followed an ivory dress shirt. He purposely left the tie on its hanger. He despised wearing them—they reminded him of a garrote he had seen once in France during the Revolution. He splashed just a bit of Dolce and Gabbana on his throat. Gideon had called the expensive cologne a *babe catcher*.

He took the stairs at a run; his anticipation of the evening ahead had caused his inner hunger to flare. He would dine as a mortal tonight, but first a reinforcement of blood. He wanted to make sure his natural male lust wouldn't aggravate the monster within.

Miranda would certainly not appreciate playing Little Red Riding Hood to his big, bad wolf.

****

Miranda's hands trembled as she tried for the fourth time to fasten the circle of pearls around her

neck. They had been a treasured gift from her
parents when she'd been accepted into medical
school. The ivory shade provided a perfect foil for the
little black number she purchased on her lunch
break. Its length was a bit on the short side for her
comfort level, but the lady at the boutique had sworn
it was all the rage. The elegant lines of the dress
caressed skin she had soaked in a jasmine-scented
bath. A spritz of the same bouquet against her pulse
points boosted her confidence. She had also made a
quick stop on the way home to pick up some silky
panty hose.

So what if she wanted to look her best? A
woman had to make some concessions when invited
out to dinner with a man like Zacke.

She pressed a hand to her stomach. Lord, he
hadn't even arrived yet, but he still managed to
orchestrate her body into a nervous volcano. She had
not eaten a bite all day; just the thought of food
made her want to run for the nearest bathroom. Her
nerves were doing handsprings on the inside of her
muscles. If that wasn't enough to make her crave a
large glass of wine, then she had no clue what
would.

She knew alcohol and a night with Zacke would
not mix well. Whenever she drank too much, she got
mellow—fluid bones and a loose mouth. She needed
a clear head tonight. She wanted to make sure the
honesty she glimpsed in his eyes at their last
meeting had been real. She wanted to trust him so
much that her heart hurt at the thought he might be
lying. This man had her flipping over him, and his
declaration that he cared for her made her want to
shout hallelujah—when she wasn't shaking in her
shoes. How could a man that sexy want her?

When the doorbell cut into her thoughts, she
jumped, almost losing her balance. The new three-
inch high heels she splurged on would almost make

her even with his beautiful lips.

She dismissed another glance in the mirror. It was too late to change even if she had second thoughts.

She grabbed her shawl and draped it over her shoulders, allowing the fringed ends to hang low in the front, before she answered the door.

"Evening, Zacke." Miranda followed her words with a smile.

"You look stunning, Miranda."

"Well, I have to admit, you don't look half bad yourself, Detective. You wash up well."

Miranda would never have believed it if she hadn't seen it with her own eyes. Zachary Kensington, Mr. Macho-detective blushed. The rose color tinged his cheeks and then inched into the strands of raven that rested against his temples.

His jacket drew her gaze to the width of his shoulders, and the shirt he wore contrasted with the smooth column of his throat. She resisted the urge to see if the dark trousers fit him as well as his jeans.

Miranda inhaled sharply; she needed to get a rein on her reactions to Zacke. She didn't plan on being sidetracked tonight. She had an agenda—one that would make him forget all about the woman in red. Miranda intended to show him a side of herself he'd never seen before. A self-assured woman who knew what she wanted and went after it. Not a wimp that fainted after a kiss or a basket case that cried because she lost her man.

"Shall we go?"

Zacke's words soaked into her "I am woman, hear me roar" mindset.

"Whatever you say." She fought the giggle that threatened to escape after Zacke's mouth dropped open. Instead, she gave him her best femme fatale look then turned and locked her door.

Zacke stared at the sway of Miranda's shapely

derriere. Lord, he would pay to have the same opportunity to cover her buttocks, as the shimmering material did. Gideon would laugh if he were here and tell him to close his flytrap.

All thoughts of Gideon and humor fled when Miranda turned after entering the elevator. She had removed the feminine and old-fashioned wrap that had covered the curve of her shoulders. The neckline of her sexier-than-sin dress plummeted in a V-shape almost to her navel.

For the first time in his unnatural life, Zacke knew what it felt like to be hunted.

****

After the waiter removed their dinner plates, Zacke wondered if either he or Miranda knew what they'd eaten. The bit of conversation they had engaged in had mainly consisted of menu choices and the humid weather—not at all what he had planned to discuss.

It seemed that his date had an agenda all her own. He did not have to delve into her mind to appreciate the trap she baited for him. However, his experiences in the past didn't tell him how to escape the seductive lure of her innocence and desire combined.

Miranda was playing with fire, her body sending darts of enticement straight to his loins. The occasional glances she gave him, when not staring at her uneaten food on her plate, had been full of flirty seduction. If she were any other woman, he would not hesitate in calling her bluff. He'd survived without a woman for a long time, but this woman stirred him body and soul as no other had or ever would. She was his, and he grew tired of fighting the war between his shaft and his mind. He might not be mortal, but the flesh that still covered his bones ached to swathe hers.

He watched Miranda toy with her wine glass. At

times, she looked tempted to gulp it down in one swallow, and at others, she barely coated her lips with the blush of the vine.

"Would you care for anything else, Miranda?"

The startled jump, almost unnoticeable, caused her breasts to push against their barely-there covering. The ample glimpse of flesh that would fit comfortably in his hands caused his erection to awake once again; a blessing to be sure that the table hid his burgeoning arousal.

"No. Are you ready to leave?"

Miranda's facial expression changed from reserved to disappointed. Zacke bit back the laughter that sought an escape. So, she hadn't given up her plan to seduce him. Good. He welcomed the dance of desire singeing his flesh, and before he took her home, Miranda would find out what taunting a beast would get her.

****

The glide of Miranda's dress over her thigh as she stepped up into the carriage hypnotized Zacke. He craved to follow the movement with his fingers. Jealousy was a new sin for him, but the need to rip the clothing from her body and replace it with his bare skin consumed him. Only his reluctance to share viewing her body with a multitude of passersby quelled his animal instincts—for now.

"Zacke, the driver is waiting."

For the second time that night and he vowed the last, he could feel heat surging into his face. The driver's smug but commiserating look didn't restore his self-esteem. At the age of four hundred and ten, he was much too old to blush.

He gave Miranda a smile and then followed her into the open horse-drawn conveyance. The carriage tours of Savannah were renown for their ambiance and historical tone. This particular excursion would take them down cobblestone streets and into the heart of the city. Although other expeditions were available, he had no desire to see the ghost and demons that made up the haunted tour. He had enough of his own without dealing with men, women, children, and monsters wandering in limbo.

He picked up the bouquet of red roses from the seat across from them and handed it to Miranda. A bottle of champagne, also part of the package, sat in an ice bucket on the opposite seat. In his opinion, the price was well worth it. Miranda's eyes glowed and the fake persona, she had previously displayed, disappeared.

"Oh, Zacke, these are beautiful. Thank you."

"No need for thanks. The flowers can never suffice for what I have put you through in the last few days."

This time a blush tinted Miranda's cheeks. "I'd rather forget about the past."

Zacke's breath caught in his throat. "So would I."

He dropped his arm over her bare shoulders and pulled her closer to his heart. A place he wanted her to remain for all eternity. He closed his eyes. He could feel her heart beat next to his and he gloried in the melody. The myth that a vampire's heart did not beat was just that—a fable. Although dead during the day, he revived when the sun set with almost all of the normal workings of a mortal's body.

Miranda's pulse quickened and then went into overdrive as she leaned into the hard contour of Zacke's chest. His scent, which had teased her senses all evening, wrapped her in its spell. The man embodied seduction. But it wasn't just lust she felt emanating from the man holding her so carefully. She sensed an aura of tranquility.

Somehow, she knew serenity and Zacke were not the best of friends. The edginess and restrained power she glimpsed at their first meeting remained—even when he smiled or made small talk. His laughter, which she loved, was conspicuously absent most of the time. The man she cared for fought more than crime; he struggled with an inner war against an obscure darkness.

"Miranda?"

She turned into the caress of his hand on her cheek. Her plan to seduce him vanished. She no longer wanted to sway him with a fabricated personality. She might be a hopeless romantic, but his gentle gesture meant more to her than words.

"Yes?"

"You have been silent for most of the evening. Are you sure you don't regret your decision to see me again?"

She sat up straighter and raised her eyes to meet the solemn look in his. She caught his palm and placed a kiss against his skin. "No, I don't regret it, Zacke. I do hate that I allowed my jealousy to make me behave like a witch. You know, I almost feel sorry for that woman."

"I assure you, she does not need or deserve your pity. She is vicious and dangerous. You need to keep your distance from Gabriella." Zacke's eyes darkened to a deeper blue. His somber gaze prompted a laugh that sounded forced even to her own ears.

"So that's her name; I wondered. So, are you telling me she might, what, come after me because we are dating?"

"That is exactly what I'm telling you. She wouldn't hesitate to hurt you because of me."

Miranda inhaled sharply—his eyes were doing the glowing thing she remembered from their first meeting. She suppressed a shiver. If the color in his eyes weren't so entrancing, she would swear their depths held more than a bit of wildness.

"Zacke?" When he didn't answer her, she waved her hand in front of his face. At last, the color in his eyes receded, and he focused his gaze on her once more.

"Forgive me."

His kiss was nothing like their first, a few days before. This one bordered on brutal, but then gentled until the flick of his tongue eased between her parted lips and bathed her in a hot spring of desire. Her hands, which she'd placed in her lap, clenched in frustration when he stopped. His second assault singed a trail of fire along the column of her throat. He raked the skin with his teeth and then kissed the gooseflesh that rose at his touch.

She grasped the front of his shirt when he tongued the flesh that covered her carotid artery. Her insides trembled when he kissed the skin; her senses reeled when he nipped her shoulder. Craving, unlike any she had ever experienced, rocketed through her. She clasped his head with her hands and fingered the silky length of his hair before pulling his face even with hers.

This time she instigated the kiss. She touched the tip of her tongue to his sensuous lips, which parted for her. She explored the inside of his mouth with a fiery need that shook her to the core. Never had a man's touch made her feel this way; she wanted to swallow him whole and then drown in the elixir of passion he stirred. Her hands slid beneath his jacket and caressed the expanse of his muscular chest. Her fingers stroked the hardness of his abdomen. His body was so perfect it should have been labeled dangerous to touch. She marveled that he allowed her such liberties without taking more of his own. She wanted him to take more and continue to take until she had nothing more to give. But she wasn't allowed that opportunity; Zacke caught her roaming hands, replaced them in her lap, and then turned away.

"Zacke, why did you stop me?"

Zacke swallowed and tried to catch his breath. He drew on all his inner strength to keep from pulling Miranda onto his lap. He craved her softness against the arousal pushing painfully against his pants. Still, he couldn't believe he had allowed things to go so far—to let her touch him so blatantly in public.

He could not risk losing control. He did not want her to see the bloodlust in his eyes or to feel his passion mix with the hunger that fed on blood. Yet, he had not been able to stop himself.

Although he had broken the skin on her throat, he had not suckled the sweet nectar of her blood. He had wanted to—the desire to do so burned like a fever. But to give in to that desire would only make him want more. Therein lay the danger. Three sucklings would be all it took to turn her into a creature, too.

Zacke turned to Miranda. "I stopped you, Little One, because I do not trust myself. Another caress from you, and I would take you as a man would a woman regardless of all who cared to look." He reached out and closed her softly parted lips.

He adored the blush that coated her cheeks but suppressed the desire to kiss it away. He had already compromised Miranda's principles. This woman, who looked so seductive with lips inflamed from his kisses, would probably suffer remorse in the morning for the kiss and the show they had put on for the driver. He could wipe the memory from her mind, but he wanted her to savor all of tonight.

"I think now would be a good time to open the champagne, don't you?" He didn't wait for her answer but popped the cork on the bottle. He poured the sparkling liquid into the souvenir glasses and handed one to Miranda. "What should we drink to?"

"I think we should drink to more nights like this and a future where we ask before jumping to conclusions."

Her serious expression changed when he laughed with elation. He stole another kiss before he tapped her nose lightly with his finger. "I laugh with enjoyment because your words echo my thoughts."

He shared the smile that crept to her lips. He raised his glass in a salute before touching it lightly to hers. Miranda took a small sip. His arousal burgeoned as her tongue darted out to touch the moisture on her lips. His first taste of the champagne resembled a gulp, and the liquid eased the sudden dryness in his throat.

He placed the half-empty glass in a holder before reaching for Miranda's and doing the same. He pulled her forward until he could feel her breasts pushing against his chest. He reveled in the sweet torture for a few moments. He needed to hold her— to reassure himself that tonight was not a fantasy his subconscious had conjured up to persecute him for wanting a normal life. For this evening at least, he would be able to actually hold his dream in his arms.

"Zacke, I won't run away if you loosen your grip just a bit."

Startled, he looked down into eyes that gleamed with amusement. He allowed his arms to ease their hold on her delightful curves but still kept her close to his side.

"Are you sure?" He injected a teasing note in his tone. He didn't dare allow the fear that chilled his spine to show. He couldn't lose her now. She helped to stave off the darkness of an eternity in Hell's flames.

"That depends."

"On what?"

"On whether or not you plan to kiss me again."

His shout of laughter spooked the horse, earning him a glare from the driver. The forward momentum of the horse's gallop threw Miranda even closer. He thanked providence for small gifts.

His lips captured and nipped at hers before his tongue investigated the sweet taste beyond. His pulse flared as Miranda joined him in a delightful dance of desire. The eagerness with which she gave herself over to him made him want to shout for joy. He fancied he heard bells ringing. The ringing continued until it filled his eardrums.

"Hey mister, could you answer your phone? It's scaring my horse."

Zacke pulled his lips from Miranda's and raked an unsteady hand through his hair. He grabbed his cell phone from the inside pocket of his coat. The display showed Gideon's number and 911 after it. He hit the button to answer it and silenced the shrill noise.

"This had better be an emergency."

"It is. Gabriella struck again—a double homicide, this time. The captain says no excuses; you have to get to the murder scene ASAP."

If his thoughts could have willed her there, Gabriella would be burning in Hell at that precise moment. Zacke's fury turned inward; nothing he had done so far had stopped her.

"Sorry, Gideon. Give me time to take Miranda home, and I'll meet you there."

The location this time was close to the hospital where Miranda worked. He doubted it was a coincidence—knowing Gabriella.

He ended the call.

"Miranda, I'm sorry. I have to go."

"Another murder?"

"Yes. This time two victims."

He hugged her briefly before tapping the driver on the shoulder. "I need to get back now."

"Yeah, I heard. Man, oh man, it use to be you felt safe here, but now it's scary to be out after dark on these streets."

"More than you can ever imagine."

Zacke's words dropped into the sudden stillness of the night.

Chapter Eleven

Miranda's intoxicating scent lingered in his nostrils—the mixture of woman and jasmine helped to cut the sweet, cloying smell of blood. The cordoned off area contained the results of Gabriella's handiwork. As before, she had not bothered to drain all the blood from the poor souls she had mutilated. She had allowed it to coat their bodies and stain the ground.

She must be feeding somewhere else. Her eating habits had been voracious in the past. She had always stolen the life sustaining fluid from her victims. He wondered where she hid the corpses that should surely be mounting by now. Or had she found another source? A willing victim from which she could feed without the need to kill.

"Kensington, get over here."

The captain's voice drew Zacke's gaze. He stepped over the yellow tape and moved to where Dr. D, Captain Myers, and Gideon stood.

"I assume you have a good reason for being late."

Zacke ignored the anger Myers's tone stirred. The captain had not actually viewed any of the previous victims before Dr. D had cleaned them up.

"Sorry, Captain, I got here as quickly as I could."

He hoped his answer would suffice without having to go into details about his evening. Dr. D motioned all of them closer, saving him from further chastisement.

"It appears that victim number one died immediately from the slash that severed his carotid artery. The blood sprayed outward and its consistency and darkness indicates he died first."

Dr. D pointed to the other body, which lay almost on top of the man. Gabriella's second victim matched her previous pattern. Her wounds were by far the worse of the two poor souls; gaping holes in her torso and multiple gashes in her abdomen and thighs.

"This young woman was not as fortunate. Most of the spatters point to the fact she lived for a good many minutes before bleeding out."

The group surrounding the bodies remained silent after Dr. D gave his assessment. Two more people had lost their lives, and they had gotten no closer to finding, much less catching, the killer.

Zacke clenched his fists. He should have searched again for Gabriella's resting place before he went to Miranda's. If he had, then maybe she wouldn't have claimed victims four and five. If he didn't find her soon, he feared she would leave off her taunting and go after Miranda.

Dr. D stripped off his gloves and motioned to his assistants. Zacke moved back to give them room to lift the bodies onto the stretchers.

"I want to see you both in my office in the morning, is that clear?" Captain Myers words although couched as a question, held an underlying command.

He left before Zacke or Gideon could respond. Dr. D packed up his equipment and departed before Gideon broke the silence.

"So, what do we do now?"

His partner's expression mirrored the frown Zacke could feel on his own features. With the double murder, the Captain would not be put off any longer with excuses. The cold reality was they had nothing to tell him—at least nothing he would believe. "We could tell him we know for a fact the murderer is a woman."

"You think he'll go for that." Gideon's voice held disbelief.

"Probably not, but at least it's the truth. It's about the only thing we can say until I find and stop Gabriella."

"I hope you took your rabies shot, partner. That is one vicious bat."

Zacke appreciated Gideon's attempt at humor, but the situation they faced didn't have a happy ending in sight if he couldn't find her hiding place.

"You make sure you stay out of her way, Gideon. I made her angry, and her tantrums make a shark's feeding frenzy look like a toddler's snack time."

Zacke moved toward his vehicle. "I plan on spending what is left of the night searching for Gabriella. After that, I'm going to swing by the hospital before our meeting with the captain, and check on Miranda."

He returned Gideon's salute and waited for his partner to climb into his truck and pull out into traffic before he did the same.

****

The sun shone brighter or so it seemed to Miranda as she guided her car through the maze of traffic outside the hospital. She had awakened at dawn, but she didn't feel tired. On the contrary, she felt energized and ready to face the upcoming day.

She pinched herself, upon rising, until it hurt, but the fear that she had imagined her wonderful evening with Zacke was unfounded. It had actually happened; he had held her close and kissed her until her limbs melted into a puddle of dissolved gelatin. She was now certain, more than ever, that she loved him and just maybe he returned that love. The dinner and carriage ride, although lovely, were not the reasons she felt he cared. The touching way he held her and the returned inflection in his tone when she teased him offered a memory she would always treasure.

She pulled into the parking lot and found a spot close to the building. With the Slash and Maul Murderer still at large, she didn't fancy becoming the next victim.

Early for her shift, she thought maybe she would swing by the cafeteria to get a cappuccino. But first, she needed to run to her office and check her messages. Stepping out into the hustle of the fourth floor, she spied Mac coming out of her office. So impressed with the surgical intern's help with her caseload, she had given him a key of his own in case he needed to access medical records for the physicians who covered her surgical patients.

"Hi Mac, how are you this beautiful morning?"

"Doing just fine, Dr. James. You sound in good spirits."

"Yes, I am."

Mac grinned before gesturing toward the open office door.

"Well then that package should make you even happier."

"What package?"

"All I'm saying is that you must rate pretty high with someone. It had to cost a bundle to get flowers delivered after hours."

Miranda didn't satisfy Mac's curiosity. She wanted to gratify her own. Could the flowers be from Zacke? She waltzed into the office and pushed back the scarlet ribbon that encased the box, careful not to tear it. The box wasn't taped, so she lifted the velum top and pulled back the tissue paper to find a single red rose.

Zacke must have sent it to make up for having to cut their evening short. Although she had the lovely roses from the carriage ride, this one deserved a special place—pressed between the pages of her mother's bible. She picked up the long stemmed beauty.

"Ouch." A drop of blood appeared on her fingertip from a thorn the florist had forgotten to trim. She took a piece of the tissue paper and tried again to lift the rose from the box.

"What on earth—?" The bud flopped sideways, its lovely head attached only by a thread to the stem. Had she broken it in her efforts to get it out? Miranda laid the crippled flower down and touched the petals. Her fingers came away wet, coated a flamboyant red.

The rose looked as if *it* were bleeding. Confusion dulled her senses for a moment, until she realized it must be the blood from her own finger coating the beautiful petals. She wiped her finger and then used another corner of the tissue to remove the stains her finger had left on the rose.

More red color came off and marred the white paper.

A few moments later, she drew back her hand. Apprehension and then outrage poured through her as she gazed at several black petals she'd uncovered on the almost decapitated rose.

****

Zacke decided to call it quits when the dawn sky awoke from its dark slumber. His search had been unsuccessful. Every time he glimpsed or sensed Gabriella's presence, she disappeared before he reached her. He was sick and tired of their childish game of hide-and-go-seek. Faced with the upcoming meeting with the captain, the only bright spot in the next couple of hours would be seeing Miranda.

He hated that their evening together terminated prematurely. But it could have been a blessing in disguise. His senses were never at full alert around Miranda. Close proximity to her luscious limbs sent his lust into overdrive. So much for thinking his lustful yearnings had died after he passed the second or third century mark. In Miranda's presence, his body stayed heated at all times. He wanted to keep her on her backside in his bed for the next two hundred years or so.

Not a possibility. Not unless he changed Miranda into a monster. Instead, she would die, and he'd be alone again. Some choice. He could love her for the next fifty years or keep her forever—enduring her hatred if he transformed her.

The past night had been humid and the coming day would be even hotter. A slight breeze would be welcome. Beads of sweat crept toward his eyes and the jeans and T-shirt he had exchanged for his suit felt damp. This particular mortal affliction still confused him, but he hoped it would pass. He'd heard rumors of immortals experiencing human traits, but he had always thought them to be myths.

He glanced at his watch. He could go home and change into something fresher, but he would have to forgo his visit with Miranda. He smiled at the thought of what Miranda's reaction might be to his unkempt appearance.

The hospital came into view just as the sun climbed out of its bed. Miranda's car was already in the parking lot and hopefully, she wouldn't be overrun with emergencies.

Zacke's descent went unnoted by the people passing on the street. He nodded to several of the hospital employees as they exited the rear of the building. After passing through the double doors, Zacke rested his head against the marble interior wall. The cold that had seeped into it from the central air conditioning helped to soothe the slight headache that had made itself known in the last half-hour or so. Zacke hadn't experienced one in centuries, and he had never known his healing spell not to work. He would have to transport himself to the station to avoid the additional pain from the sun.

Once the captain finished hauling him over the coals, he planned to get some much needed sleep. After that, he intended to hunt Gabriella again. There were only so many places she could hide, and he had scoured most of them already.

The vixen's rampage had to be taking a toll on her sleeping habits, which could work to his advantage. It might make her careless and then when he found her with a victim, he could kill her. His personal vampire code prevented him from executing her in cold blood. Eventually he would catch her and then her murdering frenzy would end.

He eased his fatigued body from the wall. His thoughts turned to Miranda and the last kiss they had shared. His craving to taste blood still danced through his veins. The demon inside had howled to get out and condemn her to life after death. Until he met Miranda, the blood he had purchased locally supplied his needs. Now he feared his daily fix couldn't rival the sweet nectar moving through Miranda's veins.

The traffic of employees intensified with the shift change. He opted to take the elevator instead of transferring his body to her office. He would just have to suffer the extra moments it would take to see Miranda.

He resisted the urge to rip the doors open when the elevator thudded to a halt on the fourth floor.

He made his way into the corridor and almost ran to Miranda's office. He expected to find her huddled over a mass of paperwork if he found her in her office at all. He pulled up short at the threshold. Miranda sat at her desk staring at a box sitting on top of it.

As he watched, she reached out with one finger and poked the contents within the white cardboard. The moment she touched the mysterious object she jerked her hand back as if something had bitten her. She repeated the gesture twice more before Zacke decided to interrupt.

"Morning, beautiful."

Miranda's body jerked and her head shot up. "Zacke, you scared me."

"I'm sorry. I've been standing in your doorway for a couple of minutes." He nodded at the box. "What has you so mesmerized?"

The gaze that now stared back at him held confusion.

"Someone sent me a rose."

"A rose?" He moved inside the office and closed the door.

"Yes."

She again reached inside the oblong package. The rustle of tissue and the volume of her sigh seemed to echo through the tiny room. She swallowed before picking up her gift.

Zacke's blood boiled. Who dared to send Miranda a token that signified love? Could there be someone else in her life? Someone from her past. Someone he would enjoy punishing.

"Was there a card?" His voice sounded gruff to his own ears. He hoped Miranda hadn't noticed. A quick glance assured him she had eyes for nothing but her precious flower.

"No, no card. I don't know who sent it."

Zacke's relief grew tenfold. Still, he wanted to tear the gift giver apart limb by limb. Upon the heel of that thought came a shame that spread over his body and poked him with guilt. He curled his hands into fists to hide his talons and cursed the demons taunting him.

"I just hope that whoever did this got their jollies for the next year."

His remorse ran so deep he had to replay Miranda's words before they registered in his mind.

"Miranda, what are you talking about?"

"The rose, Zacke. It has to be someone's idea of a sick joke."

He moved to stand by her side. Her hand cupped the head of the rose as if caressing the soft petals. He ignored how much he wanted her to caress him the same way and reached out to take it from her.

The rose head danced at the top of its thorny body before it fell to the floor in front of Zacke's feet. He stooped to pick it up. The red blush of the rose came off on his hand; the black petals Miranda's hands had hidden caused a roar of rage to build inside his chest. Shards of pain attacked his head as he tried to control the urge to release his fury.

The slight but gentle touch of Miranda's hand on his arm anchored him. He inhaled and exhaled several times before he straightened.

"Zacke, are you okay?"

Her words seeped into his brain encasing him in their gentle concern. "Yes. When did you say you received this?"

"Well, I can't say for certain. Mac assumed someone delivered it last night. It was here when he came to work."

"No one saw who brought it?"

"No, I asked him, and he said he found the box outside my door this morning. To tell you the truth, it's no wonder no one saw it. Casualties from an apartment fire had everyone up to their elbows in work."

Zacke dumped the maimed rose back in the box and saw traces of red on the tissue. It could be blood. He inhaled slightly and then released his breath in relief. Only a faint tinge was blood, the rest some type of dye. Now, he needed to find out whose blood. "Do you remember noticing any dye on the paper when you opened the box?"

"No. In my excitement, I didn't pay any

attention. I picked it up in such a hurry I didn't see the thorns until I pricked my finger. Some of the red you see is my blood."

Miranda wrung her hands and took a deep breath. "I tried to wipe the blood off with the tissue. I didn't want it to get on the petals. I thought you had sent it to me."

Pink-tinged Miranda's cheeks. His heart rejoiced at her words. Although he would like nothing better than to take her in his arms, he resisted. "Is that when you discovered the dye?"

Miranda's body stiffened. Zacke could have bitten off his tongue for being so abrupt.

"Yeah, I accidentally touched the petals, when I dabbed at my blood. The more I wiped the more color came off until the black showed through. Who would do this and why, Zacke?"

Zacke reached out, tugged her gently to her feet and pulled her to him. He eased his weight onto the wooden surface of the desk. With Miranda cradled in his arms, he kissed the droplets spiking her lashes.

How could he answer her? He believed Gabriella had sent the rose, but he couldn't share that information with Miranda. If Gabriella was guilty, then she in all probability had witnessed his and Miranda's evening together. At least the coloring on the rose had not been her victims' blood.

"Zacke, you're hurting me."

Miranda's words reached inside his thoughts. He loosened his grip around her torso. "Forgive me. I didn't intend to hurt you, Little One."

The hand that reached up and caressed his face trembled slightly, but the smile Miranda gave him reassured him she seemed to be recovering.

"So, who do you—?"

Zacke's lips cut off Miranda's question. He felt the blood rushing to that treacherous part of him that refused to be controlled when around Miranda.

The pulsating ache in his loins made him want to say to Hell with everything else, lock the door, and take what he wanted. He deepened his kiss.

He needed and wanted Miranda so badly he feared once they joined he would never allow her to leave his bed. A moan reached his passion-filled senses. He tensed. Had he once again tightened his grip? He slackened his hold, but Miranda narrowed the slight distance he put between them.

With their lips still joined, she slid her hands up under his T-shirt. His muscles quivered at the first tentative touch of her cool palms against his heated skin. His shaft lengthened and jumped against the seductive cradle of her hips. He burned with a need that could only be assuaged by burying himself inside her.

Miranda's hands traveled to his shoulders before moving downward. His breath caught—surely, she would not touch him. His woman played with fire.

He captured the taunting flesh and held it. Now wasn't the time to make love to her. He pulled his lips from ones swelled with the passion of the last few moments. He turned a deaf ear to her whimper.

"Miranda, my sweet, we have to stop this."

He watched as she opened her eyes, blinked and when pink suffused her face, his laughter came alive.

"I don't know what you find so funny, Zacke."

He allowed her to move from his embrace. It would be safer for both of them. Although the width of the acclaimed Georgia Dome wouldn't be far enough.

"I'm not laughing at you, Miranda. I'm laughing with delight. I feared we would never get to this stage in our relationship."

Miranda's lips parted giving Zacke an opening he couldn't resist. He nibbled at her bottom lip, and she launched herself into his arms once more. The impact of her breasts pressing against his chest caused Zacke to bite back a curse. He doubted he could handle much more. His body—starved for so long of sexual fulfillment—would go up in flames, burning them both in the passion he knew would follow.

He gently dislodged her arms from around his neck, before moving away.

"Zacke?"

"You have done nothing wrong Little One, but I'm only—"

His features twisted into a grimace. Only what? A beast? Human? Sorrow punched his gut so hard he shook from the blow.

"Only what, Zacke?"

He threw off the beginnings of rage at the thought of all Gabriella had stolen.

"I am only—"

The office door opened, and Miranda's assistant poked his head in.

"Sorry, Dr. James, but we have a stabbing victim en route."

Zacke returned Mac's apologetic smile.

Miranda's confusion-filled gaze turned toward Mac. "Thanks, Mac. I'll be right down."

When the door closed once more, enclosing them in a deafening silence, Zacke reached for Miranda. He ignored her efforts to evade him.

"I have to go too, my sweet. But I want you to promise me you'll be careful. The person that sent you the rose could be dangerous."

"Of course, I'll be careful. But surely it's just a sick joke."

"Possibly, but until we know, I want you to be extra cautious at night. Let someone else take the night emergencies."

"Zacke, you know I can't do that."

"I know, but think about it."

Zacke didn't give Miranda a chance to argue. He captured her mouth. Her lips parted and allowed him the access he desired. This time her whimpers evoked a bit of guilt. He shouldn't start something he couldn't afford to finish, but the softness of her tongue meeting his made him crazy.

He deepened his strokes and when she moved into the apex of his thighs, he allowed her to feel his hardened sex. Her startled gasp almost caused him to roar with satisfaction. He exulted in the fact she moved closer instead of pulling away.

He eased one of his hands from her waist to explore the softness of her breast. He cupped its fullness before gently rolling its tip between his thumb and forefinger. He ached to replace his fingers with his mouth, but if he gave in to that temptation, he would not be able to stop himself from taking her completely.

Miranda's moan competed with the jarring ring of his cell phone. Zacke broke their kiss but still kept one hand on Miranda. He wasn't ready for her to escape. He shook his head and stroked Miranda's back. His other hand found the instrument that should never have been invented.

"Kensington."

"Man, you sound like you have a frog in your throat."

"Gideon, I am not in the mood for humor."

"Good, cause I'm ain't laughing. Captain Myers wants to know why you aren't in his office for the meeting."

"Oh, Hell, what time is it?"

"Time for you to get your butt in my office ASAP, Detective."

Zacke resisted the urge to snarl back at the captain.

"Yes, sir. I'm on my way."

He cast one regretful glance at Miranda's open

mouth before placing a gentle kiss on her forehead.

"Sorry, darling. We'll finish this tonight."

Miranda still had not spoken when Zacke exited the office and closed the door behind him.

****

Zacke made it to the station only moments after hanging up the phone. The captain's snit over his tardiness grew worse when he and Gideon stumbled over their proffered explanations. They braced for the royal butt kicking they knew was imminent. As Zacke held his breath, the captain's phone rang.

"Yes, Governor, we are on top of the murders and hope to make an arrest soon."

Captain Myers motioned toward the door. Zacke and Gideon wasted no time in exiting the office.

Zacke entered the welcome coolness of his house and willed himself to his bedroom. Lassitude pulled at him, exhausting his last bit of strength. He fell across the bed without undressing, closed his eyes, and allowed the arms of slumber to hold him.

****

Clouds threatened rain when Zacke finally spotted the florist shop. He had called Miranda before she left the hospital to ask her if there was a logo on the floral box. He should have looked himself but his passion had overruled his common sense.

He wished he knew if Gabriella had delivered the gift to Miranda personally or if the florist had done so. Something he planned to ask the florist.

He timed his descent to the street to coincide with an absence of vehicle and people traffic. A cheerful exterior of yellow and green wood greeted him as he ran up the steps. A door chime announced his arrival. The man behind the counter turned when he entered.

"Evening, can I help you?"

"I hope so." Zacke pulled out his badge and laid it on the counter. He hoped the metal would induce the man to tell what he knew. But if not, Zacke would delve into his mind.

"Is there anything wrong, Detective? Officer?"

"No, sir. But I need some information about a rose your shop delivered to one of the doctors at the Savannah Trauma Hospital."

The elderly man looked confused for a moment and then awareness filled his gaze.

"I remember that order. I filled it myself. I've never gotten a request like that before. I told the lady the dye might kill the rose, but she didn't seem to care. She told me she wanted a black rose and then she wanted it dyed red. I sure don't understand why she ordered it that way. Why didn't she just ask for a red rose in the first place? Ain't none of my business though."

"A woman ordered the rose? Can you describe her for me?"

The man's face lit up with a smile. "Why sure, son. I might be a bit old, but I can still appreciate a good-looking woman. And she was one of the best I've seen in a month of Sundays." The man paused and winked at Zacke.

Zacke strived for patience. He really didn't need to hear Gabriella's attributes lauded. He wanted to know how she had paid for the rose and if she had left an address. She wasn't frequenting any of the cemeteries and that led him to believe she could be staying somewhere more conventional.

"She was a looker with all that long black hair and those purple eyes."

"Did she pay with cash or give you an address where you could bill her."

"Yep to the cash, and yep she did give me something—only not an address. She said it was a note for a Lord Kensington. Don't suppose you know who he is."

"My name is Zachary Kensington."

The man attempted to contain his boisterous laughter before he spoke again. "You must have been something if she is calling you a lord."

"Can I have the note, please?"

"Sure, ain't no need to get testy. If the two of you had a falling out, then that ain't my fault."

Zacke resisted the urge to hurry the man along. His patience wore thin, and by the time, the man went through every drawer in the old filing cabinet, it was gone.

"Here ya go."

Zacke dropped a ten-dollar bill in the man's hand, ignoring his gasp of gratitude. He waited until he stood outside before he ripped opened the envelope with a talon.

His heart stopped when he read the seven words scrawled in Gabriella's handwriting:

Next time it will be Miranda's head.

Chapter Twelve

Zacke raced through the night sky. Desperation stung him like a nest of fire ants, and he welcomed the blue haze that blurred his vision. The gloves were off. Gabriella had struck out at Miranda and threatened to steal the soft breath from her body. Never had he been more certain of one fact; any attempt to take her from him would result in Gabriella's death.

He called Miranda after reading the note. She was already at home.

"Hello?"

"Miranda, it's Zacke."

"Yeah, I recognize your voice." Her dulcet tones caressed his ears.

Zacke's sigh of relief eased the rock in his chest.

"I don't have long, I wanted to make sure you got home all right."

"Yes, I got in a few minutes ago. Is anything wrong?"

"No, I'll be there in a bit."

"Okay, I'll look forward to it. Should I cook something, I mean, have you eaten?"

"I'm fine, make sure you eat though, okay?"

"All right, I'll see you soon. You be careful out there, detective."

"You too, Little One."

The call, although short, had made him more determined to strengthen the safety spell around Miranda's apartment. He wanted—no needed—to hold her in his arms to reassure himself she remained unharmed.

His gaze caught and held the rooftop of her apartment building. He landed on the structure noting absently that some of the shingles needed replacing. It would be much easier to guard her if he could convince her to move some place with a security system—although an alarm would only make Gabriella cackle with glee.

Two shadows separated from the darkness and crept toward him, their steps hesitant and almost wary. His body tensed. Had Gabriella sent her minions to attack? Zacke's fangs and talons lengthened, as he waited. He cursed the moon when it chose to brighten the rooftop; darkness would aid his fight.

The figures stepped from the shadows. Zacke growled at their smiling faces as relief flooded through him.

Miles Dunbar and Hawk Sherwood had fought by his side in numerous campaigns.

He had not informed Gideon of all the details regarding his transformation, but they were forever etched in his mind. Gabriella had left him where he lay, weak and unable to fight. Though his wounds had already started the immortal healing process, his mind refused to accept what had happened. From folklore passed down, he knew the sun's rays would kill him and had begged sunrise to hasten its approach.

But that was not to be.

Miles and Hawk, who had gone on ahead, turned back to search for him. He still remembered the horror in their eyes as they surveyed his wounds. Their amazement that he still lived escaped their lips in myriad questions—none of which he could answer. Had he been stronger, he would have killed them for interfering. But he grew weaker with the fast approaching dawn; his breathing slowed and both men had taken it to be his death sleep.

Several hours later Zacke awakened in a shallow grave, horrified at the events that had put him there. A raging hunger shook his already quaking body. The scent of blood waffled to his nose. He was drawn to the deer's life force. His first taste of the rich elixir caused him to retch in revulsion before he drank his fill. With a strength he'd never had before, he followed the path his men had taken.

He found them—their throats crimson coated, their chests stilled. He buried their bodies and laid stones atop their graves to keep animals from digging up their corpses. Before he went underground, he placed wooden crosses amidst the stones. Though Gabriella had made his body unholy, his soul would always remain devout.

Decades later, he had risen to return to the immortal life he hated, and his travels brought him face to face once again with Hawk and Miles, who Gabriella had also transformed. Just as they had mistaken his immortal sleep for death, he had also been tricked into believing they would never rise again.

Over the centuries, they crossed paths. The bond that began as mortal men and warriors continued— now they were bound by Gabriella's blood. He tried to contact them when Gabriella first made her demonic presence known. When they failed to answer his thoughts, he assumed they had gone underground or met death, either by human hands or their own.

"Zacke, it's good to see you. It has been too long."

"I agree, Miles." Zacke pulled him into a bear hug. "I feared you both were gone forever from these earthly portals."

Hawk moved forward when Zacke released Miles. He, too, embraced his old friend. White slashed in Hawk's and Miles' faces once again, as they returned the smile on Zacke's lips.

"Come sit. I have much to tell you." Zacke motioned to the two-foot wall surrounding the rooftop. He, as well as Miles and Hawk, sat with legs dangling over the side. All three cloaked their presence before picking up the conversation.

"We went underground for a while, Zacke. Upon awakening, we opened our thoughts to any disturbances in the atmosphere and found you. Your distress drew us to this century."

"I'm glad. Gabriella Sanspree has resurfaced, and she has been on a killing spree."

"I hoped that witch had met her death and been judged for her sins before now."

"My thoughts exactly, Hawk. Instead, Gabriella is venting her spleen against me."

"The world is a big place, Zacke. Can't you just ignore her?"

"I wish, Miles. But she's not content to just plague me with the senseless killings she has committed. She has focused her hate against a woman I care about."

Zacke knew his disclosure would be a shock. Since the beginning of their friendship, all three had wined, dined, and loved without giving their hearts.

"I can't believe my ears, Hawk. The man who swore never to fall into the silken trap of love has tumbled head over heels."

"It seems so, and I anticipate meeting this woman who has ensnared his heart."

Zacke resisted the urge to reach out and strangle both men. Their remarks were nothing but the truth, but hearing the words spoken out loud, not just in his head, made them real.

"If you two could get past my love life for a moment and wipe those smug grins off your faces, we have serious business to discuss.

Hawk and Miles faces grew somber. Zacke didn't have to read their thoughts to know they considered

Gabriella and the threat she represented if not stopped.

"How can we help?"

Zacke filled both men in on the events of the last several weeks, ending with the episode with the rose.

"I agree Miranda must be protected." Miles' voice rumbled gruff and his eyes glowed with the intensity of his words.

"Tell us what you want us to do, Zacke. We will be happy to help guard Miranda and help you track Gabriella."

Zacke dipped his head in silent thanks for the friendship and support that both men offered.

"Before you meet Miranda, I have a question." Both men waited with expectant expressions for him to continue.

"As you know from our conversations in the past, I detest the creature Gabriella turned me into. I have always wanted to find a way to redeem my soul, but over the centuries, my search has turned up nothing." Zacke paused for a moment; the hope in his heart felt almost alive. "Have you heard of anyone who changed back into a mortal?"

He expected laughter but his friends surprised him.

"Yes. I'd only been a creature for a couple of decades, still learning my powers. To be honest at that time, I, too, hated what I'd become." Miles stopped and shared a grin with Hawk. "But after discovering it came in handy with the ladies, I decided to make the best of it."

"I felt the same way, Zacke, but out of curiosity, I did a bit of research. I tracked down Giles, one of the old ones, who had been changed during the Druid era. He said a druid priest told him he could change back if he returned to the beginning of the circle."

Zacke's hope dimmed with the riddle. "What circle?"

"The circle of time. You have to go back to before you were created and make sure you don't run into Gabriella."

Zacke slammed his fist into the concrete. The fissure in his hand started to close immediately. Why had he not guessed the solution was that simple? "So that is it? All I have to do is go back to England to a few days before Gabriella changed me? Wait, is that even possible? Is time travel even possible?"

Miles cleared his throat before answering. The slight rumble caused trepidation to rear its unwanted head.

"I think so. We were in the seventeenth century when we heard your call. We could move forward. I would think you could go back. But, there's more, Zacke. He said it's possible to redeem your soul by going back, but once you return to the past and are changed back into a mortal, you cannot return to this century."

Zacke's hopes fell to the ground and burned to cinders. "So, I can go back to redeem my soul but lose Miranda forever, or I can leave things as they are and pray she will not hate the creature I am." Zacke shook his head. "Not much of a choice is it?"

He accepted the nods of commiseration from Miles and Hawk. The cost and guilt of his age-old folly was his alone to bear. He could never leave Miranda—not now, not ever. He accepted the fact his hope of salvation was gone and shook off the darkness of his mood. If he couldn't regain his own soul, he would make sure Gabriella did not steal Miranda's. Forgoing human movement, Zacke transferred himself to the apartment building's door.

Miles and Hawk followed him.

With his hand on the knob, he turned and

grinned at the warriors at his side. "Before we go in, you might want to change into something more suitable for the twenty-first century."

"What, Miranda, won't appreciate our kilts?"

Zacke's vision glowed ice blue. "Our days of sharing wenches are gone. This lady, if she will have me, will be my wife."

Their good-natured grumbling sent Zacke's laughter echoing into the night sky.

****

Miranda forced herself not to run to the door when the doorbell rang. She wanted to, but after the hot and heavy interlude in her office, she just didn't know how she should greet Zacke. Shoot, it might not even be the habit-forming detective.

"Who is it?"

As she waited for her guest to answer, she clenched the hand not touching the security bolt to stop its trembling. Zacke's voice, deep and seductive as ever, floated through the wood panels and caressed her in its warmth.

"Just a minute."

Miranda unbolted the double lock that had been installed that afternoon. The rose delivery had frightened her more than she wanted to admit. After Zacke left her office—and she regained her senses— she immediately called the landlord and asked him to install the new lock. With a twist of her wrist, she opened the door; her gaze traveled up to Zacke's face before lighting on the men standing behind him. The welcoming smile on her lips died and for the life of her, she couldn't stop her mouth from flying open.

The two men stood as tall as Zacke. Their shoulders stretched the seams of T-shirts that barely confined their massive chests. Merciful Heavens, there should be a law against being so sinfully handsome.

"Miranda, do you think we could come inside

now?"

The blush that heated her cheeks only added to her agitation. She must look like a class A idiot. "Of course. Please come in."

She wondered if her small apartment would be large enough to hold the trio of giants and one mortified doctor. Did she even have enough seating—make that strong seating—to hold the Titans?

"Miranda, sweet, it would help if you moved out of the doorway."

When her feet failed to move, Zacke reached out and caught her under the arms. She found herself face to face with his dark and seductive looks, feet dangling in the air. Before she could voice an apology, Zacke slid her slowly down his body. Her nipples came to life and her core burned when she brushed against the hardness pushing against his jeans.

Positive her face would rival a stop sign in its brightness, she kicked her feet slightly. Zacke lowered her to the floor, her feet finding a not quite steady foothold on the linoleum.

She eased from his grip and turned to stare at her other guests.

"Miranda these are some friends of mine."

"Hi, my name is Mud. Nice to meet you."

Miranda's remark brought a trio of laughter.

"The pleasure is all mine, Miranda. Miles Dunbar at your service."

The chestnut-haired giant's hand enveloped hers and sent a shiver down her spine. The warmth he invoked with his touch reminded her of Zacke, although on the heat scale Miles would have been labeled hot, whereas Zacke sizzled. His eyes gleamed with laughter and a jade glow.

As she stood frozen, the second man moved forward.

"Miles, turn her loose. It's my turn."

She barely noticed Miles releasing her before her hand was taken once again, this time by a man whose hair glowed like the sun.

"Forgive my friend, Miranda. Call me Hawk."

Miranda's senses flew the coop as she gazed into eyes that burned with an amber fire. While most women only dreamed of such a spectacular group of men, her fairy godmother must have waved a magic wand.

Miranda tugged her hand free and backed up. She immediately recognized the hard surface that cradled her back and buttocks. She leaned back into Zacke's embrace enjoying the light caress of his lips at her temple. His friends might be great advertisements for book covers or cabana boys, but they would never usurp Zacke in her eyes.

"Miles, Hawk, leave off your flirting. Close the door and take a seat so Miranda can quit breaking her neck looking up."

Both men did as Zacke asked. Miranda found she had a multitude of questions and lips unable to voice them. Who were these men? In the weeks, she had known Zacke, she had only seen him with Gideon. And how on earth was he acquainted with men that sounded like British lords? Come to think of it, Zacke spoke that way at times. Those questions and more circled what was left of her already confused brain.

Her gaze darted between the men reclining on her sparse furniture and Zacke perched on the arm of her chair. Miranda wondered if she could get a picture with her digital camera. She might even send it to the hospital gazette. She had heard the disparaging titles bestowed upon her by a few of the male doctors she had refused to date—Ice Princess and Virgin Queen, to name a few. She found the name-calling distasteful but a remark she overheard by a nurse she had tried to befriend had stung her to the quick—that a man like Zacke would only go out with Miranda if she paid him.

The grin that threatened to crack her lips would not be denied.

"Miranda, you are smiling maliciously. Was it something we said?"

She pulled her thoughts back from well-deserved revenge and tried to recall what on earth the men had been talking about. "I'm sorry. I wasn't paying attention."

Her comment led to some ribbing from Miles and Hawk, but she ignored them when Zacke leaned down and pressed his lips against her ear.

"Never doubt that you are worth ten times the ones who ridicule you."

"How did you know—?"

Zacke's cell phone rang, cutting off Miranda's question.

What lousy timing. Zacke had an uncanny way of reading her thoughts and for the life of her, she couldn't figure out how he did it.

While Zacke continued with his phone conversation, maybe she should offer the men something to drink. "I have some wine in the fridge if anyone wants some?"

"That would be great, Miranda. Thank you."

She wasn't sure which of the men answered her but both smiled and all three men rose to their feet when she stood up to go to the kitchen. She could get used to manners like that.

A hasty look at the contents of her refrigerator caused Miranda to wrinkle her nose. She had to do something about cleaning it out. After a quick move and shuffle, she uncovered an unopened bottle of Arbor Mist. A bottle she had hoped to share with Zacke the night she went to the police station. She found a tray in the cabinet and thanked providence she had purchased wine glasses since moving in. She plopped the frigid bottle on the tray and added the glasses. Her hands cradled the edges of the metal in hopes nothing would slide off as she carried it back to the living room.

She turned cautiously and ran head on into Zacke. The tray tilted against the hardness of his chest and the glasses and wine began a slow descent to the linoleum. She closed her eyes and anticipated the crash. When the tinkle of breaking glass didn't assault her ears, she opened her eyes. Zacke held the tray with the glasses and wine intact.

"I don't know how you did that, but thanks." Miranda moved to take the tray but thought better of it. "If you don't mind would you take it in? I'm gonna see if I can find something for you guys to nibble on."

"Don't bother, Miles and Hawk had to leave."

"But why? I thought they wanted something to drink."

"They did, but something came up. They ask me to apologize for them."

Miranda took the tray back from Zacke and sat it on the counter, grabbed the wine in one hand, and two glasses in the other. "No problem. Maybe next time. In the meantime, I plan on having a glass of this stuff. What about you?"

Zacke rocked back and forth on the balls of his feet. He looked everywhere but at her.

"Guess this means I'll be drinking by myself?"

"Miranda, I'm sorry. I have to go into work. The captain cancelled all nights off until the murderer is stopped."

"I understand, but I don't have to like it."

Zacke's laughing gaze teased her before the depths of his eyes darkened. For the second—or was it the third—time that evening the wine and glasses changed hands. The clink as he set them on the counter registered in Miranda's mind, but not as much as the liquid heat that pooled in her center.

Zacke captured her arms and raised her to his eye level. His pupils burned with a blue hypnotic flame. Miranda wondered if one could actually get lost in another's gaze.

He bent his head just a bit and nipped her lower lip. He tortured her unmercifully as he moved his sensuous mouth in an arc of fire from her lips to her ear. The inferno blazed higher as he caressed the column of her throat. Miranda couldn't prevent a moan of desperation and suffered a total meltdown when he pulled her even closer. The burn that started with his first touch moved downward until her lower region ached.

If her bare feet had been touching the floor, she would have dug her toes into the linoleum. The pleasure of his teeth nipping her sensitive skin proved to be almost more than she could stand.

Her hands gripped the front of Zacke's shirt; she needed to ground herself in reality before she fell off the deep end. It didn't work. She could feel herself being pulled into voracious white-hot desire. Whimpers of want and need crawled up her throat and escaped her lips.

"Easy, my sweet."

She heard Zacke's words but couldn't respond. Her insides burned and her blood felt as if it boiled.

She felt like she floated on air. The taste of his kiss combined with the disintegration of her bones made her head spin.

"Miranda?"

Zacke's voice sounded far away. She wondered where he had gone. First, the adorable giants had left without a polite "May I?" and now Zacke was proving to be just as rude.

"Miranda, open your eyes. Look at me!"

His voice sounded closer this time. Maybe he felt

guilty and had returned to tell her a proper goodbye. Well she just might let him off the hook without groveling, if she could open her eyes. Strange how they felt weighted down.

"I mean it, Miranda. Snap out of it!"

He shook her so hard, her head bobbed on her neck. This time she fought the monster that held her lids closed and won a small battle—both eyes opened a bit. It was enough; she spied the man tormenting her with his loud voice.

"You don't have to yell at me. I heard you the first time, Zacke."

Miranda fought for breath as his hold tightened, threatening to crack her ribs. Before she could open her mouth to tell him to stop squeezing the life out of her, she enjoyed the sensation of floating once again. She kept her eyes closed against the encroaching waves that spun her around and around. When the torturous spirals stopped, she gave in to the lassitude tempting her body.

****

"Forgive me, Miranda."

This time Zacke's voice came in as loud and as clear as church bells on Sunday. She followed his somber tone and saw him kneeling by the couch.

"Forgive you for what? How did I get on the couch?"

"You don't remember?"

"The last thing I remember is standing in the kitchen with you."

"You passed out, Miranda. You scared me to death or you would have if I were not already..."

Zacke's words stopped, a look of what appeared to be horror crossed his handsome features. Before she could ask him about it, he jumped to his feet.

"Zacke?"

He didn't look at her as he moved away, taking his warmth with him. Chills crawled up her back to her shoulders, running the length of her arms. Her teeth began a song and dance, the chattering growing stronger and louder until Zacke turned back to her.

"God's mercy. I should have realized you would wake up freezing."

Before she could blink, he left the room. He returned with the coverlet from her bed and wrapped her up like a mummy. When she managed to free one arm, she caught his hand in hers.

"Sit." She scooted back as far as she could with her limited range of motion. "Do you want to tell me what is going on?"

A look akin to desperation mixed with sorrow turned his face into a mass of abject misery. She drew his hand to her lips. Upon releasing it, she waited a full five seconds before she spoke.

"Zacke, something is wrong, and I want to know what it is."

His sigh ruffled the fringe of her bangs and started her chills up again. For the life of her, she couldn't figure out why he looked as if he wanted to run. She was more than ready to make him spill his guts when he took a deep breath.

"Miranda, there is something, but I cannot talk about it right now."

This time he caught her hand and caressed it with his lips. "No, it is not you—never you. But there are obligations I incurred long before we met that I must take care of. I promise I will tell you everything. Just know that you give my life meaning."

Miranda, tried to hone in on all his words, but could not get past *give my life meaning*. He had told her he cared, told her he wanted a deeper relationship, but her heart had feared to hope he meant it. Now, with the truth shining right in front of her, she could put down the doubts that had plagued her. Zacke loved her. With or without the words, she knew he did. And she would wait for him to confide in her. If she could help him overcome whatever disturbed him, she would.

"I'll wait, Zacke. When you're ready, I'll listen."

****

Gabriella flew from the outside ledge of Miranda's apartment building. What a touching scene. The sweetness between Zachary and the mortal made her want to retch. How could he possibly want the pitiful and puny doctor when he could have her? Zacke's dismissal of what she offered stirred her ever-present anger. Forget having him at her side, she would pay him and his darling back in her own time and in her own way. For the moment, she would find someone else to assuage her thirst for blood.

Chapter Thirteen

Zacke braced his elbows on his kitchen table and raked his hand through his hair. He had slept but his mind still felt fatigued. His frustration stemmed from a combination of things that, for once in his unnatural life, he had no control over.

His houseguests remained asleep in two of the house's four bedrooms; it had taken little persuasion to get them to agree not to hunt a resting place below ground. Their fatigue after transcending time and a night hunting Gabriella had gained their agreement.

The results of the night's hunt had not helped his mood. Their search had turned up a few interesting snippets about a mysterious woman haunting the red-light district of Savannah. That had been what his phone call at Miranda's had been about. Miles and Hawk had been eager to follow up on the tip. But neither of them had gotten close enough to see if it had been Gabriella.

Their conversation had continued to go down hill. Both warriors had not hesitated in filling his ears with what they hated about the twenty-first century and then in the same breath they began to praise Miranda. His vexation came not from their teasing remarks that he didn't deserve her but from the sheer truth of their words.

He wasn't worthy of Miranda—especially after last evening. He had given in to his desire to steal a taste of her blood knowing it would only make it harder not to taste her again. His thirst had weakened her to the point of fainting. His actions tore at his heart as well as what Gabriella had left of his soul.

He should never have given into the insane notion he could love Miranda without touching her with his creature yearnings. Zacke again raked a hand through his hair. Would they ever find Gabriella? He had covered the area around the hospital with the hope she would attempt to leave Miranda another gift. She had not shown herself, but he knew it would not be long before she struck again.

Several times, he had checked on Miranda during the night, but she remained asleep. With her hair fanned out in a sheaf of copper and one hand tucked under her chin, she resembled an angel. He satisfied himself with the task of strengthening the safety spell and then left despite an intense craving nipping at his heels.

Zacke heard three raps on the kitchen door before Gideon entered.

"Yeah, I know I shoulda waited for you to say come in, but I don't feel like being obliging."

Zacke surveyed his partner's features. Gideon looked like an advertisement for a cold commercial. The white pharmacy bag in his hand overflowed with bottles of Lord-knew-what.

"I take it this is your way of telling me you're sick and can't work tonight?"

The sound that left Gideon's throat resembled a growl, not quite as good as one of Zacke's, but close.

"No, that's not what I'm trying to tell you, but it's your fault."

If for no other reason than to take his mind off his own problems, Zacke decided to overlook Gideon's unusual temperament. If Gideon felt half as bad as he looked, he applauded him for not taking the night off.

"I know I am going to regret asking, but how am

I to blame for your mortal illness?"

"I'm so happy you asked." Gideon's gruff words coincided with a coughing fit.

Zacke got up, took a beer from the refrigerator and offered it to Gideon, who promptly waved it away. "Can't...drink it."

Gideon *was* sick; the man never refused a beer. He wondered if he had seen a physician. When Gideon caught his breath, Zacke pushed a chair against his knees and pressed a hand to his shoulder. "Sit, before you fall on your face."

"Yeah, guess you're right. I don't feel so good."

Zacke took a glass from the cabinet and ran some cool water into it.

"How did you get sick? You were fine this morning."

"Well, with hunting Gabriella and all, I didn't get a chance to tell you about the cute blonde who just started working at the station. I decided to ask her out. When she said yes, I was kind of stuck for what to do, 'cause believe it or not, I hadn't expected her to agree." Gideon took the glass from Zacke's hand and gulped it down before responding. "Well, I decided to take her for a late carriage ride like you did with Miranda. The whole kit and caboodle, champagne, roses, ya know."

Zacke sat down in a chair opposite Gideon. Sick or not, he was wound up and this could take a while.

"Guess what, partner? It rained—not just any little bitty sprinkle but a full-fledged flood. And what were we doing when it happened? Sitting there with our champagne while Savannah rainwater popped the bubbles. Alison's roses got soaked, our clothes were drenched, and we watched the thunder and lightning show from under the canopy of a deserted gas station."

Zacke bit his lips until he tasted blood. Poor Gideon. He could imagine how those circumstances had affected his chances with the woman of the moment.

Gideon's face creased into a grimace. "And to top it all off, my date left with another driver. The only good thing out of the whole sorry night was I got a date with my carriage driver, Debbie. She and Able didn't cut and run."

Zacke waited until Gideon pulled one of the concoctions from the bag, sniffed it and then blew his nose.

"I will probably regret this also, but who is Able?"

"Oh man, Able is the horse. He was so cool, never balked or tried to run away when all the fireworks were going on. I tell you, Zacke—" At the sound of feet pounding overhead, Gideon furrowed his brow and looked toward the ceiling. "Please tell me that ain't Miranda."

Zacke's lips formed a reply, but Gideon didn't give him a chance to voice it.

"Miranda's a nice girl, not someone you can trifle with and then leave alone. Please tell me you didn't sleep with her."

"Gideon—"

"Sheesh, Zacke, I thought you knew..."

The footsteps assaulted the stairs and drew closer—louder and almost angry in the pattern that rapped on the hardwood floor. They built to a crescendo of reverberation and then stopped.

"Whose the idiot that woke us up?"

Gideon's head swiveled before he turned his body in the same direction. His first glimpse of Hawk and Miles caused the color to recede from his face, leaving only the tip of his nose red.

Zacke gave him brownie points for not wavering under the warriors' combined glares. With sleep-tangled hair, hanging past their shoulders and eyes creased in irritation, they made a compelling argument for any mortal to flee.

Gideon moved his gaze to Zacke. "Sorry, didn't know you had company."

"No problem. That's what I was trying to tell you." Zacke angled a glance toward the duo standing in the doorway. His silent warning received a slight nod from both men.

"Gideon, meet Hawk and Miles, some old friends of mine. Gideon is my partner."

Gideon stood to his feet and crossed to where the men stood. "Hi, nice to meet you."

Miles bared his teeth, displaying perfectly etched and lengthy incisors, in response to the hand Gideon held out.

Zacke's partner shrugged his shoulders and grinned. "Nice teeth."

Gideon then turned to Hawk, who shook the hand he still held out. Hawk's eyes glowed amber, but Gideon stood his ground. His brown-eyed gaze held the vampire's. Zacke wondered who would flinch first. When neither showed signs of tiring, Zacke decided to call a halt to the stare-down.

"That's enough, children. Why don't we concentrate on Gabriella?"

Hawk, Miles, and Gideon moved to the table and sat down. Zacke scanned their faces; he glimpsed consternation and guilt.

"Now, I suggest we put the animosity and theatrics away for the time being and figure out how to trap Gabriella before she kills again."

"Sorry, Zacke." Hawk's and then Miles' nods accompanied Gideon's words.

"How about recapping for Gideon what you told me?"

"We hit most of the bars in the area you directed us to, but we never saw Gabriella. I know she visited the Lady's Slipper; some of the patrons talked about a purple-eyed, black-haired woman." Hawk's nostrils flared, and his eyes gleamed with distaste.

"How long after she left did you get there?"

"Not more than fifteen minutes." Miles' tone reflected his disgust. "Zacke, when we catch her, I want to be the one to pluck her heart from her body."

"Sorry, but that pleasure is all mine." Zacke returned Miles and Hawk's scowls with one of his own. He would never allow Gabriella to die by another's hands.

He ignored their hisses and Gideon's wide-eyed look.

"Enough! I appreciate the fact you want her dead for eternity as much as I do, but I have my reasons for being the one to end her miserable life."

He waited a moment before continuing. Hawk and Miles remained silent, as did Gideon.

"Although both of you have as many years of immortality as I do, you spent a vast majority of those underground. I don't blame you. But while you got your beauty sleep, I lived through each of the detested years Gabriella added to my life. My skills have grown, as has my strength. Gabriella knows this. She will not fight fair. She will, as you have found, not be easy to stalk or to destroy."

Zacke moved from his seat. His blood churned as bile filled his stomach. He blocked the anger catapulting through his body; he could not afford to give in to the emotion. He would require every ounce of calm and skill he possessed when they found Gabriella.

He pulled the shade up on the kitchen window. His vision glazed blue. He rotated his shoulders and neck, but the tightness would not go away. It probably wouldn't until he saw the deed finished.

He turned back to the trio of men. Each met his gaze without flinching. Miles and Hawk knew death might beckon but didn't fear it. His apprehension concerned Gideon, who would not hesitate to give his life in the line of duty. His partner's sense of obligation had transformed into loyalty over the years. Convincing him to back off would not be easy. Zacke's growing talons bit into the flesh of his palms. He would not allow Gideon to sacrifice himself—not for the likes of Gabriella—not even to save Miranda.

"Gabriella is killing without her usual caution. She doesn't fear the police, and if she has any dread of my wrath, she is hiding it well." Zacke sat down before continuing. "Hawk, Miles, I want you both to cover the red-light district again. As you said, you were only a few minutes behind her. This time, God willing, you will find her."

He allowed a slight smile to cross his lips. "When you do, contact me."

He exhaled a breath before turning to Gideon. "I want you to continue monitoring Miranda's movements to and from work. Unless Gabriella has found a way to exist with the sunlight, which I doubt, I still believe Miranda will be safe during the day."

Zacke held up his hand in an effort to forestall the forthcoming protest. "Gideon, you have stood by me when other mortal men would have run screaming in horror. You have been my partner, my friend, and my brother. I know you want to do more, but you will serve me better by protecting Miranda."

Zacke clapped a hand on Gideon's shoulder. "I will depend on you to keep her safe. Gabriella knows Hawk and Miles; she transformed them. She saw you briefly at the station. I am counting on the fact she focused most of her attention on me and didn't pick up on a connection between us. If she does get close to Miranda, I hope her ignorance will give you time to get Miranda away and for me to get there before she makes a move toward her or..." His throat threatened to close at the reality of what Gabriella might do to Gideon.

"If she sees you as an impediment to her attack on Miranda, she will not hesitate to kill you."

"I know, Zacke, or worse." Gideon's lips twisted in a grimace. "I used to say in my line of work you can't expect to live forever, but since meeting Gabriella I know that ain't true."

Gideon's gaze moved from Zacke's to the others. "I'll do what I have to do to keep Miranda safe. You just make sure you kill *Wicked Woman* before she messes up my pretty face."

Disbelief, admiration, and camaraderie filled the laughter that followed his remark. After the men sobered, all four pledged an oath to speed Gabriella from her unearthly life to one of everlasting Hell.

****

At three o'clock in the morning, a shrill ringing jettisoned Miranda out of a dream world where she and Zacke made delicious love. Her frantic search for the phone sent her off the couch. While sprawled in a heap on the floor she unearthed the small device from under the coffee table.

Disappointment stalked her ten-fold when, instead of Zacke's sexy voice, she heard the impatient snap of the hospital's switchboard operator. A scarce fifteen minutes later, minus makeup but with her tangled hair in a clip, she moved through the silent corridors of the hospital's fourth floor—in what had become a futile search for her missing badge.

The emergency had been rerouted to a closer facility and she'd almost broken her neck for nothing. The new guard on duty followed hospital policy to the letter, insisting she show him her ID, which she had left at home. After he rang the emergency room desk and confirmed her identity, he had granted her entrance.

Although she had been free to leave immediately, Miranda decided to pick up a spare badge from her office. But an extensive hunt through the cluttered desk drawers, filing cabinet, and even the three lab coats that hung on the coatrack had turned up zilch. She decided to retrace her steps from the day before.

So far, she'd found her pearl earring under the desk, her favorite pen in the doctor's lounge, and her paperback novel in the atrium. The only places left to search were the deserted operating rooms.

The absolute silence of the first unoccupied room gave her an eerie feeling. Shadows from equipment-laden counters crawled up the wall and dared Miranda to enter at her own risk. With a sweaty palm, she flicked on the light switch. She entered after fluorescent bulbs banished the demons of darkness. Her search yielded nothing more than a few spots of blood that housekeeping had missed.

The subsequent exploration of rooms two and three were a bust, also. Her jitters had calmed down, but she still wanted to hurry back to a more populated area.

She crossed the corridor to the last suite and raised her hand to connect to the entry panel but stopped. A muffled noise behind her stalled her heartbeat, then sent it racing as she struggled to breathe. The terror that coated her skin in goose bumps refused to go away.

She turned her head slightly to the left and found nothing out of the ordinary. When she turned in the opposite direction, her knees threatened to buckle. Someone or something moved in the shadows surrounding the wing's entry doors.

Miranda closed her eyes and prayed her legs would support her shaking body. She discarded the idea of calling security. In the first place, she felt sure her imagination had run amok and second, she felt sure she would be pulling one of the guards away from something more important.

Although her limbs seemed only imitations of muscles that worked and her heart still had not climbed back up from her feet, she knew she had to move.

Her first steps felt surreal, as she turned in the direction of the corridor. She didn't know if pure terror caused her legs to feel numb or not. It didn't really matter. She had to get out of here.

The more she moved the easier it became. One shadow materialized into a cabinet. Another turned into a fire extinguisher. She hit the exit button. The resounding slap sounded better than a slot machine dispensing its coins.

Lingering fear and relief pricked her as she waited for the electric doors to open. She raced through them before they completely opened. Her rush sent her straight into a hard body.

"Miranda?"

Zacke's voice washed over her. The previous control she had exercised over her fear crashed and burned. She buried her head in his chest and reveled in the arms he locked around her.

"Sweetheart, I don't think you can get any closer without us making love, so come up for air and tell me what has you so frightened."

"Zacke, someone was in the O.R. suite. No one should be back there this time of the night."

Miranda's voice sounded shaky even to her own ears. Zacke replied with nothing more than a bone-wrenching hug. Maybe he had not understood her.

"Zacke did you hear me?"

"I heard you, Miranda."

The guttural tone exploding from his throat rumbled through his chest. Zacke untangled her limbs from his. He placed a kiss on her lips before thrusting her behind him.

"Stay here. Do not move from this spot."

"Where are you going?"

"I am going to see if anyone is still there."

Miranda bit her lip so hard she tasted blood. Zacke's eyes filled with that alarming color of blue before he entered the O.R. suite. He disappeared into the darkened corridor. Miranda's first inkling to how close she had been to following Zacke was the doors closing almost on her nose. She stood alone and frightened of only God knew what.

****

Zacke melted into the shadows, cloaking himself with molecules of cool air drifting from the vents. If his suspicions proved true, Gabriella had been the one frightening the daylights out of Miranda. He wanted to surprise her if she still lingered—provided she didn't detect him first.

He moved through the metal door of the first operating room. The air held a sharp smell of antiseptic and a faint smell of copper—but not Gabriella's cloying scent of gardenias.

The second and third rooms appeared the same. He wondered if the hollow sound of her own footsteps might have spooked Miranda.

He rematerialized into flesh upon entering the corridor. One room to go, and then he could go back to Miranda. He closed his eyes and listened to the air around him.

He heard nothing but the tick of the clock in the room behind him. He reached out with his mind—sought and found Miranda where he had left her.

A smile touched his lips. It seemed his ladylove had little patience when it came to waiting. She stood shifting her weight from one foot to the other and kept glancing at her watch. He would have to teach Miranda that patience could be a virtue—especially when making love.

He pushed open the door of the last room, but again nothing had been disturbed. If Gabriella had been here, she was gone.

Zacke turned on his heel, exited the room, and strode down the hallway. His mind roamed the other floors of the hospital but still nothing denoted a disturbance of Gabriella's kind. His senses went from red alert to amber, his neck muscles relaxed, and his breathing slowed.

For the moment, Miranda remained safe.

He resisted the urge to seek her thoughts. Miranda would not appreciate this particular gift if she were to find out about it.

His slightly mellow mood darkened. Someday she would find out about his gifts and his curse. His transformation was not something he could keep from her forever; it would not be fair to hide what type of creature she would be taking into her bed—when he convinced her to marry him.

His breath hitched. *What if she said no?*

"Zacke, if you're not out of there in two minutes, I'm going to hurt you."

Miranda's threat held both fear and annoyance.

He put his consternation over what might happen away. The future could wait—right now he wanted to get Miranda back to the safety of her home, the only place he knew she would be protected unless he glued her to his side twenty-four seven.

His lips turned up. That might not be a bad idea.

"Zacke?"

He took a mortal's way through the doors and drew Miranda to him. Her protests muffled as he caught her lips with his. He would seduce her into a better frame of mind and rid her of her fear. But the innocent way she gave herself to him undid his noble intentions.

His hands slipped under Miranda's shirt and found the clasp to her bra. He ached to hold her naked flesh and to take the hardened tips into his mouth. He unfastened one of the two hook front closure with haste. His fingers jerked with anticipation as he touched the second impediment to his desire only to be thwarted when his cell phone went off, followed by the incessant beeping of Miranda's pager.

Miranda's eyes opened, allowing Zacke a quick glimpse of dilated pupils. She fumbled for the device clipped to her jeans.

Zacke forced his gaze away from her seductive curves, withdrew his hands and answered the phone he was fast coming to hate.

"Kensington."

"Zacke, is Miranda with you?"

Gideon's voice resounded with anxiety.

"Yeah, she's right here. What's wrong?"

"Someone or something left a message for her in the parking lot."

Chapter Fourteen

Zacke held Miranda close to his side as they exited the hospital. The parking area, lit only by the intermittent security lights, yawned like a large hole in front of them. He tightened his grip on her waist but the tremors that had started when he told her they needed to meet Gideon only worsened.

"Zacke, what's going on? Has something happened to my car?"

"Miranda, I told you what Gideon said."

"That's not enough. Something is wrong."

"Trust me. If it is, I'll handle it."

Zacke prayed he could back up his promise. If his suspicions proved correct, and Gabriella had been behind tonight's theatrics, then she had intensified her attacks on Miranda. He knew nothing more than Miranda did; he had not given Gideon a chance to say more before clicking off his phone. He could have probed his mind or even the parking area, but fear and passion played havoc with his sensory skills.

Whatever caused his partner's cold-roughened voice to almost sing soprano couldn't be good. He spotted Gideon near the end of the lot closest to the street.

Miranda's steps slowed the closer they got to her car—her arm pulled against his, as if she sought to pull him backward. A few feet from the rear end of the Ford Mustang, she stopped completely.

Gideon moved from in front of the car toward them.

"Gideon?"

"I think maybe you might want to look at this by yourself, Zacke."

"Miranda, stay here."

The look of disbelief she launched at him did nothing to assure him of her obedience nor did it bode well for his peace of mind.

He would have to try something a bit more drastic.

The scowl he gave her, one which had frightened his enemies through the ages, only made her raise one of her auburn brows. What had happened to the trembling woman he had literally dragged through the parking lot? When had she turned into the vixen gouging the flesh on his arm with her nails?

"I assume you have a reason for trying to draw blood?"

"Yes, I do. I admit that what happened in the hospital frightened me out of my wits, but it proved to be only my imagination." Miranda paused for breath and her eyes sparked with determination. "If something has happened to my car, I can handle it. I'm a big girl, Zacke."

He agreed with her assessment but repelled the erotic scene that leaped into his mind and loins. He wondered if cajoling her with a gentle tone might get her to listen to reason. He did not want to control her with a thought command.

"You're right. It is your car but as a detective, I want to look at the damage first. If there's any evidence to show who might have done this, it needs to stay unsullied."

He watched a grimace march over her full lips, followed by a narrowing of her eyes and finally resignation.

"Fine, I'll stay here, but only for a moment."

Zacke brushed a light kiss on her pouting lips before hastily joining Gideon.

Dim lighting cloaked the windshield in shadows.

With the aid of the flashlight, which Gideon waved like a weapon, Zacke saw the letters scrawled on the safety glass. The vermilion color matched the paint on Miranda's car. The garish red still dripped, streaking the lower edges of the glass until it disappeared into the windshield attachments and the hood itself.

The pungent smell of paint did not permeate the air. He did, however, get a familiar whiff of copper; he reached out to touch it.

"Good Lord in Heaven, what happened?"

He drew back his hand and closed his eyes. He should have known Miranda would keep up with the time.

"Miranda, we still haven't finished assessing the scene."

He watched her nostrils flare with indignation. She sidestepped the hand Gideon put out to halt her progress and moved closer to the front of the vehicle.

"Zachary is mine!"

Miranda's snarl resembled one of his own. The lack of extended incisors did not prevent the words from sounding like a curse. "Who did this?"

She spun on her heel. Gideon jumped back to avoid being run over.

Zacke stood his ground. He knew that, sooner than later, she would make the connection between the message and Gabriella. When she finished pacing back and forth, her body jerked to attention. She turned around, looked him in the eyes and then advanced like a miniature Doberman.

"You know who did this don't you, Zacke? That woman. The one from the station with the odd name. She did it, didn't she?"

He thought about lying, but he knew Miranda would have the truth from him before the night sky turned pink with dawn.

He caught her arm and steered her away from

the car to a cement barrier at the end of the parking area. He seated himself before pulling Miranda onto his lap.

"Let me go."

"Not until you hear what I have to say."

She attempted to stand. Zacke countermanded her maneuver by tightening his grip on her waist.

"Stay."

"I don't appreciate your attitude. I'm not some puppy you can command at will, Zacke Kensington."

The breath he exhaled stirred diminutive spirals of escaped hair. The seductive view of the curve of her neck accelerated his breath. His teeth met with such force he feared he might snap an incisor. He needed to focus on what and how much to tell Miranda, not contemplate how many ways he could make love to her.

"I apologize. You are right. And you are also entitled to know some of the history between Gabriella Sanspree and myself."

Above Miranda's head, he caught Gideon's look of disbelief. He ignored the almost comical head shaking and rolled eyes. What else could he do but tell her part of the truth? Even if he kept his own secret, it wouldn't be long before Gabriella confronted Miranda and showed his innocent one what type of evil abounded in the world.

He prayed he would be able to prevent that confrontation.

"Zacke, are you going to sit there like a stone or tell me about this woman?"

The sharpness of Miranda's words almost brought a smile to his lips. But at the moment, he had a more pressing need.

He repositioned her to alleviate the discomfort her closeness brought his manhood by sliding her legs to the side, so they draped over his thighs. He immediately regretted his choice of action. Her soft bottom pressed more firmly against the part of him straining for release.

"No, I am not a stone, but if you keep squirming like you are, you and I are going to have a talk of a different nature."

After she froze, he continued, "And yes, I am going to tell you about Gabriella." He enjoyed the slight open-lipped expression his statement caused. "She and I met a long time ago. We enjoyed a brief liaison, but when it ended, she didn't want to let me go."

"Well, I can't say I blame her for that, but tell me something I don't already know."

He glimpsed the confusion in Miranda's eyes and could not help delving into her thoughts. The bewilderment he glimpsed ran a close second to hurt and jealousy. His heart soared with the knowledge of the third.

"Gabriella doesn't fight like you would. She is malicious and dangerous. You have no idea how much."

He pressed his lips to Miranda's temple, as he struggled to couch the suggestion she forget about the past and allow him to take care of Gabriella and the future.

"Gideon and I will take care of having your car cleaned and then returned to your apartment. I want you to get some rest and forget about—"

Miranda pulled free from his arms and wiggled off his lap causing his desire to return. Before he could haul her back, she moved several feet away.

"So, now you're telling me I should forget...what? That some woman is threatening me because of a lost lover? You're actually suggesting I back off and not bring charges against her for vandalizing my car?"

Zacke stared mesmerized at the rise and fall of Miranda's breasts before he jerked his gaze back to her face. Her temper tantrum also enhanced the blue of her eyes, turning them into a stormy sea. A slight breeze freed more of her hair, sending it swirling around her head in a cloud of copper. She resembled a Valkyrie.

He managed to pull his thoughts back from what he would rather do with her to what he must do.

"That is exactly what I am telling you. Leave Gabriella to me."

"I don't think so, Zacke. What do you take me for? That woman deserves a piece of my mind. Who does she think she is?"

"Miranda, for the last time leave it alone. Gabriella will not settle for just a piece of your mind—she will kill you!"

Incredulity from Miranda's gaze pierced him. Her agitated pacing stopped. "Are you putting me on? Why would you think that?"

"Gabriella has killed before, just as she's killing people now." He knew the exact moment her brain made the connection.

"You can't possibly be suggesting she is the Slash and Maul Killer."

"No, I am not suggesting. I am *telling* you."

He watched as horror replaced disbelief. All traces of the peach complexion he adored disappeared when her face blanched.

Still he stayed his distance. Her emotions were in tumult; so much so, he pulled his mind back from hers. He despised himself for being the one to cause those emotions. She deserved better than the problems he had caused her. He should leave and never return; Gabriella would follow him and Miranda would be safe.

"Zacke?" His name trembled from her lips, just a whisper of sound.

"Yes."

"How could someone do what she has done? It's not human."

This time he did move. She would need his touch when he told her the full truth about Gabriella.

He slid his arms around her waist and pulled her to him. His body relaxed for just a moment before he warmed the chilled limbs of his beloved. Holding Miranda restored in him something he feared he had lost long ago, a slender thread of hope.

When she relaxed fully against him, he felt the first twinge of panic slashing away at that thread. She trusted him now but what about the future?

He ignored the question—his procrastination pricked him with guilt. He could not put off telling her any longer.

"Miranda, I want you to listen to what I have to tell you. It may sound absurd, but I beg you to hear me out."

Her body jerked before she turned into his embrace and raised her eyes to meet his. He called on all the power he could beckon and prayed his words would not cause her to run screaming in terror.

"All right, Zacke, I'm listening."

"Gabriella isn't just a woman. She is evil incarnated. No sane person could visit the atrocities she has on her victims. She relishes their suffering and has no conscience about her deeds."

He paused to satisfy his need to touch something free of Gabriella's taint. His slow caress up and down Miranda's spine steadied him. He hoped the tremble he felt in her body originated from his touch and not his words.

"I've seen a lot of criminals since I came into this world, but no one as evil as Gabriella. She thinks nothing of mutilating her victims, even torturing them before delivering her death kiss."

Miranda stirred in his arms. "A death kiss?"

"She doesn't kill with a weapon made by man. She uses her teeth and nails."

The look she turned on him rivaled a child's. Her brows pulled together in a frown, and her lips formed a tempting circle as she pursed them. He ignored their innocent appeal.

"I don't understand."

He looked at Gideon who shrugged his shoulders. No help there. "She's not human, Miranda."

Zacke removed one of his arms from her waist. The hand he raked through his hair and then clenched into a fist trembled. A sign of weakness he could not afford now. He cleared the fear from his throat.

"Gabriella is a vampire."

****

Miranda waited for the elevator to chug its way to the floor of her apartment. Zacke's arm draped over her shoulders should have comforted her, but it didn't.

The last several hours held the flavor of a nightmare. *Buffy the Vampire Slayer* and *Moonlight* topped her list of television reruns to avoid.

Not only had her car been defaced, but also the woman who stalked her had more than simple revenge on her agenda.

A vampire—one of the things that made Angela Knight's romances best-sellers. Miranda enjoyed a good paranormal when she could manage the time for pleasure reading, but living in one didn't give her a warm and fuzzy feeling. The fact that Zacke actually believed in this woman—or creature's—existence troubled her. However, he could be right. There were many unexplainable things happening in the world around them but—

"You okay?"

Zacke's concerned tone caressed her right ear

sending a shiver down her back and warming her insides like a hot cup of coffee on a cold wintry morning.

She touched his hand and reveled in the sense of security it gave her. Even if all this turned out to be nonsense, knowing Zacke cared enough to be here with her made her feel safe.

"Yeah, I'm fine or I will be." The news that Gabriella had been Zacke's lover disturbed her, but Zacke dubbing her a vampire had thrown Miranda for a loop.

If anyone other than Zacke had tried to drop that irrational bombshell, she would have laughed in his face, then taken her broken and disbelieving heart and gone home.

But she trusted Zacke. Why? She really couldn't find a plausible reason. Just something inside her, call it a gut feeling, woman's intuition, or what-have-you, told her she could trust him with her life.

Zacke spirited her away from the hospital not long after telling her about Gabriella. He instructed Gideon to clean her car and then bring it to the apartment complex.

Dawn was a promise in the eastern sky, and Miranda hoped to get a couple hours of sleep, if possible, before returning for her regular shift.

Zacke disagreed with her plans to return to work.

"You need more than a few hours of rest to cope with all that has happened."

Miranda ignored the command in his tone. "Zacke, I'm not going to hash this out with you. I have to go to work. There is no one to cover for me, not on such short notice."

The elevator in her apartment building thudded to a stop. The doors opened to a dark hallway. Great, the light had burned out again.

"I'll be fine. You told me yourself that Gabriella

only comes out to play at night. I promise I'll make sure to be home long before dark."

She glanced up at his face, his lips chiseled into a thin line and his brows drew together. She reached up and smoothed the line between them.

"You shouldn't frown. Didn't your mama warn you your face might freeze?" Of course, if it did, he would still rival the hottest studs in Hollywood. His face and body both would bring an astronomical bid at the hospital's bachelor auction, the annual fundraiser for children. Maybe she could convince him to participate. He owed her that much.

"Miranda?"

"Hmm?"

"I need your key to open the door."

Miranda tore her thoughts back from the seductive lure of watching Zacke strut his stuff on an improvised runway. Her face now felt as hot as her imagination.

"Oh sure, sorry." It certainly was a good thing Zacke really couldn't read minds. She didn't need him commenting on her latest fantasy.

Zacke took the set of keys and opened the door. He always did that—something that both thrilled and annoyed her. She loved that he wanted to make sure the apartment was safe, but she didn't cotton to the idea that he thought she couldn't protect herself.

She followed him into her apartment only to have him push her back over the threshold. "Zacke?"

His response to her question was a finger to his lips and then the motion to stay put.

Had Gabriella found out where she lived? Her blood froze. Anger quickly thawed it and sent it racing through her veins so swiftly she felt dizzy. Rage collided head-on with anxiety as Zacke moved further into the darkened interior of her home. Fear followed; she *had* left a lamp on when she left for the hospital. Zacke didn't have a flashlight. He must have eyes like a cat's.

She waited poised on the threshold for what seem liked an eternity. She couldn't hear Zacke. He must be searching the rest of the apartment. The lighted dial on her wristwatch showed two minutes had crawled by—time hadn't stopped completely.

Her patience at an end, she put one foot over the doorway and then took another step. Before her eyes could become accustomed to the dark, the apartment flooded with light from the ceiling fixture.

Miranda's hand flew to her heart.

The couch had been overturned, its cushions shredded to pieces. Their stuffing covered the broken coffee table. Her two chairs had suffered the same fate. Their mutilated frames lay scattered across the carpet. The lamps were shattered and the bookcase that held her medical books rested on its side. The precious tomes of knowledge speckled the floor with torn pages and broken bindings.

Her eyes burned with tears at the wreckage.

Zacke's arms encircled her waist; his body offered a comforting support. She wanted to turn and weep all over the broad expanse of chest, but what good would that do?

Someone or something had destroyed her home.

"I'm sorry, Little One."

Zacke's soft words didn't mask the tension she could feel flowing from his body. Although his arms held her gently, they felt like corded tree branches. His chest rose and fell in agitation.

"You have no reason to be. There wasn't any way you could have known this would happen."

Miranda moved away from his warmth, her feet traversing a path toward the bookcase. The crunch of glass beneath the soles of her sneakers halted her progress.

Her gaze followed the shards on a trail that led under the overturned bookcase. Something stuck out from under the edge. She tentatively pulled on it, careful to keep her fingers away from the sharp weapons her home invader had left behind.

"Hold on a second, Miranda. Let me lift it up."

As Zacke raised the bookcase, Miranda dodged the books that lost their resting places on the shelves. They joined their fellow tomes on the floor.

The piece of wood turned out to be the lower portion of a picture frame. Her heart broke. Her parent's picture had been shredded with the skill of a surgeon. The loving glances of William and Lynda James were gone. Gaping holes stared back from where their eyes and mouths should have been.

The frame hit the floor, joining the other debris. Miranda backed away from the obscene caricatures. Her teeth chattered with the chill invading her body. Her hands trembled as they reached out in her silent plea for an explanation of why.

Hard arms caught and held her, preventing her flight to where she didn't know.

"Miranda, you can't stay here. Let me take you to my home."

His words penetrated and lodged in her mind. Miranda shook off his arms. She'd never seen Zacke's home. He had always picked her up here, or she had met him at their destination. She'd never even thought to ask where he lived or anything about his house. As much as she loved him for caring, she couldn't go home with him.

Why not, her mind taunted her. You know you'd be safe—probably the only place you would be.

Miranda ignored that reasoning. In her heart, she knew why spending time in Zacke's home would not be wise. He had been the only man to ever awaken physical desire in her. His touch all but burned her to a crisp when she gave in to the temptation of allowing her love-starved nature to take control.

Zacke had said he cared for her, but he'd never told her he loved her. He wanted to make love to her. She wanted him to but for the right reasons. Not because she was scared. She didn't want an act of sympathy. It might not start out that way, but she would always wonder if he shared his body as an act of love—or guilt.

She didn't want a one-night-stand. She wanted commitment. Something she didn't think Zacke was prepared to offer, now or ever.

"Zacke, I appreciate the offer, but I can't."

"Why not? I promise you will be safe."

Once again, she felt the comfort of his arms around her, drawing her closer until her back pressed against his chest. She tugged one of his hands free from her waist and brought it to her lips. The kiss she pressed against his palm contained all the longing for what she couldn't have. "I know, but that's not my reason for saying no."

"Are you afraid I'll try to make love to you?"

The delightful picture he conjured up with his words tempted her beyond measure, and the uncertainty she heard in his voice endeared him to her as never before.

"No, I know you wouldn't do anything I didn't want you to." Miranda continued to hold his hand. Should she tell him the real reason she couldn't go home with him?

She used her index finger to trace tiny circles on his skin as she bit her bottom lip.

His breath stirred the hair on her head and sent shivers of delight down her spine.

"I don't trust myself, Zacke."

The rumbling she felt coming from his chest developed into a rich chuckle, cleansing the air around them with its sound.

"Miranda, for the life of me I don't believe I have ever been refused so seductively in my life."

As heat scorched her skin, he whispered in her ear.

"Never mind, my love. We will think of a suitable alternative."

Chapter Fifteen

Miranda gripped the wrought iron ivy-covered railing as she walked up the marble steps of the Ballastone Inn. Zacke followed closely behind, her overnight case and garment bag containing her uniforms slung across one broad shoulder. His hand on the small of her back kept her from retreating from the opulence and old-world elegance of the inn.

Dear Lord, what a day. This morning she'd had to fight Zacke tooth and nail for the right to go to work, but she'd won that battle. Unfortunately, she hadn't fared as well in the discussion about her living arrangements. Zacke barely waited until she cleared the hospital doors before he lit into her about the B&B. She might have won that disagreement, too, if he hadn't resorted to a mind-boggling kiss that buckled her knees and left her head so foggy she could barely manage a nod. *Dang the man for fighting dirty!*

Afterward he'd rushed her to the apartment to pack her undamaged possessions. Zacke had no proof Gabriella was behind the break-in. Upon further investigation, the lock had not been tampered with.

Gaining the inn's last step, the grandeur beyond the opened doors of the inn drew Miranda's attention like a magnet. A luxurious foyer with polished wood floors fronted a lobby that beckoned. The front desk sat to the right of the wooden staircase. Scrolled newel posts, a refreshing white, reached to touch the beautiful mahogany banister. From where she stood, the carpeted treads seemed to go on forever.

Zacke went ahead to register her. He then clued the owners, Jennifer and Jim Salandi, in about the vandalism.

Miranda followed their guide to the elevator at the end of the lobby. She glanced at Zacke's handsome profile, but the stony set of his jaw and the fearsome glow in his eyes kept her quiet.

The fourth floor presented a picture of southern splendor. Polished wood floors held beautiful throw rugs. A low banister to her right allowed her to glimpse the curving stairway descending to the lower floors.

While she waited on their escort to unlock her room with the antique key, Miranda looked again at Zacke. He had spoken no more than three words to her since they left her apartment. *No more arguments.*

They crossed the threshold. A huge bed sat on a platform. The light from the small table lamp reflected off the scrolled mirror above it and skittered across the glossy wood floor. Masculine green walls served as a backdrop for a framed pencil drawing of the inn.

Zacke placed her luggage on a small table and took the key from the attendant. He nodded his thanks and ushered the woman out the door. He then walked over to the settee at the footboard of the bed and sat down. Without saying a word, he held out his hand.

Miranda hesitated half a second before taking it and allowing him to pull her between his muscular thighs. He captured her lips, and she welcomed the gentle touch of his tongue.

He deepened his kiss and her legs collapsed under her; the perch she found on his lap intensified the craving she always felt in his arms.

It could have been a minute or an hour, Miranda

had no idea—she just knew she felt bereft when he released her lips and eased her to sit by his side.

"You're a dangerous temptation, Little One. But I have to go to work, and you need to get some rest."

"Zacke it's barely twilight out. I'm not the least bit tired."

His hand touched her cheek before he stood and pulled her up. With a slight tug, her body pressed firmly to his.

"You're probably running on adrenaline. As much as I want to stay, you would be much safer without me."

He lifted his hand once more and ran the tip of a slightly calloused finger across her bottom lip. Miranda's legs betrayed her for the second time and threatened to dump her at Zacke's feet.

A deep chuckle above her head told her Zacke was pleased with the results of his TLC. "I told you, you would be safer without me." He draped an arm over her shoulder. "Walk me to door."

Miranda moved with him, glad to know her legs still worked.

Zacke opened the heavy wood door and stepped out into the hallway. He granted her one brief smile before kissing her forehead. "Lock the door and stay inside."

Before she could reply, Zacke strode to the elevator. Miranda didn't wait to see the doors close behind him; she closed and locked the doors as instructed.

Whether or not she completely believed his tale of a vampire, someone had vandalized her car and home. That alone would ensure she stayed put, at least until she had to go to work.

Miranda showered in the old-fashioned, elegantly appointed bathroom, and then decided to go to bed. She'd had a late lunch which she'd picked at and her appetite still hadn't returned. Nerves, fear, or whatever made for a great diet. She climbed the two steps onto the bed. From this vantage point she could see the panoramic view of Savannah's lights. The woman who had shown them to the room had told them the suite overlooked a courtyard filled with flowers and trees.

Maybe she would have her coffee on the balcony in the morning. The Ballastone kept a fresh pot available at all hours. Just one of the many luxuries the inn encouraged its guests to enjoy. She just wished circumstances were different and that Zacke could be here to keep her company.

****

Miranda opened her eyes to find the moon shining boldly into the room. She thought she wouldn't get any rest, but a quick look at her wristwatch confirmed she'd slept for several hours. Soon, she would have to get ready for work.

She stretched and then climbed off the bed. She didn't bother with the robe the inn supplied but slipped her feet into the soft slippers she had found earlier in the bathroom.

She padded to the tall windows and looked out at the soft glow of streetlights. She hoped Zacke's night had been an easy one. Her gaze dropped to the courtyard below. The shrubbery and trees lining the fenced area remained shrouded in semi-darkness. She could barely make out the fountain in the corner or the wind chimes hanging in the trees.

Dark clouds moved to obscure the moon. A sudden rising wind blew foliage about. Its low whine raised the hair on Miranda's arms.

She rubbed the gooseflesh and took half a step back from the window. The emergence of a shadow from beneath the tree halted her retreat. A woman's laughter filled the room. A voice screeched, "Zachary belongs to me."

Miranda recognized the voice and the laughter—

Gabriella. If she believed Zacke's story about vampires, then she should probably run for her life. But the frustration of the last twenty-four hours lit a fire and ignited a temper she didn't know she had.

"You're wrong, Gabriella. Zacke belongs to no one—especially not you."

A baying howl pierced the night. The wind picked up. A whirling funnel of leaves and grass twisted in a macabre dance.

Miranda backed away from the window. The noise grew to a deafening roar, threatening to burst her eardrums. Her feet continued their backward path until she encountered something hard and unmoving. She tried to stop her backward tumble but grasped only air.

"Ouch." she rubbed her aching elbow, which had collided with the overturned coffee table. She wished she could do the same to her abused bottom but she had worse troubles.

She glanced at the window. Tree branches outside slowed to an almost hypnotic wave, before becoming frenzied once again.

Her gaze fixated on the glass as she cautiously gained her feet. She wondered how much longer the windstorm would last. Surely Gabriella, if she was indeed responsible for nature's tantrum, would tire of the game.

Miranda's eyes burned as she stared at the chaotic melee. She blinked once and then again, in hopes her vision would clear, but nothing she saw gave her peace of mind.

The funnel of debris lifted to the windowsill. Its never ceasing twisting threatened to envelop the entire sheet of glass. The interior of the room grew dark. Miranda's instincts screamed a warning. She needed to get away from the window. She needed to get out of the room. She needed to call Zacke.

Miranda forced life into her frozen limbs. She

gave herself a mental slap on the back for bravery before she became aware of the cessation in sound. Maybe Gabriella had left?

Or maybe something worse was fixing to happen.

When the pane of glass started humming and vibrating, she knew she was right. A sharp cracking followed. Miranda's heart stopped as she watched a zigzag fissure start at the bottom, move upward, and spread throughout the glass.

Her hair whipped across her face as the wind began to blow into the room. She fought to free her obscured vision—she had to get out now. The force of the wind aided Miranda's half-turn.

The door stood only a few feet away. She had to get it unbolted.

A horrendous shriek assaulted her ears. Miranda turned back toward the window. Something struck her right temple. She fell to her knees. Her nightgown offered little protection against the debris jabbing her body.

She wiped her face. Blood stained her trembling fingers. She ignored the dizziness that caused her head to spin and started crawling toward the door.

The shrieking chorus deepened to a low rumble and then intensified to the roar of a tornado. Miranda covered her head with her hands and burrowed into the floor. She prayed the escalating wind wouldn't pull her backward. Glass shattered. Heavy pressure assaulted her chest. Her breaths came in raspy pleas for air.

The choking sensation continued until she gave up the struggle to stay conscious.

****

Zacke plowed through the emergency room doors at the hospital, his hurry so great he left off apologies to people he almost ran over. Miranda needed him. He cursed his treacherous soul and his despised powers for not alerting him to the fact she had been in danger.

His first inkling came while he and Gideon were on a stakeout. They'd been sitting in Gideon's truck observing a robbery suspect when the radio crackled to life.

Zacke knew he would always remember the words, "Accident victim, Ballastone Inn, female. Injuries undetermined."

She was transported to the Savannah Trauma Hospital, just a short distance from the inn. Gideon broke all his previous speeding records to get there. They arrived almost on the heels of the ambulance.

"I'm looking for the female victim just brought in from the Ballastone Inn." The white-coated doctor ignored him, rushing off toward another part of the hospital. Zacke resisted the urge to bare his teeth. He needed answers but scaring the hospital personnel wouldn't help.

He approached the registration cubicle. This time he used his badge and got results.

He moved a few feet down the corridor and pushed open the door to room five. Medical staff hovered around the bed, preventing even a small glimpse of Miranda.

Moments ticked by, his patience at an all-time low. One of the white coats moved and so did Zacke.

"Hey, you're not supposed to be in here."

Again, he kept his fangs under lock and key. He flashed his badge a second time.

"Detective Kensington with the Savannah P.D."

The doctor, who had a light shadow of fuzz on his face and looked like he should still be in high school, shook his head.

"I don't care who you are. This room is off limits to non-medical personnel."

Zacke's fangs pierced his gums. For the first time in centuries, he wanted to drain blood from a human.

"Hey, Detective Kensington, remember me?"

Zacke turned to the man approaching him and his newly made enemy. Mac, Miranda's surgical tech, looked pale but the slight smile on his face relieved a bit of Zacke's anxiety.

"Yes, I do, Mac."

He shook the hand Mac extended before the surgical tech turned to the man blocking Zacke's path to Miranda.

"Dr. Stone, this is Dr. James' friend. Since she has no next of kin, he's her emergency contact."

Mac turned back to Zacke, "How did you get here so fast? I just left you a message at the station."

"I heard the call over the radio." Zacke grasped Mac by the arm and pulled him out of the doctor's earshot.

"How is she? Do you know what happened?"

"She should be fine, Zacke. Her hands and upper back took most of the force from the flying glass. But the powers-that-be say most of the cuts are superficial. Her hands will be fine, thank God, and she'll still be able to operate after they heal. She has a bruise on her temple, but most of the swelling is on the outside. Doctors Stone and Slaton don't consider it to be a cause for alarm, but they plan on doing a CT scan to be on the safe side."

Zacke released the breath he had been holding. She would survive. He would wait for Miranda to tell him what actually happened, but he knew Gabriella was to blame.

"Good. Is she conscious?"

"Not at the moment." Mac scratched the bald spot on his head; his eyes held confusion. "When they transferred her from the gurney to the bed in here, she woke up mumbling about vampires, funnel clouds, and you. The doctors gave her an injection to put her out. Don't worry, delirium is a normal side-effect of trauma."

Zacke exercised more control over his wayward teeth.

"Both Dr. Stone, who you just met, and Dr. Slaton feel she will be more lucid when she awakes." Mac motioned toward Miranda; several of the medical staff had moved away. "I know she'd want you to be here."

Zacke moved to the edge of the white-draped bed. Miranda's copper curls looked like fire against the ashen pillowcase. Dark shadows under her closed eyes despoiled the magnolia tint of her cheeks, and the purple bruise at her temple marred the soft skin at her hairline. Lips that had glowed a warm vibrant cherry when he had kissed them were now pale. Zacke leaned over and placed a gentle kiss on her cheek.

He eased one of her hands out from under the cotton linen. Gauze and tape held her flesh captive from her wrist to her fingertips.

He used his free hand to lift the sheet; Miranda's other hand had received the same treatment. She lay on her side, the hospital gown a stark reminder that Miranda wasn't just sleeping. He surmised the bloodstained bundle at the foot of the bed had been her nightgown. He placed a small kiss on the tip of each abused finger before replacing her hand under the sheet.

She could have died tonight.

Zacke couldn't wait. He needed to know. He placed his palm across her forehead and closed his eyes. He scanned her mind for the truth. He saw the funnel of debris, Gabriella's temper mounting and then escalating out of control. He heard the anxiety in Miranda's voice, but also her determination when she went one-on-one with Gabriella.

He felt the first shards of glass pierced her skin as if it stabbed his own. He flinched as he witnessed the despair and fear she experienced before blacking out.

"Zacke, are you okay?"

Mac's voice infiltrated and broke the bond he shared with Miranda.

"I'm fine, Mac. How long will she have to stay here?"

"I can answer that, Detective." Dr. Stone moved toward the bed and put his hand on the spot Zacke's had just vacated.

Again, Zacke felt the urge to inflict bodily harm.

"Since she lives alone in a presently uninhabitable apartment, Miranda needs to spend a few days with us."

"I disagree, Doctor. I believe Miranda will be much happier recovering in a home environment. She will be coming home with me."

****

"No!"

"No? I believe you misunderstood me, Miranda. Staying with me until Gabriella is caught is not up for debate."

Zacke moved away from her bed. His tall form cast a shadow on the wall. With his back to her, Miranda noticed his hair seemed a bit mussed. It didn't take away from his handsome looks but regardless of how fine the man looked, he still didn't have the right to tell her what to do.

She awoke from the sedative to a furious argument between Zacke and Dr. Jarrod Stone. They had been yelling or rather, Jarrod had. Zacke's eyes glowed a blue so dark they seem almost black when Jarrod raised his voice. His stance remained sexy and relaxed, yet he appeared as if he would pounce at the least provocation.

The bickering over who knew what was best for her ended when she tried to move. Her back pulled slightly, and her hands throbbed, but the pain radiating from her temple caused her to moan. At the sound, both men rushed to opposite sides of her bed—glaring over her at one another.

She shut her eyes. A second later, the door whooshed open and then thudded closed. One lift of her lids confirmed Jarrod had gone.

It hadn't taken long for Zacke to see through her Sleeping Beauty routine and for the last half-hour, she'd been treated to a lecture.

"Why, Miranda? I don't understand why you won't stay with me."

Miranda batted at a strand of hair with one of her hands. The bulky bandage only helped to push it further into her eyes.

She felt rather than saw Zacke move to her side. With a touch that felt like a gentle kiss on her skin, he moved the offending strand away from her face and tucked it behind her ear. She tried not to look into his eyes—the stern but gentle expression she knew she would see would only undermine her determination to return to her apartment.

A gentle grasp of her chin and she gazed into eyes the color of a storm etched sky. His smiling lips beckoned to be kissed, and she hated herself for wanting to do just that.

"Zacke, you don't play fair."

His seductive laughter caused a brief smile to touch her lips.

"And why is that, Little One."

"Because you don't—you never do. End of discussion."

"Very well, why don't we talk about your lack of reason?"

The clipped tone returned to Zacke's voice. She hated when he sounded like he had a burr up his butt.

She reached for his arm to stop him from leaving her side; her fingers touched the edge of his sleeve before pain caused her to drop her hand back to the bed. Tears burned her eyes. She clenched them tight. No way would she let Zacke see her cry. He'd consider that weakness, another reason she shouldn't stay at the apartment.

"Miranda, are you all right?"

"Yes, I'm fine."

"Then open your eyes and look at me."

"No."

"Miranda, you have almost used up your allotted refusals for tonight. Now open your eyes and talk to me."

She might as well do as he asked, if she didn't Zacke would probably open them for her.

He kissed the tip of her nose; he ignored the glare she sent his way. Miranda would have given him another go-to-Hades look, but how could she stay angry with a man who even now was fluffing her pillows? After he pulled the covers up to her neck, he sat on the edge of the bed.

"Is moving in with me so distasteful?"

"No, moving in with you is plain out dangerous."

Zacke's eyes glowed, a sign of temper.

"Before you get all bent out of shape, it's not just the fact that your ex-girlfriend is supposed to be a vampire. It's..." Miranda turned away from the unspoken query in his eyes.

"It's what, Miranda? Don't you trust me?"

"I told you it's not you I don't trust."

Miranda snuck a quick look and caught a smile on his lips.

"Would you please be serious? We both know we are attracted to one another physically, but I'm not ready for that step in our relationship." Miranda took a deep breath. She could be making a total ass of herself. Zacke may have changed his mind.

"I could never change my mind about wanting you."

"I swear, Zacke, if you don't quit reading my mind, I'm going to hit you. And how on earth do you do it?"

His laughter didn't surprise her, the man found humor in her most serious remarks.

"What if I promise to keep you at arm's length?"

"Good try, Detective, but it won't fly and you know it."

His sigh ruffled her hair. "You're right, I wouldn't be able to keep that promise."

"So, you understand why I have to go back to my apartment."

"I understand why you think you do, and I think I have a solution."

"And that would be?"

"Marry me."

Miranda's mouth dropped open at Zacke's words. Surely, he wasn't serious. One glance at his face proved he wasn't teasing.

"Zacke, I can't marry you just to keep out of Gabriella's clutches. Marriage should be more than a quick fix for protection."

"I thought you cared about me." Confusion coated his words.

"I do care, but a marriage of caring wouldn't be enough for either of us."

Miranda waited but Zacke remained silent. Should she tell him how she felt? Would it matter? What else did she have to lose? Zacke already had her heart.

"Zacke, I—"

"Perhaps you are right, Miranda. Living together might not be a good idea after all. But you will not be staying in your apartment alone."

"Well, you certainly won't be staying there." She didn't care if she hurt him with her words. His abrupt change of mind hurt.

"You have made your dislike of our sharing

quarters clear. But rest assured someone else will guard you."

Miranda's mouth fell open again. Before she could ask who, Zacke moved to the door, opened it, and disappeared.

Chapter Sixteen

Miranda flexed her fingers and winced at the lingering stiffness. Three days ago, Jarrod Stone removed the bandages and assured her there would be no permanent damage. That news was a cause for celebration, however, she didn't feel much like celebrating. Jarrod's initial pleas for her to break off her relationship with Zacke had grown, along with his hints that she should date him.

Men! They should all be put in a bag, shook up, and then tossed. It still wouldn't knock any sense into their heads.

She flexed her fingers again, more forcefully this time. "Ouch!" She held her breath. When the two giants—Lords of Whatever, her nickname for the duo because they reeked of old-world manners and tone—didn't come bounding into the living room to check on her, her breath escaped in relief.

Good. They still slept. When she checked earlier to see if they had awakened, silence greeted her through the bedroom door. She doubted anything would disrupt their rest. They slept like the dead.

A shiver crossed her shoulders. She really didn't want to think about the dead. Or in this case, the undead.

After her refusal to move in with Zacke, she had stayed one night at the hospital. Her homecoming had been better than she expected. She allowed herself a brief smile remembering what happened when she returned home.

Zacke opened the door with her keys and then moved across the threshold. Miranda hated to face the destruction she knew would have to be cleaned up. With her hands bandaged, she might have to hire someone or just do a bit at a time.

"Surprise!"

Miranda peered through the doorway.

Her apartment was spotless.

"Oh my gosh, what happened?" She moved a bit further into the room.

"Well, since you remained stubborn about staying with me, Miles, Hawk, and even Gideon helped me to clean up this mess.

Everything that had been torn, slashed, and broken had been replaced.

"Zacke, I can't believe ya'll did this. It must have cost a small fortune to replace the furniture. At least let me pay you for that.

"Absolutely not. If it hadn't been for Gabriella, none of this would have happened."

Zacke gave her that arched-brow, arrogant-male look.

"Fine, but I'm only letting you get away with this, because I'm too tired to argue."

"Of course, let me help you to your room."

She welcomed his arm to lean on. As they neared the bedroom door, she spotted the picture of her parents. A new silver frame surrounded their cherished features.

"Zacke, how did you—"

"It's not important how, I just wanted to give it back to you."

Miranda slapped two of the new decorative pillows together. She owed the man so much and yet he infuriated her to no end. Why couldn't he tell her his deep dark secret? Why couldn't he commit to a relationship based on love and not just caring?

The pillows received another hardy whack before she tossed them into the corners of the sofa.

She'd awoken early this morning, and her

bodyguards had been playing cards at the kitchen table. Their larger-than-life forms seem to shrink the room. She offered to fix them some breakfast, but as every morning for the last two weeks, they declined before going to bed.

Miranda started compiling a list of candidates for the charity bachelor auction the night before but put off asking Zacke; no telling what his answer would be, but she'd gotten an enthusiastic yes from Gideon and a couple of *what am I getting myself into* nods from Miles and Hawk. The auction was still several weeks off, but some of the doctors had signed up as well as some of the nurses' boyfriends. It looked as if the children's fund would be adequately endowed.

She scanned the room; nothing more she could do in here. Her gaze strayed to the new clock on the bookcase. Good grannies, only six in the morning.

Well, she had to find something to occupy her time. She had begged and finally been granted permission to return to work on Monday, three impossibly long days from now. Zacke had not been to the apartment since he dropped her off after her release from the hospital. His orders to stay inside and listen to Miles and Hawk were issued with a scowl, and he'd left without giving her his usual goodbye kiss.

"Stupid man, and stupid me. Maybe I should have told him I loved him." Miranda's laugh held no humor. Sure, and leave myself wide open for more heartache. When would she learn? If the man cared one tenth about her like she did him, he would have demanded she marry him.

Miranda pulled a notepad and pen from her briefcase. She needed to make a grocery list. Her refrigerator had been bare when she got home, and her guests' two shopping expeditions since then had left a lot to be desired. A good majority of what she had written down had never left the store shelves. When questioned, both men had told her they didn't know what some of the items were. As if she were dumb enough to believe that.

Fifteen minutes later, she shoved the paper aside. If they followed the list exactly, she would once again have strawberry jam with her toast in the morning. She made a point to circle one item in red. Men could be so dense at times. So what if the thought of feminine hygiene embarrassed them, they could have bought them anyway.

She only hoped they would do better—

Why should she depend on the slumbering duo to do her shopping? She had her car and two almost perfect hands. She could certainly go to the store by herself.

Miranda headed for the bathroom and a shower. So what if Zacke found out? He would probably give her another one of those cold looks of his. Big deal. He should bottle the freezing glances and sell them as samples of life at the North Pole.

Her shower killed another fifteen minutes. She grabbed a towel to dry off and the shrill ring of her cell phone penetrated the closed door.

Her heart thudded a bit faster; maybe Zacke had decided to stop his silent treatment. She wrapped the towel around her body and twisted the condensation-slick doorknob. She managed to get out into the hall in a matter of seconds.

The shrilling continued. Where had she left her phone? She finally spotted it under one of the pillows on the sofa.

She grabbed it but the ringing stopped. Great! If it was Zacke, there was no telling when or if he would call back.

She checked the missed call information; maybe he had left a message. Her hope crashed and burned when the number for the hospital showed up. She hit send and a second later, the hospital switchboard picked up.

"This is Dr. James. Someone called me."

She hated being put on hold. But only a second or two later, she heard Mac's voice come on the line.

"Dr. James, we need you to come in—now."

Mac's normally reserved voice sounded frantic. "What's going on? I'm still on medical leave."

"Yeah, I know, but I couldn't reach anyone else. You're not gonna believe this, but they just transported one of the Slash and Maul victims here to the E.R."

"So, what's the problem? Why didn't the coroner take possession of the body like he always does?"

"That's just it, the body ain't dead."

Miranda sat down on the arm of the sofa, her legs weak with shock. *Someone had survived one of the killer's brutal attacks.*

"I'll be right there, Mac."

Miranda ran to her bedroom, her damp feet leaving a trail on the linoleum. She threw on underwear, jeans, a T-shirt and then clipped her badge on as she knelt down to snatch her shoes from under the bed.

Grabbing her keys and wallet, Miranda backtracked through the living room and out the door. Once inside the elevator, she pressed the button for the ground floor. The elevator almost reached ground level when Miranda remembered she hadn't left a note for her babysitters. She grinned. They were grown men. Let them figure it out.

****

Miranda swallowed the bile that crept up the back of her throat and ignored the nausea churning her stomach like the Savannah River on a stormy day. The woman lying on the O.R. table in front of her deserved better than a shaky handed, weak-kneed surgeon behaving like a first-year resident.

By all rights, the patient should be dead. Blood dripped through soaked pressure bandages, over the edges of the gurney and pooled on the floor. Only the blip of the heart monitor proved life remained within the corpse-like body.

Another glance at the monitors showed dangerously low blood pressure and pulse rate. The woman barely breathed.

Miranda quickly and thoroughly scrubbed her hands before a nurse aided her into a surgical gown, mask, and sterile gloves. Another nurse cut away what was left of the patient's clothes, then swabbed the victim's chest with betadine. Not the best surgical preparation, but it would have to do.

Time was of the essence.

Miranda lifted her scalpel and began to cut away the jagged flesh littering the woman's chest. She probed the invasive wound that tore a path almost to the woman's heart. Once she ascertained the organ had not been damaged, she placed a sterile drain tube into the wound, before stitching it closed. Next, she tended the numerous slashes crisscrossing the woman's extremities and face.

****

"You what?"

All three men standing in front of Zacke flinched—as well they should. It would do them good to see his anger.

He raked an unsteady hand through his hair. "How could you lose her? She is not a package you can misplace or a puppy that snaps her leash."

"We know that, Zacke. Miranda must have left sometime after we went to sleep." Miles' voice echoed the guilt Zacke spotted in Hawk's eyes.

A low growl erupted from Zacke's throat. "That's your excuse? Well you had better come up with a better one, and you had better pray she comes to no harm because of your carelessness."

"Zacke, if I could say something."

Zacke turned to his partner. He toned down his snarl but only a fraction. "What?"

"Well, Miranda is a grown woman. She had her keys and her car. Did you really think you could make her stay in her apartment until we catch Gabriella?"

"No, but I did think three grown men could keep up with one small woman."

"Hey, fang man, that ain't fair. I had the surveillance covered until we got called to Gabriella's latest fast-food binge."

Zacke tasted blood as his teeth caught his tongue. Hell, it was his fault as much as Gideon's, Hawk's, or Miles'. He knew Gabriella would strike again. He should have made certain Miranda knew it as well. He should have taken more precautions to protect her instead of allowing her attitude to prick him into silence.

"You're right, Gideon. I owe all of you an apology. You have already gone out of your way to do a job that should have been mine—if I had not chosen to be so..."

"Pigheaded?"

"Stubborn?"

"Too much in love for your own good?"

Zacke almost smiled. These men knew him all too well.

"So now that we have you figured out, what are we going to do about the lovely Dr. James?"

"Are you sure she didn't leave a note, Hawk?"

"We searched the entire apartment and didn't find one."

After receiving Gideon's call, Zacke had raced to Miranda's apartment. He planned to go there anyway, once he'd fully awakened.

On the drive over, every frightening scenario he

could come up with ran though his mind. What if Gabriella had gotten to her? What if Miranda, at that very moment, was being tortured or worse? What if he lost her forever?

Zacke shook off the recurring morbid thoughts and the tendrils of fear that wrapped around his body. His heart screamed for him to do something, while his mind probed how Gabriella could spirit Miranda away right under the noses of two of her own kind.

Two weeks without seeing Miranda had turned him into a mindless mortal male. After taking care of the damage at the inn and inserting the thought into the owners' minds that a tree limb had caused the damage to the room, he berated himself the first week for not telling her how he truly felt. And the last week of his self-inflicted separation, he'd gone around and around with his conscience. He should just leave Miranda alone and then maybe she would be safe. Or at the very least, tell her what he was and allow her to make up her own mind on whether or not she wanted to continue to see him.

He finally decided he would just leave it alone. His feelings toward her would not change. He wanted to be with Miranda—if nothing more than to just see her on a day-to-day basis. His continued guilt over what had happened at the Ballastone Inn had to stop. It served no purpose except to place a wall between them.

He intended to dismantle that wall brick by brick until he felt brave enough to reveal his life and death story. He hoped he would have the time to do just that.

Zacke moved around Miranda's apartment. Why hadn't the woman left a note? Had she been so angry with him, she would deliberately make him insane with worry? She could have at the very least called. He had given Miranda his cell number; he had even programmed it into—

The cell phone.

He could call her.

Zacke pulled his own phone out and hit the speed-dial button.

A muffled ringing somewhere inside the apartment shredded his hope she had the phone with her.

Hawk, Miles, and Gideon didn't wait for him to tell them; all three started a mad search for the phone. Miranda's immaculate apartment soon looked as if a tropical storm had rolled in off the coast and devastated it.

Still no phone.

The only piece of furniture that remained un-tossed or searched was the new couch.

Zacke dived for one of its pillows as the other three men fought to remove its mate.

His lungs filled and expelled air, his heart raced in beat to the joy singing in his veins when he unearthed the small silver cylinder.

Although Miranda had left the phone behind, there might be a clue as to her whereabouts.

Zacke checked the last incoming call.

The hospital's emergency department's number blinked at him.

"Well?"

"Miranda got a call from the hospital early this morning, Gideon."

"That's where they took Gabriella's latest victim."

Zacke's curses ripped the air. How could he have forgotten Gabriella's latest attack?

The crime scene had been chaotic. Dr. D finished examining the young woman's body and then blood-covered fingers caught and clenched the sleeve on his lab coat.

The next few moments would live in Zacke's

memory forever. Over the startled cries of the good doctor and his attendants, Zacke's hearing picked up the plaintive and weak voice of the victim. Her pleas for someone to help her had ripped at his heart, and his anger toward Gabriella grew even hotter.

"Zacke?"

He pulled his mind back from thoughts of earlier that day and focused on Miles concerned face.

"Are you going after her?"

"Yes, Hawk, but all of us will go. Gabriella wouldn't leave a victim alive without reason. She wants Miranda to see her work up close."

Zacke moved toward the apartment door. "Gideon you take my car. It's faster than your pickup. Hawk, Miles, and I will take to the air. If you spot Gabriella, don't approach her. She might think twice about attacking three of her kind, but she wouldn't hesitate to kill you."

Gideon saluted Zacke. "You got it! I might be from the South, but my mama didn't raise no fool."

Zacke's lips pulled up in a slight smile before all four men exited the apartment.

****

Miranda's sneakers made no sound as they traversed the basement corridor. Mac had awakened her a few moments before with grim news.

Her patient had died.

Twenty-year-old Heather Carter had succumbed to her horrific injuries. Miranda had cleaned, stitched, and prayed for almost eight hours. When the young woman survived the long and tedious surgery, Miranda *hoped* she would recover.

Heather died asking for her.

Guilt smote her; while the girl had been dying, Miranda slept.

Not even Mac's assurance that she'd done everything possible to save Heather helped to alleviate the depression sucking at her like a giant leech. She should have been with her patient instead of catching a nap.

Heather had awakened briefly in the recovery room, Miranda at her side, the young woman's gratitude poignant. As she blotted the tears from Heather's eyes, Miranda promised her she would recover. She'd also promised she would be with Heather when she awoke once more.

Miranda had lied—even if it hadn't been deliberate, she broke her promise.

She made her way to the morgue to apologize. She knew Heather's earthly body wouldn't hear her, but Miranda firmly believed her patient's spirit would know and hopefully understand.

She hated this floor. She had visited it only a few times since starting to work at the hospital. The first time she viewed the morgue had been during orientation—the second and third times were due to a mix-up in identities on two of her patients.

Miranda unlocked and then pushed through the metal door. Freezing cold air greeted her entrance. She rubbed her arms and wished she had grabbed her lab coat. Shrouded in semi-darkness, the room reminded her of several horror movies. All that was missing was the music—the kind that dropped low and then wailed a signal right before the murderer jumped out to kill another victim.

Another chill attacked her, but this one came as an unwelcome reminder of why Heather had died. The woman must have endured unspeakable horror before being found and brought to the E.R.

Gabriella, if indeed she had been responsible for the Slash and Maul murders, had to be insane. Unless she really was the creature Zacke claimed.

Miranda found the storage drawer where Heather's remains rested. She inhaled and then exhaled trying to get the courage to pull it open. Her hand reached out to grasp the cold metal handle.

She pulled it firmly and then waited for the gurney-like slab to roll out and reveal Heather's sheet-covered body.

Her heart beat triple time inside her breast. She sucked in more air and then folded the sheet back. Her breath caught in her throat at the porcelain features marred by several puckered and stitched incisions.

Death had forever locked Gabriella's gruesome handiwork into Heather's face. Eyelids now covered the once tearful blue eyes and hair washed clean of blood lay damp against a chest that bore the same crisscross pattern of death.

Miranda swiped at the tears burning her eyes and then reached out to grip chilly fingers.

"I'm so sorry, Heather."

A hideous and spine chilling laughter echoed from the darkness behind Miranda.

"How touching."

Gabriella!

Miranda's heart stopped for one brief moment. Her body froze with fear as her mind commanded her to run.

Where?

The door stood at her back, as did Gabriella.

She had only one option—she would have to face Zacke's ex and pray for a miracle.

Miranda gently replaced Heather's hand back on the slab before covering her once more. She willed her spine to stay straight as she eased the drawer back into the walled recess. She didn't want Gabriella looking at or possibly inflicting more damage on Heather's mutilated body. She closed the door after the slab clicked into place and turned around.

Gabriella sat on a metal gurney next to the door. The ruby dress she wore emphasized the death-like color of her cheeks and contrasted with her dark hair. The woman who had tried to frighten Miranda to death certainly looked the part of a killer.

Miranda hadn't paid any attention to Gabriella's eyes the night the witch had kissed Zacke, but she noticed them now.

They glowed a deep purple, but as she watched, they took on a red cast. Her fabricated courage faded as she glimpsed Hell's fires.

Gabriella remained motionless.

Miranda felt like a mouse waiting for a lion to pounce. Well, she would just have to show Gabriella a mouse could roar.

"Gabriella, I assume?"

"Yes, and you are the irritating Dr. James."

"Since I'm sure this is not a social visit, why don't you tell me what you're doing here?"

Gabriella's eyes took on a deeper tinge of red. Miranda didn't care for her hungry gaze.

"I am here to warn you once more that Zachary is mine."

Miranda clenched and unclenched her fists but kept her eyes glued on Gabriella's face. She wanted to be ready if Gabriella attacked—not that she could do much to protect herself against a vampire—but at least she wouldn't die without a fight.

"We've had this conversation before. He isn't a possession, Gabriella."

"I have seen the way he kisses you."

Miranda wasn't sure she wanted to know how Gabriella had come by that bit of information. "From what I hear, Gabriella, you did more than kiss him. Yet you have no claim either."

Miranda blinked twice. Had she just seen the woman fly off the gurney? As she watched, Gabriella moved toward the opposite side of the room—away from the door.

She needed something, anything to protect herself. An instrument table sat only a few feet away. Miranda shook off the paralysis threatening her legs.

She barely moved two feet before Gabriella swirled around. The woman must have eyes in the back of her head.

"Going somewhere, little mortal?"

The sarcasm dripping off her words goaded Miranda. "Well, yes, as a matter of fact I am. I have patients to see, and this pissing contest about a man neither one of us can claim is ridiculous."

Gabriella closed her eyes, and Miranda moved a bit closer to the instrument table.

"I didn't believe any mortal capable of your courage, Dr. James. I admire someone who can, or should I say attempt to stand up to me."

Had the woman just paid her a backhanded compliment? Miranda didn't know nor did she care. Only two more steps, and she could grasp the scalpel handle peeking out from under its sterile covering.

"So does that mean you're going to leave now? Fly back to wherever you came from?"

Gabriella snarled and closed her eyes. Miranda lunged for the table. She had the sharp instrument in her hand when she heard a guttural growl. Great, she had really angered her this time.

Miranda turned to face Gabriella and wished she could close *her* eyes. The woman's former beauty had disappeared. Her eyes now shone crimson and snarling lips revealed four incisors that would make a dentist cringe. Red tinged their tips, and Miranda didn't even want to guess if the blood-colored substance had come from Heather's poor body.

She raised her weapon a split second before Gabriella attacked.

Chapter Seventeen

Eyes closed tight, Miranda waited. Her body trembled so badly the scalpel's handle shook within her grasp, making her hold insecure. When she didn't feel Gabriella's talons tearing her to shreds, she opened one eye.

The scalpel hit the tiled floor with a clatter.

Gabriella hung motionless in midair—her arms extended, her claws curved, ready to strike.

Why didn't she? What had stopped her?

Miranda watched the horrendous caricature of Gabriella's mouth smile.

"It seems we are about to have company. I hate to break up this cozy little chat, but I must fly."

Miranda's sigh of relief lifted the hair off her forehead.

"But first!"

Miranda's heart thumped. She should have known she wouldn't get off that easy.

Gabriella struck like lightning. Her hand grasped Miranda's throat. Talons raked her neck. Bolts of fiery pain singed her skin. The wetness crawling to her neckline had to be blood. Fear surged through her. Her ears roared; her head swam as Gabriella exerted more pressure.

Miranda struggled against the vampire's hold. She tried desperately to suck in air.

The hand encircling her throat tightened. Blue starbursts exploded behind her eyelids. Miranda felt the pull of death as it tried to claim her.

Gabriella slammed her fist into Miranda's chest. The impact propelled her across the room. Her back and head connected with the cold wall. White flashes of light fled into darkness.

****

Zacke's fangs extended as he pushed open the door to the morgue. His heartbeat wailed in a crescendo of fear, hopelessness, and rage.

Gabriella had gotten to Miranda. He knew it, as did the men with him. He only hoped she was still alive and not—

Zacke froze out the thought of a torn and bleeding Miranda begging for her life before she died in a pool of blood.

He would not allow it. If he had to, he would transform his beloved. His heart and mind rebelled at the hatred she would hold for his actions, but he would embrace her abhorrence with open arms. God above, he couldn't lose her.

At first, he thought the room empty. Silence reigned; just as it should in a room meant for death. He stepped over the threshold, followed by his backup. Gideon had gotten to the hospital almost as quickly as he and his vampire brethren.

His partner found them interrogating Mac and then Gideon had taken the elevator while the rest of them had taken to the air, transforming their bodies into molecules of mist.

He sensed Gabriella—even before he'd arrived on the basement level. The evil coming from her filled his nostrils with a burning stench. The closer he drew to her, the more intense the stench became until the walls reeked with her presence.

He heard her laughter and the taunting words she spat at Miranda. Both chilled him to the core. But what froze the useless organ in his chest now was the silence.

His mind probed the confines of the room. Gabriella had gone—he hoped back to Hell. He probed again and found the treasure he sought.

Miranda's body lay prone on the floor, her neck and shoulders coated in red.

God's mercy, he *was* too late.

His keening howl echoed through the room. His eyes burned, and he felt something wet on his face. Tears—something he had not experienced for centuries—blurred his vision.

He knelt on the floor at Miranda's side but hesitated to touch her. His heart wept, and his body ached at the thought of never kissing her warm lips, never holding her vibrant body in his arms, and never seeing her eyes shine with the dauntless spirit that was Miranda.

He slipped his arms around her limp form and pulled her up against his chest. Her face looked flaxen in the dim light—the blood droplets standing out in crimson contrast. He cradled her head beneath his heart. Miranda's zeal no longer bathed him in its warmth. His hand trembled as he touched the copper curls of the only woman he would ever love. He bowed his head and inhaled the jasmine scent of her hair.

Zacke couldn't stand the thought of an eternity without her. Hope reared its bright light into the dark recesses of his thoughts. He could hold her again, but did he have the right? Did he have the strength?

A roar burned his larynx. Agony sparked his soul with a fire that would put Hell's flames to shame. He rocked back and forth, his precious burden limp as a rag doll.

In that moment, Zacke knew what death truly felt like. Without his soul mate, his nights would be as empty as the days he spent in immortal sleep.

Pain embraced him as he gave himself over to the creature he despised. He closed his mind against the dismayed cries of his friends. He could not live without her.

He dipped his head and licked the blood from her wounds; the sweet taste exploded on his tongue. Centuries without suckling nectar sent his mind reeling. He pulled back for a moment, but hunger battered past his conscience. He opened his mouth. His elongated teeth stretched to reach the bountiful harvest before him.

The first prick of incisors against the soft skin of her throat accelerated his heartbeat. His first sip caused his knees to weaken, and he dropped to the floor. The wall braced his back, and he gripped Miranda's body tighter.

He suckled faster and faster until his mouth overflowed with her blood. He ignored his heart's hope that the body he held stirred in his arms.

Hands caught and tried to pull him away from his feast. Zacke growled a warning.

"Stop it, Zacke."

"Miranda's alive, but you'll kill her if you don't stop."

"God in Heaven, Zacke. Have you lost your mind?"

Zacke heard the words coming at him as if from a distance. He released his grip on Miranda's throat and raised his head. He opened his eyes to a world of blue light. The horror-stricken gazes of his friends repulsed him, but not as much as the sight of Miranda's blood coating his hands. He knew his lips would be colored crimson also, and he despised himself as never before.

He had lost his senses! Even dead in his arms, Miranda would be better off than enduring an eternity of Hell.

"What have I done?"

He allowed Miles to take Miranda's body from him. He turned away from the look of commiseration in Gideon's face.

When a hand touched his shoulder, he flinched.

"Zacke, didn't you hear what we said? Miranda is alive!"

Zacke tried to focus on Hawk's words.

Miranda lived?

His eyes sought and found Miles. He sat on the floor with Miranda across his lap. His smile kindled an almost nonexistent ember of hope—fanning it into a bright blue flame.

He crawled the few feet separating him from Miranda. He touched the slight rise in her chest. He pressed a trembling hand to the wounds on her throat, and with guilt boring into his soul, he spoke a healing spell to close them. He did the same for her head wound.

The joy of touching her, of instilling the healing she needed, far exceeded his search for redemption—a quest he would gladly relinquish to ensure Miranda's future safety.

He rose to his feet and reached down to take the cherished gift called Miranda from Miles' arms. He accepted the claps of celebration hammering his back.

He called on all the strength he had left to blend himself and Miranda into the molecules of air. He moved through the concrete walls and allowed the night breeze to refresh his body and spirit.

The moon bathed the sky in a warm light and helped to soothe the beast his rage and fear had awakened. He shifted his precious cargo in his arms as his feet touched the roof of his home.

Zacke passed through the outside barriers and moved down the hallway to his bedroom. Tonight Miranda would sleep in his bed. And if he had his way, she would grace its lonely confines—and his soul—for every night hereafter.

****

Zacke sat in a chair he'd pulled close to Miranda's bedside. Hours had passed since he'd brought her home. Gideon had gone to work, and Hawk and Miles hit the streets in search of the elusive Gabriella. He doubted seriously if they would find her.

As much as he despised the witch, he recognized the unmistakable fact she had not endured through the centuries without a keen sense of survival. She would use that and her intellect to evade Hawk and Miles.

His gaze found the movement of Miranda's breast, stronger now than before. He looked at her throat; she would bear slight scars where Gabriella's talons had gouged.

He had thought long and hard about erasing Miranda's memories of the night's events but decided against it. Gabriella's assault would prove his warnings true and, more importantly, remind Miranda to stay on her guard.

Miranda groaned and thrashed in her sleep.

Guilt roiled in his belly. He could live for centuries more and never make up for his failure to protect her. But, at least he could ease her present discomfort. He moved to her side, caressed her brow and spoke a soothing spell.

Zacke lifted a trembling hand to pull the sheet up a bit further on her body. His room stayed several degrees cooler than the rest of his home; the tomb-like air afforded him a more restful sleep.

He rubbed a hand across his face. Dawn would soon crawl across the horizon. He could feel its lethargic pull on his mind and limbs.

The bedroom door eased open, revealing Hawk and Miles' concerned faces.

"How is she?" Hawk's whisper brought a smile to Zacke's lips. Both his friends cared for Miranda, and after tonight's events, he knew they wouldn't hesitate to protect her from all danger—including him.

He motioned them inside as he rose to greet them. His spell would thankfully keep Miranda in dreamland until after sunset. He did not want her waking up in strange surroundings with his corpse-like body lying next to her.

"She's fine." He allowed his relief to show in the arms he braced over both men's shoulders. "Any news on Gabriella?"

"No, and we searched every crevice in the city." Miles' voice shook with frustration and his lids drooped with fatigue.

"I can never repay the two of you for what you have done this night. If not for your..." Zacke's voice broke.

"No need for thanks, you would have done the same for us or any one of your men during a battle." Hawk's tone seeped with exhaustion.

Zacke knew they needed sleep as much as he did, but he had one other concern. "Did either of you run across my partner during your search?"

"Yes. We made sure he got back to his place and put a safety spell on that rat-trap he lives in."

"Thank you, Miles. Now get some rest. I'll be sleeping here, after I set spells to safeguard our rest."

After their departure and setting the spells in place, Zacke eased off his sneakers and stood for a moment beside the bed. His love still rested peacefully. He owed God his thanks, for surely his guiding hand had protected Miranda tonight.

Zacke welcomed the comfort of the bed against his limbs and shifted a bit closer to Miranda. He wrapped a tendril of her hair loosely around his finger and, for the first time in an eternity, he found peace.

****

Miranda turned on her side. Her eyelids felt weighted down as if by rocks. A faint aroma in the air teased her senses and she savored Zacke's scent. Her imagination had to be in overdrive or perhaps it was wishful thinking.

As the grogginess lifted, pain invaded Miranda's head. She rolled onto her back and gasped. Every extremity ached.

Did she have the flu? Had she fallen? Try as she might, Miranda couldn't recall anything of the last few hours. Maybe a hot shower would refresh her memory and ease her discomfort.

She opened her eyes cautiously. Her gaze focused on a quilt she didn't recognize, folded neatly at the bottom of a footboard that also didn't belong to her.

This isn't my room! Where in the Sam Hill am I?

She pushed off the sheet. After blinking several times to clear her fuzzy vision, she couldn't deny her bare legs.

What had happened to her long nightgown? She plucked at the material that scarcely covered her torso and thighs. Only one person she knew had an ample supply of black T-shirts.

"ZACKE!"

Miranda jumped when the bedroom door flew open and banged against the wall. She jerked the sheet back up over her semi-nude body and wiggled backward until the bed's headboard stopped her flight.

The identical expressions worn by the four men standing inside the threshold made her eyes cross. Miranda bit back the giggles threatening to bubble forth at their wide eyes, open-mouthed, panicked looks.

Her gaze drifted down to their hands. Gideon wielded a spatula. Miles and Hawk each brandished cutlery knives. And a most unkempt Zacke waved a large ladle. She promptly succumbed to gut-wrenching laughter.

"Miranda! Are you all right?"

She laughed harder when all four converged on the bed.

Her sides ached so badly, Miranda feared she would pop a rib. She took several deep breaths and willed herself to adopt a sober expression.

"So, which one of you galloping gourmets would like to explain why I'm here?" Silence met her question. Who would have thought all four of them could develop a case of cat-got-your-tongue at the same time? "I'm waiting."

"Well, it's like this, Miranda, uh..." Gideon halted his explanation and looked toward Zacke.

No help from Zacke. He stood silently gripping the ladle.

"You were..." Hawk's voice trailed off, and he looked to Miles.

"Zacke brought you here because..."

All three owners of the stumbling tongues turned to Zacke.

"Well, I'm waiting, Zacke. Are you going to explain what is going on? Or did you lose your ability to form complete sentences also?"

Zacke closed his mouth and hid the ladle behind his back. His heart thundered in his chest—if he were mortal, he would swear he was having a heart attack.

He thought Miranda would sleep a bit longer, and he had planned to have something ready for her to eat. His and Gideon's culinary skills along with Hawk and Miles inept help, had delayed the dinner preparations.

He finally managed to get the beef broth and vegetables to simmer on that worthless appliance called a stove. Her blood-curdling yell had not only scared a couple of centuries off his life, but also caused him to drop the saltshaker in the pot.

But at the moment, splattered soup, a sink full

of dirty dishes, and the fact he would never make it to work on time, paled in comparison to facing Miranda.

"Maybe we should go and leave you two alone."

Miles' statement seemed to be a big hit with Gideon and Hawk. Zacke's three partners-in-crime edged toward the door in a united retreat.

"Run, little mice."

Miranda's softly uttered words would have been funny in another lifetime, but right now, to Zacke, they sounded ominous.

"Don't even think about following them, Zacke. I have a headache, I woke up in a strange bed, and I want an explanation."

Miranda's words sounded brave, but the tears he glimpsed before she lowered her head revealed her confusion.

"It's not what it seems." Zacke eased down on the bed, reached out, and captured the hand pleating the sheet. He used his other hand to nudge her chin upward. "How much do you remember about last night?"

She cocked her head to one side and closed her eyes. Less than a second later, her eyes flew open.

"Oh my gosh, I spent the day at the hospital with Gabriella's victim."

Her hand clenched his so hard he felt her clipped nails biting into his palm.

"Oh, Zacke—she died. I promised her I would be there when she woke up, and I lied to her."

"You did all you could."

"But it wasn't enough. You don't understand, I promised her she would recover." She used her free hand to swipe at her face.

"Miranda, do you remember anything else?"

"Not really." Miranda rubbed her forehead. "I dreamed Gabriella tried to kill me and that you and I flew over Savannah *without a plane*. Some dream, huh?" Her hand trembled inside his.

"Miranda, listen to me. Some of what you think you dreamed did happen. Gabriella came to the hospital and attacked you."

"But, the woman flew across the room. She had fangs and claws and eyes that almost bled."

His incisors begged to stretch.

Zacke clenched his jaw to keep his temper from escalating.

"Zacke, you're hurting my hand."

He kissed the abused limb before releasing it. His vision dimmed for a moment and then returned in a blue mist. He had to keep his rage under control.

"I told you what Gabriella is. I also warned you she would not hesitate to hurt you. That is why I brought you here where you can be safe."

"We've had this conversation before." Miranda's halting breath whispered across his face.

"I understand why you refused, but things have changed. You are no longer safe except with me."

"How do you figure that? The woman isn't human."

Zacke bit his tongue before he could retort neither was he. He would tell Miranda his secret, but not now—not when he needed to convince her to stay with him.

"That's true but at least here you won't be alone."

"Right, I'll be surrounded by you and your friends. I can't live that way. It was bad enough at the apartment. They were there when I went to bed and when I got up. I like my privacy."

"Miranda, this house has plenty of bedrooms. No one will bother you."

Miranda pulled her hand free and moved off the bed. Zacke's gaze locked on the length of her legs as she paced an uneven pattern back and forth.

"I know you want to help, but face it. You said she attacked me, but I'm here, still alive. So I think the danger has passed."

Zacke's legs trembled as he moved to Miranda's side. How could she be so dense? Gabriella would kill her the next time—something he was not about to let happen.

He caught her arm and spun her around to face him. He ignored her wide-eyed gaze. "So, you think there is no reason for you to fear for your life. Well, allow me to show you just what Gabriella did to you."

Zacke pulled her into the bathroom and closed the door. The full-length mirror had been there when Zacke moved in, although he seldom used it.

"Zacke, what are you doing?"

"I am going to show you how close you came to dying last night. You can forget about thanking me, but Hawk, Miles, and Gideon deserve something besides your cynicism."

Zacke placed his hands at the neckline of the T-shirt and ripped it down the middle, exposing Miranda's neck and chest. He ignored her shocked cry. He dragged his gaze from her revealed beauty and resisted the urge to stroke her flesh.

With Miranda standing in front of him, her back pressing against him, he felt his sex stir. He hastily moved one hand to her waist and the other under her chin and compelled her to look in the mirror.

"See the marks Gabriella left on you? They are reminders that she can and will kill you when she pleases."

Miranda's trembling hand moved to her throat. He watched as she gingerly touched the blue and black marks. He saw disbelief leap into her eyes and then horror.

"Now will you agree to stay here?"

Miranda turned and pressed her face against his

chest. Her body shook with her weeping.

He caressed her back and prayed that he had done the right thing.

"Miranda?"

He felt her nod against his skin. His heart leapt with relief. "Shall I take that as a yes, Little One?"

Chapter Eighteen

Miranda smiled when her two hulking shadows fell into step beside her. She had gotten used to Miles and Hawk dogging her footsteps. And when they weren't around, she tripped over Zacke or Gideon.

"Are you ready to head home, Miranda, or do you need to stop somewhere?"

"Why Hawk, it's so sweet of you to ask. You wouldn't by any chance want me to give you another driving lesson would you?"

"Well, now that you mention it..."

Miranda laughed and her bodyguards joined in. She would never have thought she'd see the day she'd be comfortable with these two exceedingly handsome men, but Hawk and Miles had somehow managed to become the siblings she'd never had.

"I guess if you promise not to beg, I can give you a short lesson. Zacke is taking me out tonight, and I want to pick up a new dress."

"Miranda, you're not going to drag us into a dress shop, are you?"

"Hawk, your lordliness is showing, and the chauvinist piglet act doesn't become you."

"Pig?"

Miranda hit the keyless entry and pulled open the passenger door. Hawk jumped in the driver's seat, and Miles climbed into the back.

The short drive to the boutique turned into a free-for-all. Miles' ribbing and his definition of a chauvinist piglet earned him several growls from Hawk. For some reason the low growl reminded her of that night in the morgue.

Miranda ignored the goose bumps dotting her arms and told Hawk to signal a left turn. They pulled into My Lady's parking lot. Eloise, the owner, had promised the sapphire dress' alterations would be finished by tonight.

Tonight was important. She hoped Zacke would finally open up and really talk to her. She wanted to know everything about him, and she wanted him to repeat his marriage proposal. Yes, the first one had been, in her opinion, a desperate ploy to gain her agreement to move in with him. She couldn't fault the man for wanting to keep her safe, but this time she wanted him to ask for the right reasons.

Miranda wanted—no, needed to know why he couldn't or wouldn't admit how much he cared for her.

She had spent almost two months in Zacke's home. In that time, Gabriella had not actually attacked, but Miranda believed the witch had her in sight. A few times, she heard footsteps following her down remote hospital corridors. She avoided the morgue since the night of the attack and hoped the stalkings resulted from her overactive imagination. She had purposely not told Zacke.

He'd become a fanatic. Going in to work early and staying out until his shift ended. He would swing by the hospital before heading home some mornings and looked like a day-old corpse.

Her days, for the most part, kept her thoughts free of Gabriella. However, her nights dragged, except when Zacke managed to drop in for brief visits. She tried her best to stay awake until at least midnight so she could see him for just a few moments, but some nights, sleep claimed her against her will.

Miranda's worries over a non-platonic relationship had been unnecessary. The closest thing to a move by Zacke had occurred when he leaned over to open her car door. That momentous event had occurred on their first and only date since she moved into his place.

A date she had instigated and which had taken place over a month ago.

Miranda fiddled with the strap on her briefcase and recalled a note Zacke left on her pillow two nights before asking her to have dinner with him. Her heart had galloped down an avenue of what ifs. Could he be ready to say what he felt in his heart? Could he be ready to trust her with his secret past? Miranda's hopes plummeted when Zacke's attitude continued to remain distant. She hoped tonight would be different.

"Miranda, are you getting out or not?" Hawk's disgruntled tone zinged her mind back into the present. She took a quick glimpse at the car's clock and cursed her reflective thinking. She'd be late if she didn't get a move on.

"Yes." Miranda followed her words with action. She hit the door lock and twisted in her seat.

Miles' hand on her wrist prevented her exit. "You might want to take off your seat belt first, Miranda."

His low chuckle caused her cheeks to heat up, completely ruining the "don't mess with me" look she attempted.

She exited the car with male laughter spearing into her back.

The jingling of the shop bell announced her entry into a bustling but organized chaos.

"Miranda, you're right on time, my dear. Your dress is ready for you to slip into for one final inspection."

Miranda groaned; she hadn't planned on trying the dress on again. However, on the other hand, she didn't want any surprises when she got home.

"Thanks." Miranda headed in the direction of the dressing room Eloise pointed out. In her haste, she sidestepped an elegantly dressed blonde and managed to avoid a harried sales clerk.

She pushed the door open and her breath caught. The sapphire dress, even lovelier than she remembered, hung on a matching cloth hanger. Her reluctance disappeared. She stripped to her plain white undies and made a mental note to pick up something a bit more daring.

Ten minutes later, she exited the shop. The garment bag held protectively against her chest, and the designer bag containing a midnight-black corset and matching stockings swung from her arm.

Hawk jumped out when Miranda approached the car, leaving the driver's side door open for her. He took her booty.

"Please hang it up carefully, Hawk. I don't want it to wrinkle."

Hawk did as she asked, even going to the trouble of smoothing the bottom edge of the bag against the backseat. He stowed her bag of unmentionables on the seat beside it.

Hawk waited for her to slide onto the seat. He cocked one of his elegant brows, a sure sign his brain had gone into overdrive. "What is so important about tonight's date, Miranda?"

She supposed she could have told him to take a hike, but both of her oversized bodyguards had been concerned, protective, and downright sweet to her over the last several weeks. "I'm hoping Zacke is going to tell me his deep dark secret." She cast a glance up at Hawk's unnaturally stiff form and then one at Miles, whose face looked etched in stone.

"Uh, what makes you think Zacke has any secrets?"

"Because he told me."

"Zacke told you he had a secret?" Miles' voice

resembled the squeaky wheel on Miranda's first car.

"Yes, is that so surprising?"

"Zacke is usually pretty closed mouthed about certain parts of his life, but hey I've only known him a few centuries. He could have changed."

"Centuries?" Miranda shook her head, surely she had misunderstood Miles.

"Years. I meant years, Miranda."

Miles exchanged a distressed look with Hawk who had bent slightly to look inside the car. Something wasn't right, and Miranda could feel it all the way to her toes.

"We aren't finished with this conversation, you two. But, I have to get back or I'm going to be late." She had planned a long, jasmine-scented bath. At this point, she'd be blessed if she managed a quick shower.

After Hawk hopped in the passenger seat, Miranda turned the ignition key and adjusted the radio's volume.

"Miss, oh, Miss!"

Miranda looked up. A woman stood close to the car. Miranda rolled the window down just a bit. "Yes, can I help you?"

"Well, Sugar, I thought I might be some help to you." The blonde, who looked vaguely familiar, held up a badge. "You left this behind in the dressing room. I found it, and Eloise told me it belonged to you."

Miranda rolled the window down a bit more and took the proffered badge. "Thanks, I didn't realize it had fallen off my lab coat. I was in a bit of a hurry. I appreciate you bringing it out."

"Well, hon, I heard Eloise and the others talking about your big date tonight, and I just wouldn't feel right if I didn't do my part to help."

The woman smiled before giving a small wave to Hawk and Miles. Before Miranda could voice her thanks once more, the woman turned and walked down the street.

"Ready to go, guys?" When she received no response, she looked in the rearview mirror at Miles and then across at Hawk.

Both men looked slack-jawed and a bit dazed. As she watched, they both snapped out of whatever spell they had been under.

"Not just yet, Miranda. I need to do something." Hawk jerked open the car door, gave Miles a look Miranda could not interpret and then took off down the street.

"What on earth?"

"I'm sure it's nothing, Miranda. Hawk probably wanted to..."

"You're a poor liar, Miles. He probably wanted to get the blonde's phone number."

When Miles didn't reply, Miranda suppressed her annoyance with the male population, Zacke at the head of the list.

****

Gabriella tossed the long blonde wig into a dumpster near her latest abode. Blue contact lenses received the same treatment. They had helped to dull some of the amethyst of her eyes but not enough.

She laughed aloud. The precise moment Hawk and Miles' tiny minds comprehended her identity had been most amusing. The mortal twit Zachary had fallen in love with was clueless to her identity. Since their confrontation, seeking Miranda's thoughts offered no challenge.

Rage played a key part in Gabriella's decision to turn up at the dress shop. She had hoped to lure Miranda away. Then it would be sheer pleasure to tell Zacke she held his lover captive. Unfortunately, the presence of Lord's Hawk Sherwood and Miles Dunbar put a halt to those plans.

Yes, she could dazzle their thoughts for a few moments, but their wills had grown almost as strong as Zacke's. A mind wield wouldn't stay in place long, and she wasn't in the mood to fight both of them, at the moment, although she would relish a future battle.

Tonight she had more important things to accomplish.

Gabriella tossed her thoughts to the wind and found what she sought. She would call upon Jake and Tyler, Zacke's mortal enemies, to prove their sworn loyalty. After all, she had bailed them out of jail and supplied them with more riches than they could spend in several lifetimes.

If all went well, Zacke would be under her power once more.

****

Miranda held the banister as she made her way cautiously down the stairs. She reached the next to the last step and paused; the house seemed to be abnormally quiet, even for a house where the men slept most of the day.

A dreadful thought crossed her mind. What if Zacke had been called into work, and Miles and Hawk were too chicken to come out and tell her? Because of Hawk's impromptu run after the blonde, she had to bust her butt to be ready for her date.

"Hello, where is everyone?" Miranda called stepping off the final step.

Zacke stood in the shadows of the entryway, a few feet from Miranda. He had finished dressing while the water pipes still hummed for Miranda's shower. He'd been in the basement, where he had moved his blood supply, enjoying a bit of liquid dinner when he heard Miranda's tentative query. He followed her voice but instead of answering her, he stared, mesmerized by the sight of her standing on the stairs.

Never had his home been graced with a vision such as Miranda. Her copper hair reflected the light from the entrance hall and shone with a mixture of tangerine, red, and even lighter shades of peach. The lovely mass tumbled to her shoulders and then cascaded downward to contrast with alabaster skin peeking above the neckline of her sapphire dress.

Zacke's heart collided with his feet. To have this wonderful woman in his life everyday and to truly be able to love her in all ways would be more than he had ever dreamed possible.

Yet, his own stupidity in dragging his feet and his reluctance to tell her what he was could cause him to lose her forever.

He should have gone to her after he'd spoken with Hawk and Miles. Both had been visibly angry at Gabriella's bold approach.

"I'm sorry, Zacke, it took both Miles and I a moment to snap out of that mind freeze and by the time I realized it was her, then followed, she disappeared. I did find the wig in a dumpster but nothing else to show which direction she'd gone.

"She's devious. Don't blame yourselves for not being on her level. We'll catch her." Zacke grimaced. "I just hope it's sooner rather than later."

Zacke's heart moved back to his chest from where it had lodged in his throat and pounded so loudly it hurt his sensitive ears. His breath exploded with such force his incisors extended and then retracted. He had run out of excuses and time was a luxury he could not afford.

He would tell her tonight after dinner.

****

Zacke watched Miranda push the last of her prime tenderloin around the edges of the porcelain dinner plate. Despite her slightly hesitant mood, she participated in his hard sought topics during the appetizer and their entrees.

The rare steak he ordered sat in his stomach like a boulder surrounded by a red wine river.

The liquor helped to relax both of them or at least he'd thought it had. But for the last several minutes, Miranda had silently avoided his gaze.

Zacke found himself at a loss for words, a problem he encountered only with Miranda. Being with her tonight was his idea; he had succumbed to the inevitable. His strength of will had slowly eroded over the last two months, ever since he'd installed her in his home and his bed.

If he had not already been working nights, he would have volunteered just to keep his sanity. He tried to schedule his nocturnal visits home when he knew Miranda would be asleep, but some nights he had misjudged the timing.

Those moments haunted him night and day.

He didn't know what was worse; finding a football jersey clad Miranda snuggled against his pillow, or surprising her in the kitchen during her chocolate hunts.

She invaded his peace of mind ten times worse than an enemy army could invade the shores of his English home. Not to mention what she'd done to his house.

Miranda filled each room of his previously austere dwelling with flowers, pictures, and various but separate mates of footwear.

He smiled as he remembered how she would bemoan the fact that she could never find her shoes.

"Zacke, why are you looking at me that way?"

He jerked as Miranda's words penetrated his memories. "Like what?"

"Like, I don't know, maybe like I've developed the traits of a cuddly puppy or something."

Zacke's laughter burst forth, startling the waiter weaving his way behind their table.

"You, my darling Miranda, are much more

enticing than a puppy."

Miranda's gaze sparked with humor but the laughing lights quickly extinguished. Her blue eyes turned a stormy gray and her beautiful lips pulled into a taut line. "Well, you couldn't prove it by me, Zacke. I have been a guest in your home for—"

"Not a guest, Miranda, you are much—"

"If you say 'much more' one more time Zacke, I'll hit you. The entire time I have been living there, I've seen you maybe ten times. Can you explain that?"

Zacke didn't care for the turn their conversation had taken. Miranda's attitude demanded an immediate response, but he didn't want to get into that here and now.

The courage he had garnered at the beginning of the evening crawled back into its black hole. Zacke didn't know if he could coach it back.

He watched the storm clouds grow in Miranda's eyes and realized he would rather confront her anger with a bit of his own.

"So be it. If you want an explanation for my attitude, Miranda, I'll give you one." He ignored her wide eyes and open mouth. "But, I will not do it here. My alleged faults and my life history will be better told at home."

Zacke shoved his chair back and stood. He tossed a handful of bills onto the table, moved to her side, pulled back her chair and grasped her arm.

"We're leaving, now?"

"Yes." Zacke ignored the shock on her face, handed Miranda her handbag, and eased her to her feet. He welcomed the ashen look on their waiter's face when he showed him a glimpse of incisors.

He hustled her out of the restaurant and to the car. He tamped down the urge to scream out his agony to the Heavens. He had no right to expect a Heavenly host to help him out of this mess.

After seating Miranda and closing her door, he

walked to the driver's side on unsteady legs. His insides quaked with the mortal food he had consumed and with fear.

Come Hell or high water, before dawn exploded in the eastern sky again, Zacke would know if he had lost Miranda forever.

Chapter Nineteen

Miranda kicked the front door shut so hard she broke the heel off her shoe. She yanked off both shoes and threw them against the wall; the clunks that echoed throughout Zacke's house pleased her. Her handbag hit the far corner, its soft thud not quite as satisfying as she hoped. She removed her earrings and tossed them on an end table as she headed for the kitchen.

How dare he try to turn the tables? What right did he have to be angry with her? She'd been an open book to his locked diary. Did she get any answers? No! He had to go to work. Yeah right. She strode to the kitchen door then turned and retraced her steps. A drink wouldn't drown the fury inside her or the disappointment that Zacke would just up and leave—the coward.

She stalked toward the staircase and her peripheral vision caught two rather large shadows scurrying toward the back of the house. Good! She didn't need to deal with two more men afraid to face her.

In stocking feet, she thudded up the oak steps. Tears burned the edges of her eyes and blurred her sight but couldn't dispel the image of Zacke leaving her at the front door without so much as a "see you later."

Her bedroom door received the same care as the front door. Miranda hopped across the room, her throbbing toe a reminder not to kick a door while barefoot. She jumped onto the bed and stifled her shriek in a throw pillow. When the pain ebbed, she used the pillow to wipe her face. Salt tracks left her skin dry and itchy. She ignored the discomfort and crawled into the middle of the bed.

The evening had been a total bust. Zacke made stilted conversation, while she replied in kind. His mood remained so somber, she discarded any hope of talking him into acquiescence. His laughter and unexpected anger had been the only genuine emotions she witnessed.

Her stomach clenched again as it had when Zacke told her he was ready to talk. The anticipation made her limbs tremble with happiness and dread. But she had been doomed for disappointment.

Zacke's cell phone once again prevented him from spilling his guts. His explanation had been abrupt—something to do with two men out on bail.

Miranda knew Zacke had to go, but she didn't have to like it.

She looked around the room. The clock on the bedside table read almost midnight. She had to be at work in the morning and should try to get some sleep.

If she stayed awake, would he talk to her when he returned? Shoot, she didn't know if he'd even be back tonight.

Miranda eased down and pulled her knees to her chest. Maybe she would read for a bit. Hopefully that would relax her so she could sleep. A bit later, the words in her book blurred. She needed to get undressed and ready for bed. Try as she might to force her body to move, Miranda couldn't and soon gave up. She rested her head on her folded hands and closed her eyes.

****

Zacke moved through the darkness with Gideon flanking his left side. Over the years, they had developed a point position, which always placed him a couple of feet in front. Together they had refined their stalking technique to a few key hand signals. A wave of the hand or the pointing of a finger indicated which direction the other would take. Tonight, they would need silent communication as they hunted the men Zacke had arrested several months prior for drug trafficking and child prostitution.

Jake Archer and Tyler Brown had been lying low since they'd made bail. Zacke knew, as their court date approached, Jake would seek any means he could to escape the airtight charges.

The material witness had already given a written statement specifying Jake's methods of forcing teens to shake down johns for money. Zacke's own testimony about Jake and Tyler's attempts to murder a law-enforcement officer would ensure the man and his second-in-command would be behind bars until they were too old to do more than crawl to freedom.

The phone call that cut off his planned explanation to Miranda had been from an informant who always supplied Zacke with accurate information over the years. He disclosed that Jake and Tyler had thrown their lot in with a woman. Rumor had it she knew something about the Slash and Maul murders.

Zacke slowed his pace and motioned to Gideon to do the same as they neared the alley behind the hotel. He doubted seriously that Gabriella would conspire with two lowlifes like Jake and Tyler, but he couldn't take the chance. But they could know of Gabriella's whereabouts. It was worth checking out.

The further they moved into the alleyway, the darker it became. The security light stood tall but unlit at the furthest end of the alley. Zacke's vision allowed him to see the surrounding area, but since the department owned no night vision goggles, Gideon took his lead from Zacke.

Zacke exchanged a look with a tense and

impatient Gideon. He knew his partner wanted to go full steam ahead but even though the night appeared peaceful, Zacke's spine prickled.

He motioned Gideon to stand still, and he did the same. He closed his eyes and sought the elements of the night. He heard the slight rustle of a rodent as it searched for a bite to eat and the light brush of wings as a pair of birds soared overhead.

Nothing in their immediate vicinity signaled why his teeth ached to extend or why his vision tinged with a faint blue glow.

Zacke had relied on intuition for centuries to conquer ruthless killers, mortal and immortal. He wondered if the human elements he had recently experienced had weakened his self-survival traits.

He rotated his shoulders slightly to ease the tension-induced knots. He had to focus. He opened his eyes and tried once more to see the evil he sensed lurking.

A blue haze blurred his vision as he found what he sought. Two shadows hunkered down behind a dumpster on a street adjacent to the hotel. He heard the soft click of metal against metal.

A large caliber bullet hurtled straight toward Gideon.

Zacke stepped in front of him.

Fire burned the hollow below his shoulder. He dropped to his knees. Wetness saturated his shirt. An identical flame edged his temple. He looked up at Gideon through a film of red. The astonishment on his partner's face echoed his own disbelief.

He felt Gideon's arms around him, lowering him the rest of the way to the ground and then he felt nothing.

****

Miranda buried her face beneath her pillow and tried to block the shrill ringing. She desperately needed more sleep, and she wanted to bash her alarm clock.

She reached out with the intention of doing just that and found she had forgotten to set it. The obnoxious and persistent ringing came from another source—her cell phone. She clicked it on and spoke into the irritating instrument. "Dr. James."

"Miranda, this is Mac. We have a GSW coming in, and no one else is answering their pages or phones."

Miranda's jaws ached with her stifled groan. This was getting old. Why should she be the only one to respond to a call? Regardless, it wasn't Mac's fault. "That's all right, Mac. I'll be there in about twenty or so. How long before the ambulance gets there?"

"Not long. Can you make it quicker?"

Miranda rolled off the bed and stretched her one free arm over her head.

"Sure, be there in ten."

****

Mac met Miranda at the doors to the trauma unit. "Hi, Mac, I take it our patient is going to need surgery?"

"Yes, it's a chest wound with the bullet still inside. The patient has lost a lot of blood."

Miranda's lips drew together in a taut line. She'd need to remove the bullet and thoroughly cleanse the wound to prevent sepsis. She didn't want to fool with that nasty infection.

"Okay, give me a minute to get into scrubs, and then I'll take a look at him." She tried to pass Mac, but he blocked her entry to the unit. "Mac, I need to get inside."

"Miranda, there's something you need to know."

"What? That he needs me in there more than out here?"

"No, I mean yes, but there's more."

Miranda pursed her lips in an effort not to light

into Mac. Her assistant wasn't prone to this type of attitude or stall tactics—not when it came to patient care. "So, what is it? What's so important?"

"You, uh, know this guy."

Miranda looked at the discomfort, concern, and compassion in Mac's gaze. She began a slow shake of her head and saw what she had missed before— uniformed men sitting and standing in the waiting room area. "It's Zacke, isn't it?"

"Yes, Miranda."

Miranda gave a slight nod and then pushed her shoulders back into military stiffness. "Let's go, Mac. We have a patient waiting."

****

Zacke pushed open eyelids that felt glued shut. He tried to turn his head, but the ache behind his eyes stopped him. Lord above, he felt like he had centuries ago after a night of drinking and wenching. His tongue felt like sandpaper.

But the most agonizing ache centered in his upper chest. Spikes of iron stabbed him.

A groan tore from his sore throat and passed his dry lips. He closed his eyes against the pain only to be jarred back from his hope of unconsciousness by several sets of hands probing him. His distress grew and his groans became louder.

"For pity's sake, can't you leave the man alone?"

A snarl accompanied the guttural roar; Miles, Hawk, or both must be in the room. He needed to talk to them, but first he needed some privacy.

He used the pain to focus his mind on the mortals surrounding him. A moment later, they moved back and then exited the room. Zacke's breath felt trapped in his chest and the tubing in his mouth made it hard to swallow.

He used his right hand to pull out the tubing. The plastic airway produced a raw burn as it slid against his esophagus. Once the tubing cleared his throat and mouth, he sat up, took the cup Miles offered and sipped a bit of lukewarm water.

"What happened, Zacke?"

Zacke noted the extensive pallor of his friends' faces. Both men look drawn and literally ragged out.

"Guess I'm getting a bit too old to outrun bullets."

"Not funny. You were almost killed, and by a mortal. Can you explain that?"

"No, I wish I could. But for some months now I have been experiencing mortal traits." Hawk and Miles gaped in shock.

"Close your mouths, guys. It's uncommon I agree, but not unheard of."

"Where did you get your facts?"

"From one of our own, Hawk. His reign on earth lasted almost a millennium. Although the letters I located on the Internet are rumored to be myths. Basil states that he began experiencing mortal traits centuries before his demise. His theory is the longer one lives, the more susceptible one becomes."

"I've heard that, but I dismissed it as a fable."

"So did I. And I ignored the little things, like perspiring and feeling nauseous, but after tonight, I know it's not just a tale."

"So, what do you do now?"

Zacke took another sip of the water. Good question but hard to know how to answer—especially when he didn't have a clue. "I'm not sure I can do anything. I do know I have to feed so I can get some of my strength back. I can't fight Gabriella and win in the shape I'm in now."

"Well, having to feed is not really a problem."

Miles motioned with his hand toward the head of Zacke's bed. He turned and watched the slow drip of plasma make its way down the long tubing that held his left arm captive.

"Meals on wheels. What a lovely way to dine."

Miles' quip sparked Hawk's laughter and then Zacke's own. He sat holding his chest when the door pushed open and a Valkyrie with copper hair stormed in—only this one frightened him more than the ones he had met originally.

The look Miranda turned on Miles and Hawk should have turned them to ashes. His friends, the cowards, ran as they had before, leaving him alone and unprotected.

"Miranda, they were only checking on me."

Miranda took in the hangdog look on Zacke's face. His previous pallor had become a more natural color, which almost, but not quite hid the slight shadows under his beautiful eyes.

Her gaze moved to the destroyed tubing she had last seen inserted in Zacke's throat. Her mind reeled at the damage that could have been done to his seductive voice. How on earth had he gotten it out and why would he do it in the first place?

She approached the bed and almost smiled at the look of misery on her detective's face. Surely, he wasn't afraid of her? But then again maybe he should be. "Zacke, I think we need to have a little talk."

She watched misery turn into pure terror. He swallowed several times, wincing with the effort.

She perched on the edge of the bed and caught his right hand in one of her own. "Do you know how worried I've been? I expected to find you out of it and instead I find you laughing your head off. Don't get me wrong, I'm happy you're awake and able to laugh, but you scared me to death when I walked in here. What possessed you, or Lords Frick and Frack, to pull out the tubing? And how did they get in here in the first place? This is ICU, and as far as I know they can't pull out a badge and cite police privileges."

Zacke closed his eyes. When he opened them, the torment she glimpsed tore her heart into shreds.

She decided to ignore his evasion concerning Miles and Hawk and the crushing grip he had on her hand.

"Miranda, you shouldn't worry about me. I'm a fast healer."

"Sure and you can outrun speeding bullets. Well, Detective, your skills failed you last night. And why you think I'm stupid enough to believe you can get hit with a bullet and not be hurting like someone stomped on you, is beyond me."

Miranda's hand clenched Zacke's with enough force *he flinched.* "Not to mention, the graze of that second bullet to the side of your head. You know, you could have a concussion!"

Zacke withdrew his hand from her grip and then reached for the tape holding the gauze in place over his wound.

Before she could protest about ripping out her stitches, he tore off the bandage.

"This is why."

Her hand flew to her mouth as she gazed at the almost healed incision—one that should have been puffy, puckered, and red. "I don't understand. How is this possible?"

Zacke's gaze caught and held hers for a brief moment before his lids lowered, cutting off the blue glow. "Do you believe in fairytales or nightmares?"

His question made absolutely no sense. "Enough, Zacke. I'm tired, confused, and a bit ticked." She knew her voice was rising in pitch; Zacke's recoil testified to that, but Miranda didn't give a hockey puck. The man owed her. "I want the truth. Now. Not tomorrow. Not next week. Now."

Zacke opened his eyes but instead of looking at her, he chose a spot right above her head. Coward!

"I heal quickly because I'm not human. I can't die by a bullet or in any other mortal way."

Miranda had to strain to hear Zacke's words,

but she didn't have to strain to see his complexion lose all color or the tic in his jaw.

The first inklings of dread touched her heart. For whatever crazy reason he thought himself inhuman, he certainly seemed sincere. She forced her lips to move. "Zacke, I'm really trying hard to understand what you're saying, but you're not making any sense."

"I know, but there's not an easy way to tell you."

Miranda's hand plucked at the bedcovers. She didn't think she wanted to hear his explanation, but she needed to know. "Spit it out, Detective."

Zacke ground his teeth together so hard she heard them. He pushed himself forward until he sat at the edge of the bed—his face a canvas of control and determination.

"Zacke, what are you doing? You can't get up."

"No, I need to tell you something. I should have told you months ago." He grasped her hand in a bruising grip. "I am a vampire, Miranda."

Miranda shook her head to disperse the blackness threatening to engulf her. "Zacke, this isn't funny. Why would you say such a thing?"

He released her hand and then before she could blink, he jerked out the IV needle from his left hand. He moved off the bed and stood. His gaze darkened until the blue glow hurt Miranda's eyes.

Still she sat frozen, waiting for the hallucination to end.

Zacke stretched out both his hands, rotated his wrists, and then right before her eyes his clipped nails turned into talons. Her head snapped up to his face. A face she didn't recognize. His features looked cold, hard, and frightening. His lips formed a taut line, but as she stared, they curved up exposing incisors at least an inch long.

"Because I am like Gabriella."

Her heart told her he could never be a monster

like Gabriella, but her mind could not deny the evidence.

Miranda exited the bed. Her knees buckled. She slammed into the abandoned IV pole and sent it clattering to the floor. She didn't see him move, but he stood at her side. She recoiled from the hand, minus talons, Zacke extended. Try as she might, she couldn't make herself take it, even though his face held none of its previous animalistic expression.

"Miranda?"

"Don't, Zacke. Don't talk to me. Don't touch me. Don't do anything."

His gasp assaulted her heart but she turned away from it and him. Her feet carried her almost to the door when he launched his attack.

"I love you, Miranda!"

Chapter Twenty

"Miranda, stop!"

She heard the voice but didn't slow her steps. I have to get out of here. She ran past the nurses' station and out through the electronic doors into the main corridor.

I have to think. Am I losing it?

Had she imagined Zacke to be the monster Gabriella was? No, she had seen him, which meant she had fallen in love with a lie not to mention a man who had nails longer than her own. No, that wasn't right—he wasn't a man.

"Miranda, wait."

The voice sounded closer. She ran faster, gained the elevator doors, and pushed the button. For once luck was on her side; the doors opened, and she stepped in.

But so did Hawk and Miles with Gideon right on their heels.

"Is Zacke okay?"

She ignored the entreaty in all their gazes and slammed her hand on the floor button. The doors shut, enclosing her with three men she'd just as soon not see, let alone talk to.

"Miranda, please tell us, is he okay?"

For one brief moment, her heart ached for their concern. "Okay? Is Zacke okay?" She growled the words and slapped at Hawk's outstretched hand. She moved away from all three men until her body touched the back wall.

"Look, Miranda, we understand you're upset, but we need to know if Zacke is all right."

"Fine! Yes, he's okay, are you satisfied? In fact, he's recovering much faster than I dared to hope. But then again, I wasn't counting on him not being human!" She caught and held the gazes staring back at her. Their faces held relief—not the surprise she expected to see.

"So he finally told you."

"It's about time."

"Past time, if you ask me."

Miranda's mouth dropped open. The macho trio had been privy to the secret Zacke had kept hidden from her. The smile on their faces didn't assuage the mingled hurt and horror she felt. Instead, rage grew until it engulfed her.

"I'm so happy you all find this amusing. I don't! Now, if you don't mind, leave me alone."

"Miranda, look, I know this is a shock to you, but it's really not that big of a deal."

Gideon's words reached her ears. She stared in disbelief at the man who actually trusted a vampire with his life. Oh, yeah, she had done that also. Her limbs trembled as she thought of the times she had allowed his kisses to singe her and his comforting arms to hold her. All that time, she had been playing fast and loose with a soulless, depraved monster.

"Not a big deal, well I disagree, Gideon. It is a big deal! Zacke lied by omission, and all the contempt he exhibited for Gabriella was nothing but a bunch of cow manure."

"You're wrong, Miranda. Zacke despises Gabriella. He also hates what he is. In truth, he has been trying to find a way to get his soul back and become human again."

For a second, she allowed Gideon's words to touch the extinguished flame of hope and rekindle it. "Well then, if what you say is true, why hasn't he?"

"Miranda, you have a right to answers for all your questions. I'm sure Zacke will fill you in on—"

Miles words stopped when she shook her head.

"At the moment, speaking to Zacke is one of the last things I ever plan to do again."

"Then you can listen to us." Hawk's usually soft tones sounded like a growl and sent chills up her spine. As she watched, his eyes glowed a deep amber. *Oh my sweet Heavenly Father, he's one, too.*

He nodded to Miles who, with a claw-tipped index finger, pressed the stop button. Hawk waved a hand in the air, and the emergency siren stopped. Terror dispersed her confusion. Morbid curiosity overtook common sense, and she peeked over at Gideon.

"Nope. I'm too redneck to be one of them."

Her body sagged in relief against the back of the elevator. At least she wasn't the only mortal trapped inside a small box with two full-grown vampires.

The elevator started again, chugged its way to the desired floor before it stopped mechanically. The men ushered Miranda out into the corridor and over to her office, where Mac sat behind her desk shuffling paperwork.

"Out!" Miles pulled her behind her desk, barely giving an open-mouthed Mac time to vacate her chair.

"Miranda?" His concern warmed her, but she shook her head.

"I'm fine. Zacke's fine. I just need a few moments with his friends."

"Sure, I'll be in the lounge if you need me."

The look he gave her unwanted escort smacked of bravado, and she knew he wouldn't hesitate to stay if she asked.

Again, she shook her head and managed a slight smile.

When the door closed against further intrusions, Hawk and Miles sat on the corners of the desk, and Gideon sat in the chair opposite hers.

"There are some things you need to know about Zacke before you condemn him, Miranda. He never wanted to be a vampire. Gabriella turned him and left him for dead centuries ago because he lost interest in her."

She looked at the blond-haired giant. Tears sparkled in Hawk's eyes; the amber glow dimmed.

"We found him, me and Miles. He had gashes and wounds that equaled what you saw on Gabriella's latest victim. We buried him, Miranda, and then we left. We were on our way to complete a mission for King James when Gabriella attacked us."

Hawk's head dropped forward just a fraction and his shoulders slumped.

"This time, Zacke found us. He returned the burial favor. We hooked up several decades later, but Zacke, instead of embracing the immortal life as we did, decided to do all he could to prevent Gabriella from turning others." Miles rubbed his eyes before looking again at Miranda. "Sometimes he was successful, sometimes he wasn't.

For the first time since the elevator, Gideon spoke up. "Because of Zacke I'm alive today. We'd only been partners for a few months when a stakeout went bad. I took a bullet to the gut and bled like a stuck pig. I didn't think I'd make it, but Zacke took care of me then just as he did tonight. The bullet you removed from his chest was aimed at me."

Miranda struggled to find her voice. "How did he take care of you?"

"Zacke sat right down in that filthy alley, dead center in broken glass and garbage and hauled me up in his arms. I couldn't see worth a damn, but I swear his eyes were wet. He told me it'd be all right, and then he opened this awful gash in his arm and made me drink from it."

Gideon shared a grin with the fang men. "I have

to tell you, the taste of blood ain't nearly as good going down as a Coors Light. He didn't let me take much but it helped ease the hurtin'. I must have blacked out after that cause I woke up in the hospital. Zacke told me what he was and that he would kill me if I told anyone."

Gideon's laughter sparked Hawk's and Miles'. "Come on, Miranda, I'm kidding. Zacke, in the decade I've known him, has never killed anyone. The man is too sweet for his own good."

Miranda's sigh of relief dislodged some of Mac's carefully arranged papers. "Okay, so sue me for being scared and confused. You have to admit all of this sounds like something out of a—"

"*Horror* flick?"

"Yes, Gideon." Miranda returned the grin he gave her. "All right you three, you've given me more than enough to think about, so how about getting out and letting me get to it."

After all three exited the office, she dropped her head onto her hands and closed her eyes. Instead of seeing darkness, she saw the brilliant blue flames of Zacke's eyes.

****

Zacke paced around the confines of his room, hands clenched into fists, his nails grew and retracted with his emotions. Why had he told Miranda the truth? He could have hidden it from her for a few more years, by then she would love him the way he loved her and it wouldn't matter.

Yeah right, she would do just what she had done earlier, run from him in horror. His heart felt split in two. All he'd succeeded in doing was frighten Miranda. Forget frightened, she had been positively terrified.

And she remained so, from what his partners in crime and fang had told him. No wonder she hadn't been back to see him. He couldn't blame her.

Learning the men who guarded her from Gabriella's fangs and claws had some of their own must have shocked her. But discovering the man who proposed marriage was a vampire must have stoked every nightmare she'd ever had.

It would be a miracle if she ever spoke to him again.

He should just leave her alone, but he couldn't. Miranda certainly wouldn't consent to continue living at his house, and he really doubted the woman would allow Hawk and Miles to continue to guard her.

Ha! She would probably give even Gideon wide berth after this. He would have to come up with another way to keep her safe until he found Gabriella.

He just prayed he found her before his powers became nonexistent. God's precious tears, his hope of becoming mortal again seemed to be coming true, but the timing reeked to high Heaven. He would need all the strength he could master to defeat Gabriella.

The door whooshed open. Zacke cursed under his breath. If Mac came in one more time to check on him, or to confide his concern about Miranda, he would not be answerable for his actions.

"Zacke?"

His body jerked, his heart thundered so loudly he swore it kept time with the infernal monitor that still blinked and bleeped at him.

Miranda moved past the half-opened door. Her head tilted sideways just a bit, allowing copper curls to slide over one shoulder. She glanced around the room before her gaze came to rest on him. His muscles tensed as he waited for her previous look of repulsion; instead, her beautiful eyes shimmered with tears.

"Zacke, I'm sorry."

"Forgive me, Little One."

For the rest of his days, Zacke couldn't say who spoke or moved first. But he knew nothing could ever be better than having Miranda back in his arms again.

Miranda rubbed her cheek against his chest. The softness aroused his senses, but the trust she gave him rivaled and won against desire. He allowed himself one sniff of her jasmine-scented hair before he gently pushed her away.

"What's wrong, Zacke?"

"Nothing's wrong, I just want to make sure this isn't a dream."

His heart mended with her laughter. He had believed he would never hear her voice ring with amusement again.

"I assure you this isn't a dream. For a while I thought it was a nightmare."

He pulled her so close he could hear her heart beat. "It was and is a nightmare, Miranda. I would gladly have pulled my fangs out with pliers before hurting or frightening you. For centuries I have been resigned to living my nights alone. Love seemed a blessing beyond my reach, undeserved—"

"Zacke, don't." Her hand found its way to his lips and silenced his words. "You do deserve it. Your secret came as a shock to me, but I know you aren't a monster. You care about your job and protecting people. You've protected me from Gabriella, and you have tried your best to do right. No one, not even a mortal man, could be a better person."

Her words touched and healed a place inside him that had ached since Gabriella had transformed him.

"Miranda, does this mean you forgive me?"

"Yes, and I hope you can forgive me for not trusting you in the first place. I'm sorry I allowed my fear of Gabriella to touch what I know isn't possible about you. You are nothing like that witch."

She raised her head, and with her hands, she pulled his face down to hers. He anticipated the expected soft caress her lips would bring and the sweetness he would once again explore.

The whooshing of the door stopped their lips from meeting. This time he would kill Mac.

"Hey guys, I hate to break this up, but has anyone noticed what time it is?"

Gideon's words caused Miranda to twist in Zacke's arms. She flipped back the cuff on her lab coat and looked at her watch.

"Oh my gosh!"

"What is it, Miranda?"

"No time to talk, Fang Man. Do you still want to marry me?"

Surprised, he barely nodded before she clutched his arm in an iron-grip.

"Then I suggest we get a move on. There's no way, I'm going to let sunrise turn you into toast and cheat me out of a bridegroom."

Chapter Twenty-One

Miranda meant what she said. She hustled him into a wheelchair, and wheeled him past attendants, nurses and even her own boss. Her pat answer of "I'm taking him home to recuperate," met with open-mouthed stares and silence. It seemed no one wanted to mess with his little Amazon.

Once in the car, she broke every speed limit between the hospital and his driveway.

He enjoyed a brief hour or so of listening to Miranda order a wedding cake, beg church space, and cajole the minister from her hometown to officiate at their wedding before she turned those drill sergeant eyes on him.

"I think you would be better off resting in bed or don't you need your sleep?" Her question knocked him for a loop.

Was she really taking his death-like rest in stride?

Even as he swore, he would never become a hen-pecked or de-fanged husband, Zacke mumbled, "Yes ma'am."

****

A week later, from his perch at the end of the counter, Zacke watched Miranda smile and avoid the outstretched hands of his vampire brothers and Gideon. Mac joined them at the kitchen table amidst the clutter of dishes, wineglasses, and the crumbs from his and Miranda's wedding cake.

Guffaws from Gideon as Miranda rapped Miles on the knuckles with a spoon brought his thoughts back to here and now.

"Keep your hands to yourself, Miles, or lose them. I mean it!"

Her words brought a smile from both Hawk and Mac.

Truly, his new bride had grown some fangs and claws of her own. Zacke couldn't be happier. His house finally felt like a home, filled with hope and the possibility of happy ever after. The only glitch in the mix—Gabriella's continued evasion.

Tonight, however, he planned to forget all about Lady Sanspree. He had his own lady to woo.

The boisterous laughter grew even louder, and Zacke decided to put an end to the antics. Besides, Gideon's rendition of "*Boot Scooting Boogey*" had hit a flat note.

"Say goodnight, gentlemen. We appreciate you being here, but it's time to go."

Five gazes turned to stare at him, each one with a different expression.

Mac looked apologetic, and Zacke almost felt bad about kicking him out. The man looked prouder than a peacock as he walked Miranda down the church's short aisle. As he joined her hand with Zacke's, he whispered, "You better not hurt her, Detective, or you'll answer to me."

Gideon's gaze held bafflement. He had gone over his quota for drink, but he had been as staid as a judge when he had stood as best man.

Hawk and Miles would see he got home okay. They had both taken a room at the Ballastone Inn for the next couple of days. Their gazes spoke congratulations and envy. They had taken part in the ceremony by acting as ushers to the numerous guests from the Savannah P.D. and the hospital.

Miranda's gaze held just a bit of trepidation mixed with shyness. And a bit of satisfaction lurked in her eyes. Before the night ended, he would make sure she was completely satisfied.

"Night Mac, Hawk, Miles and Gideon."

Miranda's combined goodbye had the men vacating their chairs. Her cheeks shone a deep peach after each man leaned down and kissed her.

"Congrats again, Detective, and remember what I said."

Zacke returned Mac's handshake. "Don't worry, Mac. I would give my life for Miranda."

Gideon weaved a slightly uneven path to Zacke's side. "Well, old buddy, you finally did it. S—so happy for you."

Zacke caught him before he stumbled over the kitchen threshold. It was a good thing the captain had given Gideon the night off for the wedding.

He smiled and braced himself for Hawk's and Miles' hearty back slapping. Their slight nods indicated what all the others said and more.

A moment later, he and Miranda were alone.

She gathered the glasses and plates from the table. After she placed them in the dishwasher, Zacke wiped off the table while she rummaged around in the utility closet.

"What are you doing?"

"I'm looking for the broom."

Zacke pulled her into his arms. "Why don't you let me get that? You go get ready for bed."

****

Miranda tied the matching robe to her almost non-existent nightgown. Lord, she was nervous. Tonight she would share a bed with Zacke. Her knees began a slow tremble. She sat down on the edge of the tub. Had she done the right thing? Could she forget her new husband wasn't just a man?

The past week had been surreal. From the moment, she learned Zacke was immortal, her mind had been at war with her heart. She realized she loved him almost from the first moment they met. She still loved him, yet a part of her feared him just a bit.

The bathroom's fluorescent light caught the gold of her wedding band. She stiffened her shoulders and tossed out the disloyal and utterly ridiculous thought that she might be bedding a monster. He trusted her enough to keep his secret. She would trust him.

She stood up, took a deep breath, and opened the door. Her mouth promptly dropped open.

Lit candles adorned every available surface of the room. The covers of the bed were turned back and a single peach rose rested on the nearest pillow. But the rose didn't hold her attention as much as the man reclining on the bed.

The white towel that covered Zacke's lower body emphasized his masculinity.

She averted her eyes. He looked nothing like the male bodies she had seen in the E.R or surgery. Zacke's body was firm, healthy, and totally aroused. The blush heating her cheeks actually burned.

"Miranda?"

She dragged her gaze from the floor. The smile on his sinful lips touched his eyes, which deepened to sapphire as she watched. "Yes?"

"Are you coming to bed?"

"Of course I am. I just thought I would get a drink of water first." Way to go. That had to be the lamest excuse she'd ever come up with.

"Wouldn't you rather have champagne?" He gestured toward the ice bucket and glasses sitting on the table next to the bed.

"No, actually water would be better."

She forced her feet to move across the floor. She avoided Zacke's outstretched hand. She really did need to get some water. Alcohol would fuzz her brain, and she wanted her mind clear tonight. What if she couldn't live up to the women Zacke had been with before?

The soft whisper of satin halted her in her tracks. Zacke's arms circled her waist, preventing further flight. His lips nuzzled her neck encouraging her to relax in his arms. The hardness pressing against her backside started a trembling deep inside.

Zacke moved his lips from her neck to her ear. The gentle but oh-so-seductive caress of air caused her toes to beg for a piece of carpet. His hands untied her robe. Through half-closed lids, she watched it fall to the floor.

Zacke turned her slowly until she faced him. The tip of his erection quivered against her belly and her inner flesh dewed. His hands slid one strap and then the other off her shoulders until the material created a silken trap, pinning her arms gently against her sides.

Dipping his head, Zacke suckled her beaded nipples. The moist patches on the satin cooled her skin, and his heated mouth caused an erotic sensation so intense her breath rose and fell rapidly—hyperventilation became a real danger.

He removed his lips and his fingers became instruments of sweet torture as he tugged on her responsive flesh. Her blood heated to global warming.

"Please tell me you no longer want that water."

Yeah right, and bullfrogs fly too. He makes my insides boil, my flesh burn, and then asks a stupid question.

Zack's deep-throated laughter ruffled her hair and the arms around her slackened just a bit.

"Stop reading my mind. It's not fair."

His laughter silenced. "Little One, you are right. I shouldn't use my gifts this way. But you can't blame me for wanting you in bed anyway I can get you there."

His apologetic tone touched Miranda. This man,

who had sworn to love, honor, and protect her had to be the sweetest man alive.

"You unman me. After all I have put you through, all the hurt and harm I have caused, and you still love me."

She caressed his chest with her cheek. The tantalizing smell of Dolce and Gabbana wafted to her nostrils. The man didn't need lessons in seducing a woman. He could do it without lifting a finger.

He lifted more than a finger. He scooped Miranda into his arms. Her head rested against his chest and the accelerated beat of his heart matched hers.

Her back soon touched the satin covered bed and Zacke followed. He lowered his mouth. Miranda's breath hitched as he taunted and nipped at her bottom lip. His tongue seared the inside of her mouth as his hands skimmed down her body. His touch turned her insides into liquid fire.

Miranda could feel corresponding waves of warmth from Zacke's body. His fingertips grazed the column of her throat, as they swept downward to remove her gown. She closed her eyes and turned her head slightly. The coolness of the pillow relieved some of her embarrassment.

Zacke scarce dared to breathe as he gazed on Miranda's peach tinged flesh. The lovely color in her cheeks had moved in a provocative path down her throat and beyond, taunting, enticing him to follow its path. He gave in to the temptation. His hands cupped and then caressed the twin mounds.

Her soft whimper caused his erection to pulse in time with his heartbeat. It had been centuries since he felt flames of passion this hot. He resisted the urge to sheathe himself within her core. He would control the beast urging him to take her without care. He wanted Miranda's first experience to be memorable. His skin burned from the brush of her crowning nipples. He nudged her chin until she turned her head. Her cheek carried the crease of the pillowslip. Her eyes glowed deep cobalt. His lips captured hers once more.

Miranda returned his kiss with such passion he pulled away. He wanted to shout with jubilation—she desired him, but... What if her passion caused the beast lurking within to break free?

"Zacke?" Miranda's hesitant voice pulled him back from the crimson flow invading his thoughts.

"Do you have any idea how much you touch my soul?"

Miranda's eyes, almost black with passion, told him she did know.

His hands grasped her legs and gently tugged her body closer. The lush bed of copper at her center beckoned him. His hand caressed her lower lips. His fingers sought and then found the moisture of her desire. Miranda pushed against his hand, and his erection hardened like ice-forged steel. He eased a finger inside the wet folds. The tight haven suckled him with heat.

Miranda moaned. Her body twisted and arched. He allowed a moment more of the pleasure touching her brought before he reluctantly withdrew from her soft wetness.

"Zacke, please."

"Soon, Little One." Zacke turned his attention to her breasts once more and paid homage to first one and then the other before lifting his head. "Are you sure, my love?"

"Yes."

Zacke kissed the lips that spoke the reality of her trust. The soft and raspy sound of that one word made him feel like a king. His hand trembled with passion and wonder as he caressed her face.

Then he allowed his desire free reign.

Zacke paused for one moment at the opening of her passage, but Miranda's body pushing against his engorged rod crushed his restraint. Her tight sheath resisted his entry, and Miranda winced. He tried to pull back. His incisors dug holes into the inside of his lips. His jaw ached from resisting his desire to take her. Zacke fought the voice within urging him to plunge forward. He won the battle, but Miranda opened her eyes glazed with need. She caught his hand in hers. The soft kiss she bestowed fired his heart and shattered years of emptiness.

He eased his straining sex inward and then pulled almost out of her seductive center before he pushed again—this time a bit deeper. He caught the slight moan of distress from her kiss-swollen lips with his own. He softly plundered the inside of her mouth before he captured her tongue. The walls of her sex tightened. She raised her hips to accommodate his length. Again, the trust she gave him threatened to unman him.

Zacke braced his hands on the mattress and began a slow thrust in and out of her narrow passage. The dew of Miranda's passion inflamed his until his vision filled with a blue haze.

When her body joined his in a dance older than time, he knew the ultimate triumph.

"Zacke!" He caught her frantic cry and drew it deep within his mouth. Miranda's body clenched and her sheath tightened around him. He eased his hand between their bodies and touched her. Her body shook once, twice, and he felt her release. A breath later, he followed her into ecstasy—his groan of fulfillment a promise that he would always be there to catch her.

Zacke waited until Miranda's breath slowed and her pulse stopped racing before he eased out and away from his vixen bride. He placed a kiss on her red lips before moving off the bed.

"So much for pillow talk."

"I heard that, Miranda."

"I meant for you to."

Her entry into womanhood had given his wife a bit of brazen courage.

"I'm going to the bathroom. Don't tell me you can't do without me already."

Miranda's cheeks turned an enticing shade of pink, and she closed her eyes.

Zacke smothered his chuckle. His woman might be a bit braver than before, but she retained some innocence.

"Uh, no. Don't mind me, I'll just lay here and breathe."

Zacke couldn't resist the urge to read her thoughts.

The man had certainly stolen the breath from my lungs and the things he did with his hands, lips, and other parts of his body were awesome.

Zacke cut off the link to Miranda's mind when his manhood, which he thought drained of any immediate response, stirred to life once more.

It never paid to eavesdrop on a woman's thoughts. They were more lethal than a stake in the heart.

Yes, it would be safer to put a moment of distance between him and his seductive wife. He turned on the bathroom taps and removed a plastic bowl he had previously placed under the basin cabinet.

Once the water reached the warmth he desired, he turned it off and added a couple of drops of aloe to the liquid. He grabbed a washcloth and a small towel from the linen rack before returning to Miranda's side.

"Zacke, what are you planning to do?"

He smiled and dipped the cloth into the water. He squeezed out the excess and traced a gentle path over Miranda's center.

Her blush deepened but she remained silent. He wondered if she enjoyed the intimate act as much as he did. An outdated custom to be sure, but he wanted Miranda to know he cherished what she had given him.

After a final pat of the towel, he pulled the sheet up to her waist and set the bath materials aside. He removed the cork from the champagne and poured the golden liquid into fluted goblets.

Miranda scooted backwards and reclined against the bed's headboard. She pulled the sheet up to cover her breasts and tucked it behind her. She accepted the proffered glass. The first sip caressed her tongue and helped to quench the renewed dryness coating her throat.

Zacke stood by the bed. His dark hair, free of its usual bond, reminded her of a pirate the way it fell against his shoulder. He certainly knew how to plunder. His skill had threatened to melt her toenail polish.

Her husband placed one knee on the bed and then sat by her side. She resisted the urge to share her sheet with him. Maybe, in a zillion years, she would get tired of looking at his body, but she doubted it.

She raised the goblet to her lips and gulped. The alcohol burned her throat but gave her some relief from her wanton thoughts.

"Miranda, if you've finished your drink and your perusal of my body, I would like to give you something."

"Zacke, I'm not sure I could handle anything else at the moment."

His chuckles turned into a full-fledged roar. "Close your eyes."

Instead of the warmth of his lips against her own, Miranda felt the cold touch of metal on her finger. Her eyes blinked open. "Zacke?"

"This ring belonged to my mother, Miranda. My father gave it to her when they wed." His lips caressed her ear sending heat radiating to her toes. "I hope that one day our son will give it to his beloved."

Her heart contracted. The ring's Celtic design held a small ruby. The soft rose glow mesmerized her and overshadowed the simplicity of her gold wedding band. Tears crept to her eyes when she saw the uncertain look in his blue gaze.

"Oh, Zacke. I don't know what..." She caught his hand and pressed kisses against his palm. "I love it. Just knowing it belonged to your mother is a gift."

"I know she would have wanted you to have it. Her last thoughts were of me, that I had found peace with death."

"Were you there when she died?"

Zacke's breath brushed the top of Miranda's head. Silence followed her question. She worried her index nail with her teeth. Maybe she shouldn't have pried. Perhaps the past was still too painful for him to talk about.

"I was there. I held her in my arms as she drew her last breath. She thought I was a spirit, an angel sent to guide her home."

Her previously unshed tears dripped onto their joined hands. "Zacke, you don't have to say anymore. I shouldn't have asked."

"You are my wife. You have a right to know." Zacke tightened his grip on her hand. "You know how I died. I want to tell you about my life after death."

Miranda buried further into his side for her own comfort, and she hoped his. Zacke might never admit it, but she knew he hurt. She wanted him to know she would always be there for him. Finally, some of the tension eased from his body.

She forced words past the lump in her throat. "I'm not going anywhere, Detective, so don't skimp on details. I have a lot of centuries to catch up on."

She wanted to shout at the smile tugging at his lips.

"After Gabriella turned me, I was angry, my life as I knew it—gone. The king sent a messenger to inform my family I had died. Someone must have found the marked grave. After I rose, I stamped the earth back down. I didn't know what to do. I was sick with hunger and didn't know how to stop the pain until I smelled the blood beating through a defenseless deer's veins. I fed from it. I couldn't help myself. I rushed back to Kensington Hall. I arrived in time to see my parents grieving."

Miranda willed her heart to settle and took a sip from her glass. She savored the reprieve from Zacke's history lesson. How horrid and so sad to give up all he held dear because of one woman—or creature's—rage. And to go through it alone. Her heart cried for the injustice he had endured.

"It's okay, Miranda. I've had ages to accept what cannot be changed."

He caught her hips in his hands, lifted her slightly, and lowered her between his outstretched legs. He drew her back against his chest so her head rested under his chin.

Miranda decided to ignore the fact he had read her mind once again. "Zacke, I don't understand. Why didn't Hawk and Miles take your body back to your home?"

"Miranda, as a doctor you know that bodies decay rapidly without embalming. I'd been killed miles from even a remote crofter's cottage. They had no means to take my remains home, although if they had, maybe they would have escaped Gabriella's venom."

Miranda caught his hand and brought it to her

lips. She kissed the talons that edged his fingers. "There wasn't anything you could do. This wasn't your fault."

"But it was. If I had not bedded Gabriella then she would not have turned me or the others."

"Well, Fang Man, I'm not sure what you see when you look in a mirror, but I doubt you would have escaped Gabby's attention for long."

"Gabby?"

"It's shorter, and I don't want to spend anymore time than I have to on her."

Zacke's laughter was contagious. When Miranda caught her breath, she patted his hand. "See, you are more human than you think."

For her comment, she earned a quick kiss. "You make it so easy for me to forget the creature I am. Thank you. So far I have managed to keep my bloodlust in check but who is to say it won't escape?"

"I say it won't, Zachary Kensington. Have you ever killed in rage? Have you ever drank blood from a victim?" Miranda craned her neck to look up into Zacke's eyes—eyes filled with silver droplets. "Zacke?"

"Yes. God forgive me I did! When you were near death in the morgue, I took your blood. I tasted its sweetness. I drank until Hawk and Miles stopped me."

Miranda ignored the nightmare quality of his words. Instead, she turned, scooted onto her knees and pulled Zacke's head to her chest. He thrust her from him so violently she lost her balance and her backside hit the mattress.

"Don't you see, I would have turned you into what I am."

Miranda stifled the horror his words brought. There had to be a logical reason. The man she loved would never do something that horrific without good cause. "Tell me why you did it, Zacke."

"Why? Because I couldn't face a future without you. You were dying. Your lifeblood flooded the floor like a crimson river. I didn't want to let you go."

Her heart bled with his pain. Would he have continued to drain the last bit of life from her, or would he have stopped himself? Her money and her future life would be on Zacke. He'd shown he'd go to any lengths to protect her.

"Well, just in case you forget, I'm not going anywhere. In fact, I may call in sick for the next two years."

Zacke's arms gripped her closer. His lips captured hers, and she returned his no-holds-barred passion with some of her own. She caught his pillaging tongue and turned the tables.

His groan thrilled her. She exalted in the fact she could make him lose control. His response fired her blood, and then he lifted her onto his beckoning erection. Her glee disappeared when Zacke thrust upward. Miranda reveled in the erotic sensation of his sex filling her. However, this time she wanted control. She would set the pace, and her detective was in for the ride of his life. One way or the other, Zacke's mind would be off his past and back to the present.

His hands cupped her breasts. His fingers teased her nipples. Her head dropped back and her eyes blurred with the orgasmic rhythm of their movements.

In a frenzy to attain the satisfaction just beyond her grasp, Miranda swiveled her bottom against Zacke. His hips lifted off the sheets as she continued to raise and lower her body. She forced her eyes to stay open. She wanted to see his face when he reached his release. She wanted to see if his eyes would glow the heavenly blue she loved.

Miranda lost her focus when Zacke's hand teased the curls between her legs and then caressed her aching core. Her eyes closed and her mouth flew open as a storm of hurricane proportion rocked her.

A soft growl near her ear assured her Zacke was trapped in the same tempest. Her body felt as if it would shatter. Miranda's world went black before red spheres of light crisscrossed her eyelids.

Her breath tangled with Zacke's in a kiss that superseded any kiss they had shared before. She gave in to the inevitable and rode the wave of desire until it swallowed her whole.

****

Gabriella shredded the skin on her fingers until blood dripped to the earth below. She consumed the shriek clawing its way up her throat. Even in the throes of ecstasy, Zachary would no doubt hear her. She didn't want that—not now. Although, she would love to rip out the mortal's throat, she would pick the time and place.

Zachary's intense search had forced her to go underground. Her body had trembled with the need for human blood. The rodents running in the underground sewers had not provided enough sustenance. She owed Lord Kensington much for his interference.

Zachary would die, but not before he watched his bride suffer the tortures of the damned.

Chapter Twenty-Two

Miranda tossed the cover back on her side of the bed and then moved to Zacke's side. Her husband of four weeks was asleep—his features stiff as marble, the body she loved to cuddle next to after lovemaking, cold as a block of ice. She doubted she would ever grow accustomed to this facet of his nature, but at least now, she didn't shriek like a banshee. She'd never forget the first morning she'd awakened next to his corpse-like body. Screaming, she fled their bed. On her way out of the room, she glimpsed Zacke bolting upright. His shocked gaze pulled her back to sit on the bed's edge.

Zacke told her it was the first time he'd ever been awakened so abruptly. He tried to reassure her with a smile, but his blue-tinged lips had not helped to ease her peace of mind.

"Miranda, I'm sorry. I should have warned you that I sleep like the dead."

His feeble attempt at humor had not swayed her to be any less concerned, but it wasn't his fault—she should have asked.

"It's okay, Zacke. I should have known that you wouldn't be exactly—"

"Human?"

"Yep, that's the word. I just hadn't thought about it. You felt so warm when we finally fell asleep that I kind of forgot—"

"Maybe I should sleep downstairs."

Miranda forced herself to ignore the icy blast of his skin as she climbed over him to sit by his side. "Oh, no you don't. If you think for one minute I'm going to sleep in this bed all by myself, then you can forget that idea, Detective."

His smile and the kiss he gave her had heated up her cool skin; her insides flamed and then caught fire when he made love to her in a sexy, slow manner—quite unlike the night before.

She had stayed put, enjoying the aftermath of passion until Zacke's breathing slowed and he had gone under once again.

The first full day after their marriage had stretched out like a desolate island. She rushed through her shower, ate breakfast, and then rinsed and placed the dishes from her morning meal into the dishwasher. After that, she had tackled the bedroom Zacke had used before their marriage. By the end of the day, she'd taken down the bed, moved in a desk and turned the room into a workable office. She completed the redecoration by adding her laptop and lining bookshelves with new medical tomes, courtesy of Zacke.

He had found her there, and after making love by candlelight, they decided to purchase a daybed as soon as possible.

Hawk and Miles moved back a couple of days later, but only after she and Zacke pleaded with them.

"We have plenty of room here. I won't listen to your nonsense of moving out."

Zacke backed her up. "With Gabriella still at large, it would be better to have a united defense against whatever she pulls next.

****

Miranda returned from work that night before sunset to find Zacke still asleep. Poor man, he was probably exhausted. He and the boys had been out past dawn hunting Gabby.

She'd let him sleep a bit longer before she went in and gave him his evening wake-up kiss. After booting up the computer in her new office, she started checking email and decided to pay some bills online. Before she was halfway through the utilities, she looked up to see her husband propped against the door's threshold.

"Hi darling. I didn't know you were up."

Zacke didn't reply to her words. He just stood there.

"You okay?"

After several deep breaths, he staggered into the room.

Miranda jumped up, caught him under one arm, and guided his reeling body to the daybed.

"Zacke, what's wrong?"

"I'm fine. I just got up too quickly." He brushed away the hand she placed on his forehead.

"Since when does the man who mumbles, 'Let me sleep a bit longer,' get up too fast?"

"Look, I'm fine now. I need to get a shower."

Miranda leaned down close to his face. "You're not going anywhere until I get an explanation. Now, spill it."

After baring his incisors at her, he finally spoke. "It's nothing to get alarmed about. Several months ago, I started having some dizzy spells, usually when I don't take sustenance right after I get up. And I also started the annoying habit of sweating when I go for a run."

Willing her heart to slow down, she took a deep breath. "I assume this is not something normal for vampires?

"No, it's not. As long as it only happen every once in a while, I just ignored it."

"Are the episodes getting closer?"

"Closer than I would like." Zacke raked a trembling hand through his hair.

Another symptom that frightened Miranda.

"Why don't you go get that shower and I'll warm

up your dinner."

Zacke complied, discarding her offer to help. He'd injected two syringes of blood and then gone to work.

She had no idea what type of problems in his makeup could cause his symptoms, but she planned on using her previous major of hematology to help her find answers.

After several hours of opening book after book, she was no closer to a breakthrough than when she had first started. Her eyes burned from reading small print. She turned off the desk lamp and hauled herself to bed.

****

The next morning, Miranda tucked the sheet around Zacke's body and then moved to the bathroom. She cast a fond glance at the hot tub. She would forever cherish the memories of champagne, candlelight, and making love in the spacious depths until their skin wrinkled like prunes.

She turned the shower tap on full blast, pulled her hair up into a topknot, and stepped under the spray.

Miranda soaped, rinsed her skin, and turned off the tap. Five minutes later, after brushing her hair out, applying makeup, and dressing, she retraced her steps to the bedroom.

Zacke, even in almost death, made her heart pound like a jackhammer and still managed to turn her limbs into useless appendages. She crossed the floor and leaned over to place a kiss on his frigid lips. If she didn't know better she'd swear he smiled. An improvement over his actions of last night.

Today, she'd planned to spend the morning poring over more hematology books, but a phone call from Mac ruined her plans.

She glanced at her watch and then scrambled for pen and paper to leave a note. Hopefully, she would be home long before he awakened.

****

Zacke awoke while the sun still reigned over the western sky. With the curtains drawn tight, he couldn't see its rays, but he felt its heat.

He awoke earlier and earlier each night but had kept the fact hidden from Miranda. His lovely wife had almost gone ballistic when he described the problems already plaguing him. It would not do for her to find out his dizziness came more frequently or that some days his body felt like it had been run over by a semi. Those facts along with the additional symptom of his insides feeling like an ignited flamethrower would cause Miranda to fly off the deep end.

Zacke sat up and propped his pillow against the headboard. With his desire to sleep gone, he might as well think about his next move concerning Gabriella.

The witch had been missing in action for over a month. Zacke would love to think she had met her demise but he knew better. Gabriella was too smart to die by human hands. And the only vampires capable of finishing her off had not seen fang nor claw of her.

She had made herself scarce, but he feared it wouldn't be long before she came after Miranda again. He felt certain she knew of their marriage, and he'd bet Gabriella was fit to be tied. Gabriella had a penchant for owning people and things. She would never sit back and idly accept that he now belonged to another.

He planned to intensify the search. He would stake out the red-light district of Savannah tonight, as soon as he checked in at the station. If Gabriella remained among the missing tonight, he planned to check out some of the cemeteries again. She had to be resting somewhere. He also wanted to see if he could find out what had happened to Jake and Tyler. After getting out on bail, they had become as elusive as Gabriella. Although, he'd bet his incisors they were behind the shooting incident.

A car pulled into the drive. Zacke smiled. Miranda's home.

It never ceased to amaze him how much he loved her, and how she had turned his lonely house into a home. Since she'd become Mrs. Dr. Kensington, Miranda had done wonders to the barren and utilitarian furnishings. She redecorated Hawk and Miles' rooms, using medieval as well as modern furnishings.

She planned to redo the basement next; she wanted a safe haven for him in the event Gabriella decided to stalk him instead of her. He shook his head. How on earth did his petite wife think she could hold off Gabriella? But Lord love her for wanting to.

The door eased opened and the object of his love and thoughts rushed in.

"Hey you, what are you doing up? Shouldn't you still be napping?"

Zacke chuckled and the sound brought a smile to his lady's eyes and lips. He really didn't want to tell her his symptoms had grown. "Can't a man wake up to see his wife?"

"Yes, but not you. You have to work tonight, Detective or have you forgotten? You need to rest."

"Yes ma'am, but I might rest better if you get into bed with me."

"Nope, not gonna fall for that again."

Miranda stood with hands on her hips and a delicious pout on her lips. "Every time we lie awake in bed, I don't get any work done and you, my darling husband, lose valuable sleep." She walked closer to the bed but still not close enough for him to capture her.

"Well, you don't hear me complaining do you?"

"No, but you will come morning when your eyes are glowing red with fatigue and not the beautiful blue I love."

Miranda sidestepped his grasping hand and moved a step back. "Besides, Hawk and Miles are still snoozing, and we don't want to wake them up. They're worse than you are when they don't get their beauty sleep."

"Please. Come to bed. I promise to be a good boy if you lie down. I miss being with you at night."

Damn it. A husband and wife should share the night hours together.

Miranda shook her head but toed off her sneakers and pulled off her hair band. He watched her walk around to her side of the bed. The gentle sway of her hips encased in jeans made his manhood throb in time with his heart.

"Fine, but just for a bit and only until you doze off."

He caught the waist of her jeans, tugged once and then cuddled her against his body. Soon, he began to feel drowsy.

He forced open his heavy lids to see if Miranda had noticed. The woman who loved to say I told you so, had fallen sound asleep. Zacke pulled her even closer before he too succumbed to slumber.

****

Miranda awoke to the sound of groaning. For a moment, she thought she was back at the hospital, but the soft glow of lamplight highlighted the furniture in their bedroom.

She rolled over and found an empty and cold expanse of bed where Zacke had been. "Zacke?"

Another moan of pain brought her up on her knees. "Zacke!"

A glance over the side of the bed sent her scampering off; in her haste, she landed hard on her knees. She stifled the scream of terror crawling up the back of her throat at the sight of Zacke's writhing body. "Zacke, tell me where it hurts." She hesitated to move him until she knew.

He didn't answer but his hand moved to rest on his abdomen.

Miranda placed a trembling hand on his forehead. No sign of fever. She gently cupped his limp wrist and counted his pulse. It was normal—at least for a mortal.

Maybe he just had a stomach virus. Did vampires have viruses? His face creased in pain again. "Zacke, I need to get you on the bed. I'm going to get Hawk and Miles to help me."

"No. Just give me a minute." Zacke shrugged off her hand, pulled himself to his knees, caught the bedpost, and then gained his feet. She caught his arm to steady him. His slow topple onto the bed sent her sprawling as well.

"Zacke, please, let me call one of them." Her voice shook just as badly as her hands.

"No, there's nothing you or they can do. It will pass."

A few moments later, Zacke lay against his pillows with a damp cloth on his forehead. His color had gone from waxy to lightly creamed coffee—not the rich bronze she loved, but she would take what she could get.

"Now, tell me when the pains started and how long has this been going on." Miranda knew her voice sounded sharp—she didn't care. The man had literally scared years off her life, and she didn't have any extra lives to call on.

"The stomach pains just started tonight."

"Did you eat anything different?" Miranda knew he rarely consumed mortal food. Maybe something he ate caused an adverse reaction.

"No, nothing in the way of human food, not since

our midnight picnic and even then I didn't eat much."

"Maybe you need to have something now, I mean besides your injection of blood." Miranda pushed her hair out of her eyes and moved to the side of the bed. "I'll broil you a steak."

"I'm not hungry."

"Zacke, we have to try something."

He nodded his head and closed his eyes. Relief flooded her weak limbs when his breathing returned to normal.

****

"Zacke, hon, wake up. Your dinner is ready, and I brought you a syringe of blood. You need to eat."

Zacke stirred a bit and then opened his eyes. He raised himself up and when his back rested against the headboard, she placed the tray on his sheet-covered lap. Zacke eyed her culinary offering with distaste.

"Miranda, I really don't want anything."

"Zacke, please. Even a vampire needs sustenance. Just take a bite or two of the meat and if you still don't feel like eating, then that's okay.

Zacke picked up the fork lying by the plate, speared the most minuscule bite he could find and brought it to his lips. He forced back the revulsion clogging his throat and tried to keep it from his features. Miranda looked like she was on her last nerve, and he didn't want to add to her distress.

He tasted the lukewarm meat and his stomach roiled. Under Miranda's watchful eye, he forced himself to continue to chew. The more he did the larger the bite grew. The grate of meat sliding down his esophagus caused his gorge to rise. When the meat hit his empty belly, nausea rose in waves as high as the Savannah River in a tropical storm.

The tray went flying as Zacke tossed the sheet off and forced his legs off the bed.

"Zacke!"

He heard the anxiety in Miranda's voice, but the black storm of dizziness prevented a response. His legs felt like a landlocked sailor's as he zigzagged toward the bathroom.

He would not throw up in front of his wife.

Zacke returned to the bedroom to find Miranda smoothing fresh sheets over the mattress. The tray had been removed; he assumed she had carried it downstairs after he told her to leave him alone. No matter how much she pleaded for him to let her come in, he refused to have his wife hold his head while he puked.

He might be a creature, but his pride still held the stamp of man and warrior. However, he did owe her an apology for shouting.

"Miranda?" She ignored his entreaty and continued making the bed. The pillows came under fire with a vigorous fluffing.

Apparently, his wife was still upset. "Miranda, look, I'm sorry. I should never have yelled at you."

Miranda's head snapped up; she glared at him but said nothing.

He forced his spaghetti legs to move, his gait a cross between a baby taking its first steps and a drunk. When he gained the lifeline of the bedpost, Zacke grasped it with both hands and lowered his body to sit on the edge of the bed.

Miranda skirted her way around him, keeping a good foot away from him. She picked up the syringe she must have placed on the bedside table.

"You have two seconds to inject yourself, or I'll do it for you."

Zacke heard the tears beneath her abrupt words. "I'll do it." He held out his hand, and she slapped the cylinder onto his palm. The tremble of her hand as she pulled back matched the tremors in his own as he uncapped the syringe and discharged the air pockets. A moment later, the needle bit his skin, and he shot the blood into his jugular. The injection lacked its usual euphoria—instead he felt shame. Never before had he allowed Miranda to witness the appalling act.

He turned away to hide the heat stinging his face.

"It's okay, Zacke. I'm okay. I would much rather you yell at me than be ashamed." Miranda moved to stand between his legs. "You're not a monster. Your choice of how you take the blood you need to survive is admirable."

Miranda's words touched his heart, and when she embraced him, her body helped to repel the cold. Much too soon she drew back and took the syringe from his grip. She recapped it and placed it in the biohazard container she had brought from the hospital. Then she again cradled his head against her chest. She made him feel loved. It had been so long since he felt that way. He only wished he knew if there would be many more moments like this.

Zacke shuddered as a chill speared the skin of his back. For the first time in centuries, he wondered if his immortality might be ending.

****

Gabriella rubbed her hands together in glee. Lord Kensington had an Achilles heel, one besides Miranda. Zachary's usual mind block against her had slipped, not only that, it seemed he could no longer sense her—probably due to whatever illness he suffered. It didn't matter to her how he'd gotten sick, but his weakened state meant her next move would be even more interesting. And if all went well with her human minions, the next full moon would see her exact her revenge on Zachary and his mortal wife.

Chapter Twenty-Three

Miranda closed the medical book and tossed it on the foot-high stack resting on the desk in her home office. She rubbed her gritty, fatigued eyes; she didn't need a mirror to know red had overtaken the white sclera.

Zacke had returned to work over a week ago. He wanted to go to work the night he became ill, but she'd threatened to stake him to the bed. Lucky for her, Zacke hadn't been sure if she meant tying all four limbs to the four-poster or a stake through the heart.

Miranda would laugh if her insides didn't still quake with terror. She had studied, taken vials of blood from Zacke's already weak body, and still she was no closer to finding a way to help him.

Turning off the desk lamp, Miranda stretched her arms above her head. Muscles screamed in protest to the movements she forced upon them to work the kinks. Her neck popped as she rotated it and then her back did the same when she bent at the waist.

When she straightened up, a wave of dizziness caught her unaware. Heaven's bells, all she needed was to catch the stomach flu going around. She inhaled and exhaled and soon her head cleared— thank the Lord. She needed to check the blood samples she took earlier in the week against the ones she had taken tonight. She prayed the white blood count hadn't increased.

She had taken a week off despite the protests of the hospital administrator. To salve her conscience and to keep the hospital happy, she had finalized all the arrangements for the charity auction. Tonight was the night, and she would be happy to have it finished. The money the bachelors would bring in would go a long way toward aiding the Children's Cancer Ward, but she wanted to concentrate all her efforts on Zacke.

Almost every waking moment she spent analyzing samples, watching Zacke as he slept, and giving him transfusions with the blood Mac had swiped from the blood bank. She hadn't told him about Zacke but Mac had not questioned her requests, either.

She knew stealing was wrong, but she didn't care. Zacke grew consistently weaker, and she feared one day he wouldn't wake up.

Tonight, when he'd awaken, his features had been the color of milk. Miranda wasn't the only one worried. Hawk and Miles cornered her several times over the last week, their eyes full of fright and desperation. She had no more to tell them than she had Gideon in his numerous secret calls.

Although unspoken, she believed all four of the people who loved Zacke felt it to be best to keep their fears and anxiety from him. He had been like a man possessed in the last several days, leaving as soon as he fed to hunt Gabriella. Each morning he returned without triumph, his mood went from surly to rock bottom depression and then to rage.

A few nights before Zacke withdrew from the auction. Nothing she tried could convinced him to change his mind.

"I'm leaving for work Miranda." Her husband's words broke into her thoughts.

"All right, Zacke, but I wish you would change your mind. The auction is important, and I don't want you out there without backup. You know Hawk, Miles, and Gideon will be tied up. Can't you wait before going? You could at least come to the auction with me and just watch." Miranda held her breath waiting on his reply but nothing prepared her for his tone.

"Miranda, I'm a cop. This is what I do. I don't tell you when to go to work at the hospital, even if it means I don't see you for almost twenty-four hours."

"Zacke, we're not talking about me. We're talking about you. You're not well, and you could end up injured, even killed."

"Gabriella is the only one that can kill me, Miranda. Although your incessant harping could if you don't let up."

Miranda fought the stinging tears his words brought.

"Okay, you win. Just promise me you'll be careful."

Zacke nodded his head, his gaze almost cold as he turned and left. For the first time since their marriage, he left off his goodbye kiss.

She used the back of her hands to scrub her face. She still had work to do before getting dressed for the charity event. The symptoms Zacke experienced along with the elevated blood count smacked of leukemia. But she wasn't even sure if the blood disease could affect a vampire.

At the beginning of the week, she installed a mini refrigerator in her office. Now, she pulled out a syringe, depressed the plunger, and squirted a few drops of Zacke's blood onto a slide, which she then placed under her newly acquired microscope.

Minutes later, Miranda's shoulders slumped in defeat. The white cells had multiplied compared to the sample she had taken right after Zacke had first become ill.

She discarded the slide and replaced the unused blood back in the refrigerator. At this rate, Zacke would quickly become too weak to work, to walk, and finally to live.

"Miranda?"

Hawk's voice cut through her hopelessness. "Hi, Hawk. You off to feed before you have to be on the runway?"

"No, actually Miles and I did that earlier. I came back to check on you." The stunningly handsome vampire wore a hesitant smile as well as a tux. "How are the tests going?"

"Not so good. His white blood count is still too high, and I don't know what to do about it. The transfusions aren't helping him, Hawk. He's growing weaker by the day."

Hawks amber eyes filled with horror. "You don't think he could die, do you?"

Miranda reached out and touched his arm. "I don't know. If he were mortal, he would already be dead. I just don't know enough about his body's chemistry to know how long he can keep going like this."

Hawk dropped a trembling arm across Miranda's shoulders. Miranda raised her gaze to meet his. "Will you and Miles be going out to hunt Gabriella later?"

"Yes, Zacke says she won't stay down long before she tries something again. Which reminds me, I should be getting to the hospital. The woman handling the walk-ons until you get there says we have to practice our strut. Not sure what that means but guess I'll find out."

Hawk removed his arm and caught her hand in his. "Make sure you stay inside until Gideon picks you up. Good thing he isn't being auctioned off first. At least he'll be able to take you to the hospital. Stay safe. There's a full moon tonight and vampires aside, it brings out the crazies."

Miranda knew he spoke the truth. The emergency room always filled up with attempted suicides, stabbings, and gunshot victims when the moon reached its fullness.

"Don't worry about me. I plan on staying barricaded inside until Gideon gets here."

The house became too silent after Hawk left. Specters of a future without Zacke haunted Miranda as she hurried through a quick shower and dressing. What would she do without him?

****

Miranda toed off her shoes and propped her feet up on her desk. The auction had gone off without a hitch. All three of her candidates had pulled in mega dollars for the worthy cause.

"Miranda?"

Gideon stuck his head in the door of her office. "I checked out all the doors and windows. Do you feel like coming down and locking up after I leave?"

"Sure, it's the least I can do for one of the stars of tonight's show."

Gideon's face turned a light pink but his grin lit to one hundred watts. "I had a great time, Miranda. I never thought this redneck boy could look so good in a tux." His smiled dimmed a bit. "I just wish Zacke could have been there too."

Miranda got up and moved to his side. "I know. So do I, Gideon." She squeezed the hand he held out and allowed him to lead her downstairs.

"Don't let anyone in unless it's one of us."

"Yes, dear. I promise. You be careful too!"

She shot the bolts on the door after Gideon left and started back toward the stairs. The shrill ring of the house phone, Zacke had the phone company install, broke the silence. She picked it up, vowing nothing could make her go to work tonight.

"Hello?" Silence greeted her ears. "Hello!" Miranda's patience thinned when still no one answered. "Fine, don't talk to me." She slammed the phone back on its cradle. Probably a wrong number, but whoever it was could have said so.

Miranda made it to her office this time without interruption. Halfway through the latest copy of Medical News, the doorbell rang. She ran to the front door. "Who is it? If you're selling something, there's a law about soliciting after hours!"

"Miranda, it's Gideon."

Her heart stopped. Zacke! Something must have happened to him. She undid the deadbolt, the chain, and turned the lock. She yanked the door open with such force it narrowly missed her nose. "Gideon, is Zacke okay?"

Gideon's grin disappeared and she watched remorse settle into his gaze. "Sheesh, I'm sorry, Miranda. I didn't mean to scare you. Zacke was fine when I left him. His mood is a bit wolfish, but hey, that's a good sign, isn't it? Of course it's kind of hard to talk to him when he acts like someone pulled out his fangs with a rusty set of pliers."

Miranda laughed. "I assume you forgot something."

"Naw, Zacke sent me back to babysit, uh, that didn't come out right."

"Don't worry about it. I'm actually getting use to having my almost every move watched. Come on in."

Gideon raised one foot to step over the threshold but stopped. "Did you hear something?"

Miranda cocked her head, straining to pick up any sound outside the usual. "No, maybe it's just a car on the next street over."

"Yeah, maybe." Gideon started into the house. Rustling in the bushes to his right caused him to stop again. Two men came from out of nowhere.

All Hell broke loose. One man shoved Gideon against the outside wall. The other took out an extremely large gun.

Miranda waited for the explosion but she heard only a thud. Gideon's body slumped to the porch floor. She stepped back from the door and slammed it shut. She couldn't help Gideon by fighting his attackers but maybe she could get to the phone and call 911. She cursed the ice coating her hands in fear as she reached toward the lock.

The door slammed opened and sent her flying backward. She landed in a painful heap on the hardwood floor. The men with ski masks covering their faces now stood inside her home.

"What do you want? Money? I have some in the safe. I'll go get it." When the men didn't jump at her offer, Miranda's spine tingled in fear.

One of the men moved toward her, and she scooted backward on the floor. He dogged her movement and outdistanced her frantic attempt to escape. An arm encircled her chest and a rough cloth covered her mouth. Her nostrils burned from the sickening sweet scent. Chloroform—she knew it well from surgery. She tried to wrestle the material from her face, but his other hand moved to force her nose and mouth further into the cloth. Darkness swirled before her eyes and then pulled her into its grip.

****

Zacke pulled into his driveway. The Lexus had become his mode of travel since the dizzy spells had grown worse. Nothing like taking a freefall to earth from the clouds to jar a vampire into reality. No matter how much he hid his escalating illness from Miranda, he could no longer hide it from himself. He had sworn a scared speechless Gideon to secrecy after he landed in a heap at his partner's feet.

Gideon was the best friend a man or vampire could have. Zacke should never have sent him to see if Miranda was still angry with him. He should have bitten the bullet and gone himself. That's why he blew off their captain when he wanted to have a one-on-one about the case's status.

Zacke exited the car and walked around

Gideon's truck. Parking had never been a talent his friend had acquired. As he moved around the half-on, half-off the driveway vehicle, he noticed the porch light was off. He had asked Miranda to keep it on when he wasn't home, maybe the bulb had burned out.

Zacke hurried up the porch steps. His foot slipped in something near the wall. He knelt down and dipped his index finger in the liquid. He brought it to his nose and inhaled the sweet, tangy scent of blood.

His neck tickled with apprehension, his talons stretched as his senses went to full alert. He stood and inserted his key into the lock. The door moved silently inward. Something was bad wrong. Miranda would never leave the door unlocked.

He moved his foot over the threshold, anxious to find Miranda, but a soft groan forestalled his progress. The sound came from behind him. The azalea bushes Miranda loved stood as silent sentinels to his search. His hand scrabbled to find an opening in the dense growth and then he brushed a sleeve-clad arm. An arm attached to the body shoved beneath the bushes. A pain filled moan assaulted his ears.

"What the—"

"Zacke?"

"Gideon! Can you stand?"

Zacke helped Gideon to his feet then scanned the house and surrounding area for disturbance, which he should have done in the first place. He blamed his lapse on worry and guilt. All was quiet.

Too quiet.

Miranda's gone.

A few moments later, Gideon rested on the sofa with an icepack propped against the back of his head. Pain pulled his features tight, but at least his gaze remained clear, no sign of a concussion—yet.

The bleeding had also stopped.

"What happened?"

"I'm not sure. Miranda unlocked the door to let me in and something hit me from behind." Gideon, his face frozen with dread tried to sit up. "Where is Miranda? Is she okay?"

"She's gone."

"Ouch!" Gideon swung his body around and put his booted feet on the floor. "Are you sure?"

"Yes, whoever struck you must have taken her."

"Well, we can't just sit here. We have to find her."

"I know, and we will. Hawk and Miles will be here shortly. One will stay with you and the other will come with me."

"Hang on, Zacke. I'm not staying here. It's my fault Miranda's in danger. I'm going with you."

Zacke knew arguing wouldn't do any good. Injured or not, Gideon would follow Zacke even if it meant he had to crawl on his hands and knees.

"All right, but you will stay back."

Gideon bristled but Zacke's mind churned with the potential dangers Miranda faced. Men who he had helped lock up for their crimes wouldn't hesitate to use Miranda to get to him. Yet, he had the sinking feeling that a mortal wasn't behind his wife's abduction.

A couple of light thuds on the front porch signaled his vampire brothers' arrival.

"Hey, we got here as quick as we could. Any news?"

"No. I was hoping you two might have learned something."

Hawk crossed to Gideon's side and placed a hand on the goose egg protruding through his hair. In just a moment, the knot subsided to the size of a pebble.

Zacke cursed his weakness; he should have been

able to do that for Gideon. "Thanks, Hawk. I owe you one."

"No thanks needed. I caught the last of your argument. Vampire hearing." This he tossed out at Gideon's puzzled look. "I agree with you both. Zacke, it would be best to have all the backup you can get considering the shape you're in." Hawk shot a grin at Gideon. "Mortal or not, this man has proven he has the heart of a warrior."

"I agree with Hawk. At least four of us will assure someone is there to take care of Miranda. You know she will be right in the thick of things if..."

If she's able. Zacke finished Miles sentence silently. Yes, Miranda would be more than ready to fight if she could.

The ringing of the phone prevented him from telling them he agreed.

"Hello!" Zacke's tone matched the way he snatched the receiver off the cradle.

"Zachary, I believe we have some unfinished business." Gabriella's sugar-sweet tones sent a shiver down his spine. She had Miranda.

"If you want your sweet little bride back in one piece, be at Johnson Square at Midnight. And leave your minions at home if you don't want their blood on your conscience."

His growl of fear and fury coincided with the click on the other end of the line.

"Zacke?"

"Our plans have changed. Gideon you are not to step one foot outside this house. Hawk, Miles, that goes for you, too!"

"You can't mean that."

"Yes, Miles, I do. Gabriella has Miranda and if it's a fight to the death she wants, it will be her death or mine, no one else's."

****

Zacke allowed the rising wind to do most of his

flying. Gabriella's call, received a few minutes before midnight, made traveling by car and arriving on time impossible. Dark clouds moving across the horizon forebode a late summer storm. He prayed that by the time it hit, Miranda would be back at home, unharmed.

He left a disgruntled trio behind. Gabriella was a loose cannon and anything could set her off. He didn't want his friends' well-meaning efforts to cause them or Miranda their lives. Lord above, he knew that Gabriella would welcome the chance to kill on a technicality.

Johnson Square came into view.

The wind picked up speed the closer he got to touching down. The sky turned a deep purple slashed with black streaks. Lightning speared the night with macabre fireworks; the streaks reminded him of a corpse's fleshless fingers. Thunder rolled across the Heavens; its faint rumbles increased to the resonance of a metal drum clattering down a graveled road.

His eyes picked out a bit of color right at the base of the monument. Gabriella had tied Miranda to the stone. The ropes criss-crossed so tightly across her body she could only move her lower legs. His talons grew longer.

Miranda's tear-filled eyes testified frustration. His heart pulsed with a proud beat; his wife would never show fear in front of Gabriella. He landed a few feet from Miranda.

"Zacke, you don't have to do this. Cut me loose and then give me a knife. I'll kill the witch myself."

He kissed her silent. Their minds linked for a moment. Zacke allowed her to see his pride, his appreciation, and his love. She returned the favor by allowing him to see what he already knew. She loved him more than her own life.

With a motion of his hand, he released the ropes

holding her captive. He knew she wouldn't leave but he had to try. "I suppose if I begged you to go home, you would defy me."

"You've got that right, Detective. Even if vamp woman would let me leave, I'm not leaving you here alone. Why didn't you bring a posse?"

"They wanted to come, but were amenable to my suggestion they stay behind."

"That's what you think, Zacke."

Zacke turned as Miles and Hawk, holding Gideon between them, landed beside him.

"You didn't expect us to listen to that dime-store drivel that your death should be the only one." Miles grinned but his words sounded forced.

"Besides, mortal man here needed a lift."

Gideon steadied himself against the stone monument. "Evening, Miranda. Next time, don't answer the door when you know it's me." He leaned over and kissed her cheek.

Zacke appreciated the show of force from his friends but show was all he wanted from them. "I can never repay any of you for your support, but if you stay, you will do nothing. Miles, Hawk, if something happens to me, you two have to get Miranda and Gideon to safety."

"Well, well, well. Isn't this touching? I suppose they just wouldn't listen to you. It really doesn't matter. I changed my mind. I prefer to have an audience to testify how and where you and your wife die, Zachary."

Gabriella's mouth opened wider to show fangs flecked with red. Since she had already fed, she would be stronger than ever and ready for battle. Zacke thrust Miranda into Miles' arms only seconds before Gabriella struck.

Chapter Twenty-Four

Zacke slammed into the monument. The impact forced the air from his lungs. His back screamed in pain.

Gabriella swiped at his face.

Blood seeped from the furrows her talons left behind. She missed his eye, but his cheek stung as if an army of red ants nested there. He caught her wrist before she could sink her talons into his neck.

Her eyes glowed a fearsome red.

Never had he seen her in such a fury—not even the night she had attacked him centuries before.

Zacke shoved her with pain-enhanced strength.

Her body somersaulted through the air, stopped by an ancient oak.

He heard the combined gasps of the men behind him. He appreciated Miranda's self-control; her anxiety would not help his concentration.

He had mere seconds to regroup before Gabriella attacked again. She shot through the air like a stealth bomber. Zacke sidestepped her lunge. She crashed into the monument. He hoped her pain mirrored his.

Zacke leaned over her crumpled body. He flipped her over and reached for her chest to rip out her poison-filled heart.

Gabriella's eyes snapped open. She bit deep into his arm. Pain roared through him. Her poison, strong with centuries of malice and evil, polluted his body.

Dizziness engulfed him. He ripped his arm free. Blood gushed from the wound. Lethargy began to take hold. As he shook it off, Gabriella edged away.

Bloodlust radiated from her gaze. She had grown tired of playing.

Zacke knew her next strike would be a deathblow. If he died, Johnson square would become the scene of a bloodbath. Hawk and Miles' combined strength would not stop her from killing Miranda and Gideon. He held little hope that his vampire brothers would survive either.

He had to get back into the game.

Gabriella flew toward him. Her claws aimed for his face.

Flesh and muscle tore as Zack's talons anchored in her chest.

Howls of pain ascended from the square. Birds and small animals scurried for safety.

Gabriella's face wore a grotesque mask. Ruby eyes glared at him. She tore from his grip.

He had hurt her, but her heart remained untouched. Would her pain give him the advantage or would it fire her rage even more?

Her gaze darted to the tree limbs overhead. An ominous crack ripped through the night. A thick branch splintered from its trunk.

Thank Heaven, Hawk and Miles had pulled Miranda and Gideon to safety.

Pain dulled Zacke's senses. His strength oozed through his wounds like water through a slow moving drain.

Gabriella's shriek of rage signaled an end to what patience she possessed and snapped Zacke from his stupor.

In the blink of an eye, she gained his side. The first flick of her nails dug deep within his chest, narrowly missing his heart. Her exultant shout rang in his ears. Zacke's blood stained his shirt and dripped into the waistband of his jeans. In a matter of minutes, her poison would start to fester.

He had to kill her now.

Triumph shone from her eyes as she stepped back. She knew the last wound, so close to his heart, would weaken him further.

He cursed the illness that had stolen so much of his strength. Had he been healthy, he would have killed Gabriella before she struck her first blow. Drained but not defeated, he slumped to the ground.

"Zacke!"

Miranda's agonized cry hurt his heart more than Gabriella's wound. Through half-closed eyes, Zacke watched Miles hold his wife back and Hawk restrain Gideon.

"So, Lord Kensington, you underestimated me once again. How does it feel to know you are going to die?" Gabriella leaned over him. "What a pity you won't be around to see me kill Miranda."

Her fetid breath fanned Zacke's cheek. Her talons grazed his throat.

He knew she would go for his jugular before she tore out his heart, yet her attack surprised him. Like a wild animal, she tore a path from his throat to the flesh of his stomach and downward to his thighs.

Pain exploded throughout, but he willed his body to stay prone. He slowed his breathing to reduce the agony. His hope—Gabriella would think he had succumbed.

The air currents swirled when she turned toward Miranda. "And you, little mortal, how does it feel to know all your skills as a physician can't save him? Does your heart beat with fury? I hope so, though soon it will beat with fear. I shall enjoy toying with you before I send you to follow your dead husband."

Propelled by immortal strength, Zacke hurled himself off the ground. He caught Gabriella's shoulder and spun her around. Her look of surprise gratified him.

"If anyone is going to enter the jaws of death, it will be you, Gabriella." He welcomed her struggle, but she had sealed her passage to Hell when she further threatened Miranda.

Zacke reopened her chest wound—this time wide enough to insert his fist. He felt the pulsating and quivering of a heart gone wild with fear. His hand tightened around the evil organ before he ripped it from her body.

Gabriella's eyes dripped blood yet she still thrashed to get away.

He helped her in her quest. His shove spun her though the night air to land twenty feet away.

Blood gushed from the cavernous hole. The grass beneath Gabriella's body withered and died.

Zacke's hand, which held the still-beating heart, blazed like fire. He needed to burn it before he took Gabriella's head.

His eyes lit on a pile of debris near a garbage receptacle. A wave of his hand sent the leaves and litter in an upward dance and then a downward spiral. He waved again and smoke rose from the can. Flames soon followed. He tossed the heart into its final resting place.

He moved to Gabriella's body. Her eyes remained open, frozen in hatred and fear.

"You need to take her head, Zacke."

"With what?" Zacke looked to Hawk, who lifted his hand in a flamboyant gesture. A serrated piece of steel materialized from under his coat. Zacke caught the handle of the dagger Hawk tossed to him. With one stroke, he separated Gabriella's head from her body, which then met the heart's fate.

His wife's and his friends' shouts rose, but they sounded as if they came from a distance. Zacke's strength faltered. He slumped to the ground. The dagger clattered onto the cobblestones of the square.

Miranda's mind reeled against what she had seen. Her heart rebelled against the physician within, who knew no one could survive such wounds. Yet, Zacke couldn't be dead. She broke free of Miles and flew to Zacke's side. She reached out toward the furrows cleaved in his chest.

"Miranda, stop!" Miles gripped her hand.

She looked up into his face drawn with grief, horror, and compassion. "Miles, let go of me. I have to at least try to help him."

"I don't think you can, but even if there is a hope, you can't touch him. The poison from Gabriella's talons will burn your flesh."

Miranda looked toward the woman who had torn her world asunder and watched Gabriella's rotting corpse disintegrate into ashes before her eyes.

Hawk moved to the pile of remains. With a flick of his wrist, he sent the bits of soot swirling into the steadily rising wind.

The approaching storm would wash away the night's battle but not the desolation lying like a rock inside Miranda's heart. She turned once more toward the man she loved more than life itself. Zacke's eyes remained closed, and she could not detect even the slightest movement of his chest. Anger rose within. He couldn't be dead. She wouldn't allow it.

"Gideon?"

Her cry broke Zacke's partner's trance. He kept his gaze aimed at her face rather than Zacke's body as he walked toward her.

"I need you to go to the hospital. Tell Mac I need biohazard bags, peroxide, alcohol, bandages, gloves, tape, scissors, and more plasma. Oh and tell him I need some IV tubing." She hoped she hadn't forgotten anything in her haste. "One other thing. Ask Mac if he can get me some morphine and antibiotics. Tell him to forge my name to the orders, and I'll take care of it later."

She turned to Hawk next. "Can you fly Gideon there?"

"Yes, but Miranda—"

"Just do it, please."

Hawk nodded and Gideon pulled a ballpoint from his pocket and wrote her list on his palm. Both men squeezed her shoulder in silent commiseration.

Miles stood silent guard next to Miranda, who sat on the dew-soaked ground and fought the desire to touch Zacke. He needed to know she was here, that she loved him, and he would be all right. Desperate to reach him any way she could, she sent her thoughts on the wing of a prayer. *Hang on Fang Man, not much longer, and I'll have you back at home in bed and at my mercy.*

She fought the stinging in her eyes. She wouldn't think about what if. She had to believe he would recover.

Time crawled by as she waited for Hawk and Gideon's return. She had no doubt Mac would come through for her. He had been a good friend, far beyond the dictates of being her aide. She would make sure he didn't get into any trouble for helping her.

A slow mist teased her face and kept her from falling into a stupor of despair. The sky soon grew darker and the drizzle became a deluge that soaked Johnson Square and its inhabitants.

She moved to cover Zacke with her body, but Miles still wouldn't let her touch him. His gaze reflected the misery she felt in her heart. They were both helpless, and they both hated it.

The wind gusted, swirling wet leaves and dirt all around the perimeter of the square. Miranda closed her eyes against the debris. She reopened them when the wind slowed and then stopped.

Hawk and Gideon had returned.

Urgency, concentration, and hope reigned for the next few moments. From the satchel Mac had packed, she took one of the large red bags, split it and spread it open. She ignored the blood soaking the ground near the bag—she couldn't afford to think about how much Zacke had lost. She needed to get him ready to travel and to prevent him from losing more. She split another bag and placed it open on the ground beside the first before pulling on two pairs of the latex gloves.

She motioned Hawk and Miles forward. She handed them each two sets of gloves. "Put these on before you pick him up." Both men did as she asked and a moment later, she directed them to place Zacke on the second bag.

She connected the bags with tape, then stood and stretched her back.

"Can you lift him so I can wrap the bags and his body with tape?" Both men looked confused. "We have to get him home and that means one of you will have to carry him."

Comprehension flickered in their gazes.

"Unless I miss my guess, his contaminated blood will burn your flesh, also. I don't know why Gabriella's blood is that way, but I don't want any more patients, no offense, and I don't want to risk further infection."

After she secured the makeshift barrier, both men lowered gently. All three of them stripped off their gloves, and tossed them into the still smoldering flames of Gabriella's funeral pyre.

Miranda repacked the medical supplies and closed the bag. "I guess that's it. There's nothing more to be done here until we get Zacke home."

Her words roused the haunted faces around her. Gideon picked up the bag and looped the strap around his neck. Miles and Hawk exchanged looks and then Miles stooped and lifted Zacke into his arms—his touch as gentle as if he handled a newborn.

Hawk held his hand out to Miranda, and she moved to stand near him. She assumed he would be flying her out, but who would take Gideon? For the first time since the battle, Miranda spied a hint of a smile on her husband's vampire brother.

"Trust me, Miranda. I am much stronger than I look."

She almost laughed at the sheer ridiculousness of his statement. Hawk's girth rivaled a mature tree and muscles corded his arms. Of course he could wing a duet flight.

She reached up, caught a lock of his hair and tugged gently. He bent to look her in the face, and she kissed his cheek. "Thank you, my friend." Miranda sought and held first Miles' gaze and then Gideon's. "Thank you, all."

****

Miranda sat in the chair she had pulled to Zacke's bedside almost forty-eight hours before. The sheets had been stripped, and the bed layered with a multitude of biohazard bags as soon as they'd arrived home. She cut the tattered clothing from Zacke's body and then poured a mixture of alcohol and peroxide into the numerous wounds. When he lay silent instead of thrashing, as he should have, her heart died a bit more. She had slathered on copious amounts of antibacterial ointment before applying bandages.

She watched in silence as bag after bag of plasma, with a strong dosage of morphine and penicillin added, emptied into Zacke's arm. Still her husband didn't stir.

Miles and Hawk ripped open their wrists and pleaded with her to take their blood for Zacke.

Gideon's numerous trips to the hospital for more supplies, with a quick stop at the police station to tell them he needed to take a week's vacation told her how much his partner meant to him. Considering his haggard features and red-rimmed eyes, Miranda understood why Captain Myers had not pitched a fit.

She had talked to Zacke's superior herself and explained Zacke had come down with a viral infection.

If only it were that easy.

Her head jerked as she fought to stay awake. She didn't dare sleep. The last time she had dozed off, the fever that still held Zacke in its grip had started.

She expected his temperature to rise, but the ugly, pus-filled blisters that covered ninety percent of his body surprised her. His handsome face suffered the same fate, but she didn't care. She would love every inch of his scarred body if he would just wake up.

"Miranda?"

She turned toward Gideon's voice, which echoed through the darkened room. The moon had not yet risen, and the night sky offered no stars she could wish upon.

"What is it, Gideon?"

"Miranda, you have to think about what you're going to do when..."

No! She wouldn't think about it. Zacke would get better. He had to.

"Gideon is right, Little One. Zacke is growing weaker and all you are doing is prolonging a life he wouldn't want."

Miranda's heart stalled at hearing Zacke's endearment spill from Miles' lips. What she wouldn't give to hear those words uttered against her ear as Zacke held her close after they made sweet and passionate love. Would she be forever cursed with the pain of never hearing his seductive voice again?

"No, there has to be something we can do! Miles, Hawk is there nothing you know of that will help him. Something that will heal his body?"

Hawk moved to squat by her chair. His gentle touch renewed the flow of tears she had fought to dam. "Miranda, we can do nothing now. Zacke made his choice months ago."

"What are you talking about?"

Miles and Gideon joined Hawk at her side.

"Do you remember at the hospital, you asked why Zacke didn't do what he could to redeem his soul?"

Miranda nodded. "What does that have to do with now, Miles?"

"It has everything to do with the decision you have to make, Miranda. Zacke did have a way to return to human form."

"But—"

Miles placed a gentle finger to her lips. "Let me finish. In order to get his soul back, Zacke would have to go back in time to the days before Gabriella transformed him." Miles looked at Hawk and shrugged his shoulders.

Hawk laid a hand on her shoulder, sending a chill of dread into her bones. "He wanted to go back and kill her so she wouldn't be able to turn him or anyone else into what we are."

Miranda's eyes burned as she looked at the faces of the men trying so hard not to tell her something. "So why didn't he go back?"

Hawk squeezed her hand slightly before clearing his throat. "Zacke had one reason and one reason only."

Miranda wanted to pull the words out of Hawk's mouth. Her impatience to know ate away at her. She inhaled and exhaled deeply. "And that was?"

"You, Miranda. Zacke knew if he went back and became human again, he wouldn't be able to come back to you."

The ramifications ricocheted inside her brain then traveled straight to her heart. She had caused this. Because of her Zacke lay dying now. He had loved her so much he had willingly given up his centuries-old dream.

Silent sobs shook Miranda's shoulders. Her heart felt as if it had imploded. She knew what she had to do and prayed God would forgive her for doing it.

"Again, I thank you all. You have no idea what it means to me to know how much you love Zacke. He returned that love. He was so proud to call you his brothers."

Miranda scrubbed a fist across her wet cheeks. Her throat clogged with heartache. "I need a few moments alone with Zacke before I let him go."

The men filed out as tin soldiers, their bodies stiff with the same ache drumming an incessant rhythm inside her.

She kicked off her shoes and knelt by the bed. "Lord God, I know Zacke is not a creature of your making, but he was at one time. He has never given up hope of finding redemption for a soul that evil stole from him. I ask you, Lord, to please, when you take him from me, give him a home with you. Zacke is a good man, and I humbly ask that you allow him to finally know peace. Amen."

Miranda crawled up on the bed to sit beside Zacke. She tore the tape and the bags from his body. If she had to let him go, then she would be there beside him, holding him in her arms when he drew his last breath.

****

Zacke traveled a path glittering with light. The golden glow hurt his eyes, and for a moment, he wondered if some enemy had staked him in the sunlight. His body throbbed, and he wanted to stop and rest but some compulsion kept his feet moving forward.

As he drew closer to the source of the light, his vision cleared and his body stopped aching. If this was a dream, then Zacke wished it wouldn't end. For the first time in centuries, he felt none of the guilt, shame, and despair that plagued him. He moved with strength, though he knew not from where it came. He remembered a battle fought and barely won, before darkness shrouded his mind and soul.

He reached the perimeter of light. The bright beams dazzled him and bathed him in warmth that felt like his mother's arms wrapped lovingly around him. He stopped, afraid to go farther.

As he waited, conflicted on the decision to flee or stay, two forms moved toward him. Although Zacke stood taller than most, these men—or beings—towered over him. He should probably fear them but he didn't.

"Zachary Kensington, welcome."

Zacke's peace fled. What he had always dreaded had now come to pass. He would be judged for his sins. He dropped to his knees, closed his eyes, and awaited his sentence.

"You are not here to be judged. You are here because someone loved you enough to pray for your soul."

Strong arms lifted Zacke to his feet. He wondered again if he was dreaming.

"The creator of Heaven and Earth knows also that you became a creature by another's choice. He also knows you did all you could while on earth to stop evil. Therefore, you are being given a second chance to live."

"But why? I am not worthy."

"Look at the clouds of Heaven and see your future, Zachary Kensington. Is this not reason enough for you to return?"

Zacke's gaze moved to the soft swirls and watched them separate. Miranda stood in their midst, surrounded by small children. Bright sunlight turned her hair to the copper he loved, and she laughed when the children begged her to let them open the presents. His gaze fixed on the table behind her. It appeared piled high with wrapped parcels.

His beautiful wife shook her head. "You must wait until your dad gets home."

As he continued to watch, a man strode through the backyard. The closer he moved to Miranda and the children the clearer his features became.

Zacke gasped. The man walking in bright sunlight carried his features. Surely, that wasn't possible.

"Anything is possible if it is God's will."

The clouds moved away, and Zacke felt his limbs begin to dissolve beneath him. Before he could thank the angelic beings or the Heavenly Father, he found himself falling through space.

****

Zacke awoke to a dark room. His body ached once again. Not the horrific pain he suffered after his battle with Gabriella, but a dull reminder of what had happened. He stretched his limbs and all but his right arm responded. He looked over and saw Miranda's head resting on that shoulder. Her arm, splayed across his chest, held him prisoner.

He glanced around the bedroom. Hawk, Miles, and Gideon sprawled in chairs. Their heads touched their chests and their faces appeared drawn from exhaustion.

Zacke reached out and touched Miranda's face. The sheer joy of being able to caress her cheek would have brought him to his knees if he were not already prone.

His prayer of thankfulness drifted toward the ceiling. He knew it would be heard.

Miranda stirred and then her eyes flew open. "Zacke!"

"It's all right, Miranda." He touched her face once more before allowing his hand to fall back to the bed.

Her blue eyes darkened as she turned and gazed at him. She jerked upright on the bed. A moment later, her hands moved over his body in a frantic and incredulous fashion.

"Oh, thank God!"

Her cry roused the men from their sleep, and his friends joined her with their exclamations.

He allowed all four a moment more of astonishment before he spoke. "It would be more prudent to give a sick man some peace and quiet, don't you think?"

"Zacke, I can't believe this. Last night you were dying. What happened?"

Miranda's question echoed in the others gazes. He caught her hand and brought it to his lips. "Last night I did die. Today I have my mortal life ahead of me."

"Mortal life? Zacke, what are you taking about?"

"I am saying that upon my immortal death, I received my mortal soul back."

Miranda wondered if the fever had returned. Maybe delirium had overtaken Zacke. What other reason would there be for his statement? Then again, nothing about his awakening made sense. The blisters on his body had disappeared except for one on his face. The wounds had stopped seeping and most importantly, his eyes appeared clear and focused.

"I know this is a lot to take in. I'm still not sure it wasn't a miraculous dream." Zacke's eyes filled with the light of determination.

"I know of only one way to prove it." He turned his head and looked at Hawk and Miles. "Is the sun high in the sky?"

Miles moved forward, placed his hand on Zacke's shoulder, and nodded. "It's midday and the sun burns strong. Hawk and I fought the lassitude as long as we could but finally succumbed to our death sleep."

Zacke's smile included Hawk. "You two have stood by me for centuries, and I now ask you to stand by me again by leaving this room and not returning until Miranda calls you."

"Zacke, you can't possibly be thinking what I think you're thinking."

"Yes, Gideon I am. I ask you also to step outside."

Miranda turned tear-filled eyes to the men in a silent plea to help her convince Zacke to forget the insane notion that he had become human. But all three men ignored her and walked out, leaving her as the only witness to what surely would be Zacke's second and final death—given his already weakened state.

Zacke kissed her lips before moving away from her frozen body. He exited the bed and walked to the window facing directly toward the sun. He turned and grinned at Miranda then grasped the heavy drapes and jerked them open.

She shut her eyes. She didn't want to see his flesh burn. She covered her ears to muffle his shrieks of pain.

The room remained silent. Miranda forced her lids open. Zacke's silhouette drew the rays of the sun like a sponge draws water.

A bare second pass before he caught her suddenly limp body in his arms. "Zacke, if you tell me this is only a dream, I swear I will kill you myself."

"It's no dream, Little One. I no longer have to cover up to be out in the glorious rays of the sun. I no longer have to live my life as a creature of darkness. God has been merciful and in that mercy He has given me back my soul."

Miranda gasped as Zacke caught her lips in a kiss that sucked the breath right out of her lungs. Mortal he might be but the man could still kiss. She wondered if he could still read her mind. "Zacke, does that mean you won't have access to my thoughts anymore?"

"I'm afraid not, Miranda."

"So that means you won't know all my secrets ahead of time."

Zacke carried her to one of the vacated chairs. After seating himself, he held her even tighter. His lips caressed her ear as his hand moved to her belly.

"I wouldn't say that, Little One."

Zacke's laughter echoed in the room. The sound carried to the men waiting outside and to the very gates of Heaven, where angels stopped their Heavenly chores and smiled.

About the author...

Faith started her journey to publication when she joined the Romance board at iVillage.com, where she has long since become a community leader. She has written book reviews for Bridges Magazine, MyShelf.com and, for the past six years, Romantic Times Book Reviews. She also pens a column for a local magazine. Her path veered into editing and marketing for a small press before she joined The Wild Rose Press staff. Her dream of having her own work published is a blessing and an honor. Faith resides in the South with her daughter Amanda, memories of her now-angel husband Rick, and a special zoo crew of furry babies.

Visit her at www.faithvsmith.com

Other books by Faith V. Smith:
Beware What You Wish

To my readers,

I hope you enjoyed reading Zacke and Miranda's tale of love as much as I did writing it. Please look for Miles' story, *Dunbar's Curse*, Book 2 of "Bound By Blood, The Legends" coming soon from The Wild Rose Press.

~Faith V. Smith